T0149380

PICTURE WINDOWS

Mike Robertson

authorHOUSE®

AuthorHouse™
1663 Liberty Drive
Bloomington, IN 47403
www.authorhouse.com
Phone: 1 (800) 839-8640

Published by AuthorHouse 11/19/2018

ISBN: 978-1-5462-6834-5 (sc)
ISBN: 978-1-5462-6833-8 (hc)
ISBN: 978-1-5462-6832-1 (e)

Library of Congress Control Number: 2018913633

Print information available on the last page.

THE PREQUEL

May 1954

Richard's first memory of the neighbourhood in which he would spend most of his childhood involved a tractor pulling a large sled carrying the family's belongings up a muddy road in a newly constructed housing development in Pointe Claire. This was a newly constructed suburb on the western island of Montreal. His family's new home, a three bedroom bungalow stood alone in the middle of the property, its borders measured out in a rough rectangle by ropes attached to yardsticks plunged into the ground like warnings. Its geography, like every other of the dozens of in the area, was entirely untended. There was no driveway, no lawn, no hedge, nothing on any of them. The houses, currently in the process of being inhabited for the first time, just sat on mounds of dirt awaiting new residents to animate them. He recalled following the tractor up the unnamed, unpaved street in the back seat of the family's Pontiac Pathfinder, listening to his parents, Rene and Frances Matthews, discuss their futures with an exuberance likely shared by millions of recent escapees from decades of depression, war and general dismay. Although he could not remember with any clarity the family's previous home, Richard was certain that it was a great deal less comfortable than the one that was awaiting them. Decades later, when he was over sixty years old, he visited the old family homestead in Verdun, a working class section of Montreal where his father had grown up and where his parents had started their family. It made the suburban house in the sea of mud in Pointe Claire look like a paradise, which he guessed had been the objective all along.

That day, the visit was intended to introduce the family to their new home, now that it was finished. It would also ensure that their belongings, which were sitting in a moving van at the bottom of the street were handled properly. His father and mother had spent the last week carefully calibrating the floor plans of the three bedrooms, the living and dining rooms, and the kitchen with pencil drawings of the location of the furniture in each room. For their part, Richard and his two brothers, Hugh and Kevin, tried to stay out of their parents' way as they planned their future. Their father parked on the other side of the street from their new home and instructed them to get out of the car. He told them to follow their mother and himself up to the front of the house, demanding that they be careful to walk on the planks that had been laid out between the street and the front door. Kevin, Richard's youngest brother, almost fell off the plank but was saved by his father who didn't know whether to laugh, hit him or let him fall into the mud. The front door of the place was three or four feet up from the ground, a planned veranda was yet to be installed. Makeshift stairs had been erected and all five of them entered the house through a small porch.

His brother Kevin and he were led into the smaller bedroom in the north east corner of the house where they stood at its door awaiting further instruction. This was to be their room, complete with the same bunk beds they shared in the old place in Verdun. Hugh was to bed down in the other small room, equipped, as his father pointed out in a strangely theatrical voice, with an entrance to the attic. He had followed with a low cackling laugh, as if it were some sort of jest. Richard thought that Hugh suddenly looked a little scared, as if there was something sinister waiting for him in the attic. Richard walked into his new bedroom, the one he was to again share with his baby brother. He stood at the window, looked out at an empty yard of dirt, mud and nothing else. It was curious. About twenty yards from the rear of the house was a tall, faded wooden fence beyond which was a large clapboard structure that appeared to have been built early in the century. It stood on another street, a street that had been there long before the new Matthews house was even on an architect's drafting board. It was part of the Valois Village of the old Pointe Claire, back before the subdivisions invaded a community that had been the residence of cottage owners and families whose breadwinners worked at places like the local brick factory. At one time, all that the longstanding residents of the village used to see beyond their backyards was acre after acre of wooded fields with the only civilization in evidence being the brick factory. Beyond that stood an exclusive golf club frequented by Montreal executives. That pastoral view had now permanently faded from view.

Richard stood at that window, almost mesmerized with the house, and wondered who lived there then and who lived there now.

The family completed their move into the house within a week although mother often said that it should have taken a month. This was a reference to the delivery of new furniture, which unexpectedly arrived within days as opposed to weeks. Richard happened to be standing at his own bedroom window as the summer light had started to disappear into the horizon. Having already developed a curiosity regarding the history and present status of the large clapboard structure beyond the fence behind their house, he had become even more interested when he noticed that someone lived there. He had seen a young boy standing in a window on the second floor of the house looking out into the neighbourhood that was no longer acres and acres of woods. Richard was, however, not really be sure. The figure was standing still, almost transfixed, staring out of the window as if he had seen something so fascinating that he could not look away. Richard stood in his own window, himself staring, as inquisitive as any six year old boy could be. He tried to persist in his curiosity, as any young boy would. He must have stood there for about five minutes, like he was at prayer, his head empty of any other thought. He even felt his knees starting to shudder until he turned away from the window, still wondering what the kid in the window was looking at. As he went to bed, his brother Kevin already tucked in the top bunk, he did not know it but he would soon be dreaming of the figure in the window of the house beyond the backyard.

For the next couple of weeks, Richard did not look out at the window on the second floor of that clapboard house. Fact was that he had forgotten about the boy in the window. Like any six year old, events, including observations that he may have been curious about, did not stay in his mind very long. Even now, he sometimes had to be reminded of his own memories. With the boy in the window temporarily overlooked, Richard was busy becoming acquainted with the new neighbourhood. The street name was Columbus. Until Richard was about eight years old, he had been misled about the street's origins. His father, who was sometimes a bit of a comedian or at least he thought he was, maintained that the street was named after a local hardware store owner named Norm Columbus and not after the man who discovered America. Richard believed him until one of his classmates in grade three, a guy named Kenny Keon, told him that his father was wrong regarding Columbus Avenue. It soon developed into a serious difference of opinion between the two eight year olds. He couldn't remember when the argument started but their grade three teacher, Mr. Clark, had to settle the dispute. Richard soon realized that he had been quite gullible in believing the story about Norm Columbus. He did not own a hardware store but did work in one, a joint down in Valois Village.

Richard had been driving his new tricycle, a classic red model with one partially defective pedal up and down Columbus in his investigations of his new neighbourhood. It was not exactly a new trike. That was obvious, the defective pedal, peeling paint, and a model name partially erased being the obvious clues. Richard was to eventually find out that his father had picked it out of the garbage of a house on Broadview Avenue. He said that he had intended to repair the trike but apparently never got around to it. After that first month pedalling up and down the new street, Richard had managed to confirm that all the recently constructed houses on Columbus Avenue were occupied. And every one of the houses were now populated by families, parents with children, many of whom were possibly around Richard's age. He would likely find out for sure when school started in September.

He befriended two boys around his age during those initial travels around the street. There was Peter, who lived four doors up on the same side of the street as Richard, and Brian, who lived across from Peter in an identical house. They had already seen each other several weeks previously, both families having moved in on the same day. Peter was a short, thin boy with black hair while Brian was a taller, heavier boy with blonde hair in a brush cut. When Richard was cycling past the two of them that first day, Brian asked about Richard's tricycle. They were sitting on the lawn of what Richard would come to know as Brian's place. It was a Saturday.

"Hey, kid, isn't that a new trike?", more a comment than any sort of question. Richard didn't respond at first. He had, however, stopped pedalling. "It doesn't look new." Obviously, Brian had a sharp eye. Pete nodded, got up and walked over to examine the trike. Both he and Brian had been sitting in the dirt in front of one of their houses. It later turned out to be Brian's place. Behind them, a man who turned out to be Brian's father, and another man were laying sod. Half of the lawn was still composed of dirt. Neither of them looked up at the new arrival.

For a moment, Richard wondered why the lawn in front of his own house was still barren of grass. He then answered Brian. "It isn't new, my dad just gave it to me a couple of days ago." Brian and Pete nodded in unison. Pete then spoke. "How come your dad didn't get you a bike?" Richard gave the only answer he thought he could. "I don't know."

"Maybe he thought you couldn't ride a bike." replied Pete. "Can you ride a bike?"

"I don't know. I never have." said Richard, admittedly an embarrassing admission that elicited a couple of giggles from his new friends. Richard then attempted to change the subject without really knowing it. "Where do you guys live?"

Pete pointed across the street while Brian threw a thumb over his shoulder toward his own house. "I guess you moved in a little while ago too." said Brian. "Yeah, we did, four houses down." said Richard, pointing south.

＞

Richard become fast friends with Brian and Pete that day, a relationship that lasted for decades. They discussed their origins, in so far as they could actually exchange information on where they lived before they found themselves on Columbus Avenue. Brian said that his father had told him that they used to live in a place called Lachine, a Montreal suburb that it was not very far away. Their house was smaller than their previous house, suggesting that maybe they used to live in duplex. Pete said he wasn't sure where his family used to live although he seemed to know that they had lived in an apartment building. All he would say is that the place they had lived in had an elevator in it. The location of that building with an elevator remained unknown until Pete was ten years old and he discovered that the family used to live in Notre-Dame-de-Grace. Richard informed his new pals that his family used to live in another section of Montreal called Verdun. He knew this because his grandparents, on his mother's side, still lived down the street from where they used to lived. The family usually went over there for dinner on Sunday. The grandparents were not exactly pleased with the family's move to the suburbs but understood.

THE CURRENT STREET

It was Richard Matthews' first week of retirement. After more than thirty years toiling anonymously and perhaps pointlessly for the government of Canada, he had graduated into his emeritus years with the predictable reactions of relief and at times regret. For the last several years of his so-called career, he was having difficulty taking anything he did or said seriously, so cynical he had become with the situations often surrounding him at work. As he sometimes reminisced with colleagues of similar durations, he regretted no longer working for bosses from the "good old days", members of the so-called "greatest generation", those graduates of depression, war and then boundless optimism. While not every boss from that era was worthy of such compliment, many of them were. They seemed to have had honour, integrity, and wisdom, qualities that Richard often thought were sometimes absent in many of their successors. For the last years of his career, Richard reported to a variety of overbearing, irritating, or outright feckless individuals whose deficiencies as managers were enough to prompt Richard to contemplate retirement almost daily. On the other hand, on reflection, he had to admit to himself if no one else, that those bosses for which he had such disdain were actually smarter, better qualified, and socially more acceptable than he was. Maybe it was envy.

Fittingly, none of the last few directors that Richard had the misfortune to endure attended his retirement event although, as pointed out by several of his colleagues who were there, they may have been uncertain as to whether they had in fact been invited. Or maybe, and this was the more likely explanation, they were just as relieved not to be attending his retirement party as Richard was when they didn't attend.

His wife Jean, nine years his junior and married to him for over thirty years, was initially worried about Richard. Despite his growing reluctance about his job, he still put in the time. Unlike some of his co-workers also headed toward retirement, Richard did not start to limit his hours, showing up late and leaving early. Some did not bother to even show up for work, particularly those whose indolence was already well known. On the other hand, Richard continued to put in his eight hours a day, arriving in his cubicle at seven o'clock in the morning and leaving at five o'clock in the afternoon, the two missing hours invested in lunch, almost always out of the building, one of the few who actually went out for lunch, a habit that all the bosses he admired invariably pursued without fail. Sure, some of them, quite a few of them actually, would use the extramural lunch to make respectable progress toward inebriation but Richard never minded. Aside from those who returned from lunch completely unable to proceed with their duties, Richard found most of them to be more congenial than they normally were, which was considerable before they had even touched a drop of alcohol at lunch. For Richard, his custom seldom involved alcohol, the exception being the occasional beer if he happened to have a luncheon companion.

Jean had long been worried that once retired, Richard would fade into inertia, not to mention sloth, possibly spending most of his time watching television, his collection of more than two thousand DVDs an excellent source of diversion. In addition, Jean was also concerned that Richard's lack of enthusiasm for domestic chores, the daily drudgery of laundry, vacuuming, dish washing and the like, would continue despite the dramatic increase in his free time. With Jean still working, she had reason to hope for a change in his behaviour but was doubtful nonetheless. So after a week or so of her husband going to the gym every day, watching movies on television and otherwise lounging around the house waiting for her to come home and prepare dinner, Jean did the only logical thing she could. She convinced him that they should get a dog.

She was a hound/collie mix with a gentle though generally nervous disposition. There wasn't much of a discussion regarding the pouch's name. It would be Margie, a derivation of the moniker given to their one previous dog, a ginger coloured pointer named Maggie, who was much beloved and much missed by the family, particularly by their two boys, Jay and Tyler. They still mentioned their regret with her passing, that is whenever Richard and Jean saw them, which wasn't that often now that they were both out on their own. Thinking that her husband would benefit from assuming some sort of responsibility for the care of their new pet, Jean assigned him the duty of walking her twice a day, the other daily constitutional being her obligation. Richard was a little surprised that he got the call to walk Margie, seeing as how both of them had long acknowledged that Jean was better equipped to handle canine care than her husband, he more a stumbling Dagwood Bumstead than Cesar Milan when it came to dogs. So the schedule was established. Jean would guide Margie around the neighbourhood in the mornings while Richard would walk her at noon and around dinner time. As a final inducement, Jean suggested that the strolls with the dog would give him an opportunity to become more familiar with a neighbourhood that was changing, new and remodelled houses emerging all over an area that was coming to define gentrification.

While Richard was not particularly enthusiastic about the opportunity to assess the neighbourhood, he reluctantly took up his new duties with a certain inevitable curiosity, just as Jean had advised. After all, perhaps being more enlightened about the neighbourhood would certainly provide Richard with enough material to begin one of his longstanding though hardly practical ambitions, to start writing again. He had at one time pursued a literary aspiration, particularly in university where he found that passing himself off as a writer, whether it was accurate or not, had certain social benefits, not the least of which involved women. For a few years in university, he wrote poetry, generally because he found it less work than prose. It was enough to allow him to consider himself a writer, unpublished and unbowed, at least until he found himself compelled to work for a living. He had basically forget about literary pursuits for almost forty years. Perhaps his daily walks with Margie, passing previously unstudied houses and people, would prompt a return to that ambition. So, after several sessions with a dog trainer, classes arranged and also attended by Jean, Richard began to appreciate his walks with the dog.

He and Margie usually began their walks heading west on their street, the oddly named Lakeview Avenue, odd because there was neither a lake nor any other body of water close enough to merit any reference in a street name. Richard had thought of inquiring about this oddity of some of his older neighbours, particularly the Italian couple who lived across the street. But he never did, keeping his curiosity about the name of his street to himself. Regardless of its name, Lakeview Avenue was exemplary of the reinvention of the neighbourhood. There was an influx of new homes being built over the sites of old homes that were being demolished and then forgotten, an advance of affluence that seemed inevitable. It was a process called infill development, a process of constructing new houses on vacant or underutilized lots, the inevitability being that every second house in the neighourhood seemed to be too large for the property it was built on and too modern for the neighbourhood more generally. There were massive single family dwellings with four or five bedrooms, at least three bathrooms, living rooms, dining areas, family rooms, laundry rooms, and enclosed garages that seemed to be invariably occupied by people with expensive European automobiles. They were usually built about a foot from the house next door, close enough to be almost attached. Some were called houses, some were called condominiums. They were all called expensive.

The Matthews, who had moved into the neighbourhood over twenty years ago with their two sons, had occupied one of the few infill houses that were on Lakeview Avenue back then. Their house was hardly the size of the newer houses that had since been constructed or were still being built on the street. Richard and Margie did not pass any of the newer infill homes until they were half way up Lakeview on their walks. Each one of the dozen or so houses going west on Lakeview from the Matthews place were of an older vintage, different models, different styles, most with relatively new roofs, new windows, resurfaced driveways, new backyard patios, some surrounded by large oak trees, some surrounded by fences, others with carefully manicured hedges and lawns, most probably improved to contend with the newer houses being constructed around them.

It was not surprising that only five of the dozen or so older houses, all likely built in the 1950s and before, were still occupied by their original residents. There was the sweet Italian couple from across the street. They were both profoundly elderly, blessed with kind faces, snow white hair, and an insatiable appetite for neighbourhood gossip, which was surprising given that neither of them were mobile, their ability to collect information evidently based on neighbours dropping by for chats on local developments. They grew tomatoes in their backyard and grapes on vines over a trellis attached to the garage. Except for the winter, they would sit outside by the side door of their house, an uninspiring brick duplex which they had long shared with one of the old man's cousins from the old country. They would sip coffee, enjoy Italian pastry and presumably leisurely reflect on the changes in the neighbourhood. They had moved in directly from some town in southern Italy sixty years past. Sometimes, maybe once every two weeks or so, their daughter, who was never accompanied by a husband or a boyfriend, and two young boys would visit, usually in the afternoon. The daughter would park her expensive automobile across the street from the Matthews, stay for a couple of hours and be gone before dinner time. Sometimes but not always, the old cousin and his wife would join them. The only time Richard and Jean ever seemed to see the cousin and his wife was when the daughter and her two boys visited.

Next door to the elderly Italian couple, still on the other side of the street, was a pair of older women who supposedly had lived together for over forty years, a couple who until quite recently had gone out of their way to disguise the actual nature of their relationship, which was that of two women living together as romantic partners. Despite the masquerade, they were well regarded on the street, pretty well friendly with all of the neighbours. In addition, everyone liked their two dogs, two black pointers who were so well behaved that they made Margie look like a jungle beast in comparison. Going further east on that side of the street, Richard and Margie would then walk by the ramshackled, weathered clapboard cottage owned by a retired man and his grown son. Both were strange individuals, the father easily qualifying as the street busybody, constantly annoying neighbours with senseless observations and strange comments about issues as diverse as the weather and the political situation, not to mention boring rhetorical questions about mail delivery and the bus service. He also seemed to have an endless supply of junk, mainly useless electronics, which usually found their way to the bottom of their driveway with a large sign informing the public that these items were free. While his father was certifiably irritating, his son was simply strange. Although he was likely in his mid-thirties, he was neither employed nor had anyone ever remembered him being employed. He didn't seem to have any friends, any hobbies, or any other activity that he pursued with any regularity. Aside from riding his bike, even in the winter, the son was seldom seen by anyone, prompting the kind of conjecture and rumour that were usually associated with local eccentrics. Richard and Jean could not have been alone in their speculations regarding father and son, often wondering, like presumably many of the neighbours, about what they did inside their clapboard cottage. They just never came to any conclusion nor had they heard anyone else coming to any conclusions either.

The two other houses on the street that were still occupied by their original owners were situated on the Matthews side of Lakeview. Living next door was an elderly woman who was seldom seen outside the squat little bungalow that sat on one of the largest properties on the street, a tract that was likely, once the current occupant passed away, to fetch a handsome windfall for the old lady's two middle aged sons. The two sons, who evidently had taken after their father, a local restaurateur who was as disagreeable as he was overweight, would routinely drop by their mother's house, to tend to the lawn, put out the garbage, and presumably make sure that their investment was still breathing. Jean thought that her husband was being unnecessarily cynical about the apparent devotion of the woman's sons, suspecting that the sons were your basic mama's boys. On the other hand, Richard always though that the two boys were waiting for their mother to pass so they could sell the property, divide the spoils of her estate, dump their wives, that is of course if they had wives, and replace them with exotic dancers. Not only did Jean think that assessment misanthropic but cruel.

The other original resident was actually the son of the first owner who had grown up in and still occupied the small Cape Cod cottage next to the old woman's place. No one, including the old Italian couple who lived across the street and the weird father and son act who lived across the street from the son in the Cape Cod cottage, seemed to know anything about him. The prevalent theory was that he accepted, repaired and sold stolen automobiles, a large structure having being built in his backyard after his father died being the key evidence, that and the occasional sounds of machinery emitting from the building. Several women and at least one ten or eleven year old boy seemed to live with him although not simultaneously. Like most of their neighbours they assumed, Richard and Jean were convinced that something questionable was going on in that little cottage. Richard had his suspicions confirmed one afternoon when an obvious prostitute, a young blond girl with an array of colourful tattoos and an inviting outfit mistakenly rang their doorbell rather than the one two doors down. Richard also noticed a scary man waiting for her in the street, behind the wheel of a big black car with the motor running. When he told Jean, she expressed neither surprise nor dismay. Richard didn't mention the incident to anyone else.

The rest of the neighbourhood, principally the three streets, including Lakeview, on which Richard walked Margie, was primarily constituted of relatively new houses built by several construction companies and designed by four or five different architectural firms, a curious fact since most of the new buildings looked to be replicated somehow, as if the plans for most of these new homes were plagiarized from the same source. Every house, which could qualify as mansions compared to the rest of the neighbourhood's abodes, had similar, ultra modern characteristics, many of which suggested designs for recently constructed ecumenical churches: floor to ceiling windows, floor to ceiling doors, flat roofs, chrome, steel, ostentatious Scandinavian wood, perfect lawns, stone walks and patios that looked like they were counterfeit marble, the occasional balcony, some houses had garages, some had anachronistic carports, some had parking spaces in the back instead of a lawn. One could speculate, if not conclude that most of the new house buyers also shared similar characteristics, the principal aspect of which was affluence. While wealth was common to most of the occupants of the newer houses, not all of them fit the same description. In fact, the local dacha owners seem to be either rich millennials, middle aged yuppies with huge mortgages or retired or soon to be retired baby boomers trading up from homes in other regions of suburbs. The neighbourhood, which at one time was populated by former working class heroes climbing the social ladder one suburban rung at a time, was now inhabited by citizens who for the most part were already entitled.

He had forgotten which day of the week it had been when he and Margie first came across a man standing still in the window, on the second floor of one of the monster houses on a parallel street directly south from Lakeview. To Richard, it seemed quite familiar. The sighting came around lunch time, the usual time for his turn for walking Margie. The second floor window was in the rear of a house on Belcourt Avenue, a main street that ran east-west for more than four blocks between two larger streets that ran north-south around a neighbourhood quadrant that included three other thoroughfares. Richard and Margie were walking on Coolbreeze when Richard noticed the man staring from that second floor window on Belcourt Avenue. Margie was doing her business when Richard was looking over the fence containing the grounds of that house on 233 Coolbreeze Avenue into the backyard of the house on Belcourt Avenue. It was there that a motionless man was standing in a second floor window, apparently staring in a north easterly direction. Although Richard did not get a decent look at his countenance, not being close enough for any sort of accurate impression, he was reasonably certain that the apparition in the window was a man, a young man who did not seem to be wearing a shirt. Richard invested some time considering the thought of a spectre in the window, this one staring without purpose, almost like a statue. Margie, having finished her business, had commenced barking at another man walking his dog, an inquisitive pug that seemed similar in appearance to its owner. Margie was straining at the leash, pulling toward the pug and his owner, two targets towards which Margie would invariably launch her canine ire. As was usually the case, Richard immediately began to tug Margie toward the opposite direction. She struggled against Richard's guidance, as she usually did, until he was able to produce a liver treat from a small plastic bag that both he and Jean always carried on their travels with Margie. The dog then calmed down and they both continued on their walk.

Richard returned, when he and Margie reached the corner of Coolbreeze and Hawthorne, to the thought of the man half silhouetted in the window on Belcourt Avenue. For a moment, it reminded him of something.

On the corner of Coolbreeze and Hawthorne, on both sides of the street facing Hawthorne, were two large Edwardian era mansions which may have been home at one time to two very prosperous families. However, at least according to the elderly Italian historians across the street from the Matthews, the two houses were home to a succession of tenants over the past few decades or so. One of the houses was a large white stucco building with three floors and dozens of different size windows while the other was a sprawling bungalow encircled by trees, thickets of vines and a grand veranda that would not have been out of place surrounding an older resort hotel. Most of the time, there were signs on one or both properties advertising either apartments or rooms for rent. The identity of the building was evident: an apartment building or a rooming or boarding house. Instead of a front lawn, the white stucco building featured a large asphalt lot in which eight to ten cars were usually parked. Across the street, the bungalow mansion did not provide a large parking lot, there being only enough space for two or three cars. Their conclusion, at least based on the few residents who Richard and Jean happened to see coming and going from the place, was that it was some sort of group home, addicts, ex-cons, and handicapped adults being among their most frequent conjectures.

Sometimes, depending on the dog's behaviour on her walk, Richard and her would sit on the stone palisade in front of the bungalow/apartment/rooming house with the grand veranda as long as there was not an abundance of traffic on Hawthorne Street to bedevil Margie into a paroxysm of barking, only buses being exempt from precipitating Margie's barking compulsions. While Margie attempted to sit quietly, her determination assisted by the continual provision of liver treats, Richard stared at the front door of the bungalow, considering the identity of tenants in the house and wondering why he, Jean or anyone else for that matter, seldom, if ever saw any of the residents. While he was contemplating that mystery, suddenly another mystery arrived in his head, a fading thought of the man in the window on Belcourt Avenue. It was cut short by a man and a dog walking by on the other side of the street. Being short of liver treats, Richard had to direct Margie forcefully back to Lakeview Avenue.

THE PREQUEL

September 1954

It was the morning of his first day at school, grade one actually, there being no kindergarten in those days. Richard was standing in the backyard of the family's new house in the five street housing development recently built by the McGill Construction Company. It had been four months since the Matthews family moved into their three bedroom bungalow on Columbus Avenue. In place of the mud landscape that had been there when they had first moved in, a rudimentary grass lawn, conceived from a mountain of grass seed, new fences, hedges, and patio stones had been installed by his father with the help of one of the brother-in-laws and Mr. Simpson, who had moved in across the street a week after the Matthews had.

Richard remembered watching the moving men unloading their furniture off a sled. He had laughed and pointed at the moving men allowing a refrigerator to slip off the sled into the mud. My father, who had been tinkering with the car, his head under the hood, had looked up at the disturbance and yelled at Richard for laughing.

But on this day, the first day of school, Richard wasn't laughing. He was just staring into space, standing in the backyard, holding back tears, waiting for his mother to walk him to the bus stop to school. He was five years old and, like most children his age, had never been been away from home, except for the time he had run away from home for a couple hours in the old neighbourhood. While he waited, he happened to notice someone staring out out of the window in the top floor of the old house that sat on the property directly behind the Matthews' place. He recognized him. The face staring out of that window belonged to a boy who he may have seen before, a couple of months ago, when the family had first moved in, a boy that he had thought might have been his age. It looked like the same boy. He had been staring out of the window.

Neither Richard nor anyone else in the Matthews family knew anything about who lived in the old house that sat beyond the Matthews backyard, even though they had now been living there for several months. Richard did not know the family name of the people who lived behind them although he might have heard his father mention it. He had been told by his parents, however, that the house was home to a family of two parents, and four or five children. Perhaps his parents knew more about the family that lived beyond their backyard but had not related any such information to him. Nonetheless, Richard somehow knew or thought he knew that there was something strange about that family. On the other hand, he was only five years old.

But that morning, he was only wondering about his first day at school. He was scared although his fear could have been ameliorated if Brian and Pete, the friends he had made that summer were able to attend the school with him. However, both of them were not old enough to register, both of them being well underage. Richard's mother was also apprehensive. The day was grey, rainy and foreboding. His mother escorted him to the corner of Columbus and Broadview where they joined three or four pairs of mothers and their children, waiting for a school bus which would transport them to school, an older, predominately French speaking elementary school named St. Louis. It was a relatively small school, a crumbling brick building old enough to have been constructed sometime in the previous century. Richard and his soon to be classmates were temporarily attending a French school because the families moving into the newly constructed suburbs courtesy of the McGill housing development all had children. They were almost all English speaking. No one had neither the time nor the foresight to build a new English school to serve the newly arrived English speaking kids. On the other hand, the St. Louis school, its French speaking student body having been recently dwindling for mysterious demographic reasons, was a convenient temporary option for English speaking intruders. The St.

Louis school was suddenly half French, half English, an idea that would seem quaint, if not ironic in view of the developments in the area in the years to follow.

Like most of the kids waiting to enter school that day, grade one represented for Richard the first taste of life without mother. The trauma of separation was almost too much to bear. Richard and every other kid entering first grade that day were in tears most of that morning. And if that wasn't frightening enough, as if to further punctuate the gloom already enveloping them, there was a stern old bat of a teacher awaiting them. Her name was Miss McCarthy and she looked like she could play the role of the Wicked Witch of the West if asked. After rendering their final tearful farewells to their mothers who were apprehensive enough to accompany them on the bus to school, the first graders, of which there were several dozen including Richard, were asked to line up two by two for their march into school, military provision being an important component of education in 1954.

As students in the more senior grades entered the school, one of the boys in Miss McCarthy's class stepped out out of the line for a moment to say something to somebody else in line. Richard remembered the sound of Miss McCarthy's yardstick landing on the boy's head. He looked like the boy he saw in the window of the house behind his that morning. He remembered the incident for the next sixty years it seems, its recollection sometimes coming to him anytime he saw a six or seven year old crossing the street near the school in his neighbourhood. The boy immediately let out a cry, bringing both hands to his head as Miss MsCarthy commanded the rest of the class, in a voice that frightened anyone who heard it, to stay standing in line or face similar consequences. Most of the class, still not recovered from the departure of their mothers, eventually walked into the school with another scary thing to worry about, their tears barely dry.

Once in their classroom, the boy who had been hit with Miss McCarthy's yardstick, the boy who may have been living in the house behind his, was seated at a desk that was directly in front of Miss McCarthy's, the spot that Miss McCarthy explained was for "troublemakers", a designation that hardly seemed justified. Richard remembered that the boy, whose name he was eventually told was Scott Vessey, only attended Saint Louis for a couple of days.

Apparently, as his father speculated, Scott Vessey had behavioural problems that could not be remedied or controlled despite the constant application of Miss McCarthy's yardstick.

THE STREET AGAIN

Not surprisingly, the image of the man in the window on Belcourt Avenue appeared in his thoughts as he strained for sleep that night. During his contemplations, it seemed more like history than a short term memory. Since he had retired, he had been taking afternoon naps, a benefit that he certainly could have used when he was working, and many of his colleagues did use. But now the afternoon naps were disrupting his normal slumber, sometimes delaying sleep by the few hours he invested in rest that afternoon. Although he would sometimes read, a practice he regretted not pursuing with more enthusiasm now that he was no longer working, he usually just lay there, wrestling with the pillows on the bed, thinking about the events of the day, as trivial as they were, rediscovering or re-engineering his memories, mainly about old girlfriends it seemed, and talking to himself about whatever emerged in that addled, sleep deprived brain of his, mostly about arguments he had lost to Jean, which was fairly regularly.

So after the day he saw the man in the window, it was predictable that the afternoon's excursion into voyeurism and perhaps memory would find its way into his head at some point. He remembered having pursued a fascination with a man in the window previously, now pretty well certain that it was not the first time he had that feeling. It was a long time ago. All he could remember now was that his boyhood friends Brian and Pete may have had something to do with that feeling, that possible memory. It was odd he thought, the selectivity of memory, particularly at his age. He could recollect or he thought he could recollect, with what he usually assumed was a certain precision, all sorts of events from his childhood, having presumed that what he was attempting to remember at the time

21

was a memory from his childhood. It had to be he thought, had to be. And he was reasonably certain that further details of the memory would eventually come to him.

Richard woke up the next morning with the thought of the man in the window still settled in his head. He mentioned his experience to Jean over coffee and asked her if she ever came across a similar circumstance. Jean gave him a shrug, a quiet giggle and told him a story about a girl who had the habit of taking Polaroid snapshots of people she saw standing or sitting in the front windows of houses in her old neighbourhood. The girl's unique habit was understandably not very popular with the neighbours. The people in the surrounding houses reported that the girl, who was commonly regarded as the neighbourhood weirdo in any event, gave up her strange hobby once the police got involved. Jean said that she was never told about the fate of the Polaroids or the reason for her adventures with her camera. Jean added that her mother and her sometimes speculated that she might have gone on to a career in fashion photography. Jean laughed again. They then discussed the case of the Belcourt window man. Jean suggested that the most sensible explanation for a supposedly shirtless man standing in the rear window of a house on the next street was simply a matter of someone looking out of window for no apparent reason, a moment of dumbfounded contemplation, a sort of temporary meditation, something that Richard himself had sometimes found himself pursuing, just staring for no particular reason. As usual, Richard found himself agreeing, or being compelled to agree with Jean. He did not mention that he had had a similar experience many years ago, when he was a boy.

After breakfast, Richard picked up Margie's leash and started making the arrangements for her walk, specifically the plastic bag full of liver treats and the poop bags. Jean was surprised. The morning walk was part of her schedule, not his. The morning was a slot which Richard refused to even consider. Fact was that her husband was reluctant to take Margie on her walk at any time, his hesitation to walk Margie a function of his inability to control the dog's behaviour when the two of them came across the situations that harried her, mainly the appearance of a man or a large dog. But this morning, he was practically rushing to get Margie out of the door for her walk. As dumbfounded as she was, Jean did not need an explanation. The thought of seeing the man in a rear window in a house on Belcourt Avenue again too much of a motive to resist, even though he did not really expect to see him at this time of day. His enthusiasm to confirm yesterday's sighting of the man in the window was difficult to resist.

He was out of the door before the dog, another first, at least for Richard. They turned left on Lakeview, then turned left again, and were quickly walking west on Coolbreeze, heading toward the house at number 233. After getting two doors up, Richard spotted a circumstance that caused him to delay their walk by shepherding Margie up the driveway at 239 Coolbreeze, to shelter Margie from reacting poorly to two dogs being walked by two men. More importantly, the two men and the two dogs were standing there in front of the house next door to 233 Coolbreeze, casually talking. Richard was tempted to wave the two men and their dogs off the spot that was holding Richard and Margie from continuing their walk. He and Margie huddled in that driveway for at least ten minutes, shuffling the liver treats into Margie's gob. Richard briefly wondered whether the treats contained some sort of tranquilizer. Sometimes, Richard wished that Margie could go back on that tranquilizer that her veterinarian had proscribed for her nerves when she was first adopted by Richard and Jean.

Richard and Margie must have waited for ten minutes, sometimes an eternity if Margie had been stressed, a condition that Richard was attempting to relieve with liver treats. Once the two couples ended their conversations near 233 Belcourt Avenue, Richard and Margie started back up Coolbreeze, their pace quickened somewhat, Richard being worried that they might run into another problem for Margie before he ran out of dog treats. The two of them did, however, slow down and then stop when they arrived in front of 233 Coolbreeze and looked beyond its backyard into the grounds behind the house on Belcourt Avenue. He didn't see anyone or anything in any of the windows in the rear of the house. He wasn't surprised, just disappointed. Just as he had expected, the man wasn't there. After all, on the previous day, he had passed the house four hours later, at around noon. But this day, it was eight o'clock in the morning. Richard just stared at the empty windows on the second floor, empty of thought, at least for the moment. He would eventually return to his ruminations, however fruitless they may have been. He would return at noon. He was confused.

Margie had started to get a little fractious standing there in the driveway of 233 Coolbreeze waiting for her bewildered master to continue her walk. Richard turned and started up Coolbreeze again. The two of them would be back in four hours.

He returned to their place on Lakeview without incident. He offered no comment to Jean who was still wondering, however dimly, why he insisted on taking the morning walk of Margie. Richard put the dog's equipment away and sat down in the living room to watch the television news. It seemed that the news was pretty well the same every single day. He didn't know why he continued watching the television and reading the paper. It seemed the same every day. It was like walking the dog every day.

He had nodded off for a couple of hours or so in front of the television. Jean shouted from another room. It was time for Richard to walk the dog, that is if he wanted to take his usual shift. He did. Jean shrugged to herself. She could hear him collecting the bags and cutting up some more liver treats for Margie. He would likely need a fairly large supply of treats to sustain them on this walk, that is if Richard managed to spot the man in the window. For some unfathomable reason, Margie started to bark before they were able to get out the door. Something had spooked her but when Richard stepped out of the door and looked out into the street, he saw nothing either way, no men, no dogs, nothing. Perhaps there was something in the air. Richard had to invest three liver treats just to get her out the door, then two more to get her to the bottom of the driveway. Finally, fortified by liver treats, almost constant admonitions and the occasional tugging on her leash, Margie was finally walking east on Lakeview toward the next two lefts that led to Coolbreeze Avenue and the backyard.

She seemed relatively serene now, as if she was convinced that she had already received her limit of treats. By the time they got to the corner, the two of them were conducting themselves like every other proper dog walking duo, however temporarily. They both started up the south side of Coolbreeze, their pace quickening with Richard's anticipation. There was no one else on the street, allowing them to approach their objective address without any further distraction. Margie was walking ahead of him, looking back at him like she knew something.

They arrived in front of 233 Coolbreeze, stopped at the bottom of the concrete walk that lead to the front door of the house, stood to look to ensure that there would be no witnesses to his curiosity, which he may have thought inappropriate. Once he was certain that there was nobody in the house, nobody on the property, he moved to the driveway to look behind the house at the rear of the house on Belcourt Avenue. Having moved up the driveway, he was standing next to the garage when he noticed that the garage itself offered a unique perspective on his target, the man he hoped would be standing in the window at 240 Belcourt Avenue. He stood between the garage and the house and looked beyond the backyard at the Belcourt window. After ensuring that no one was around to witness his trespassing into the backyard at 233 Coolbreeze, he and Margie crossed the yard, stood at the fence, and looked up to see the man in the window. He was there. The man in the window did not see Richard and Margie which was surprising in a way. Richard and Margie were no further than twenty meters away, behind a fence over which they were clearly visible or would be clearly visible if the man in the window were not resolutely staring off in space, transfixed it would appear by something in the horizon, perhaps by a house on the other side of Coolbreeze or more likely, by the high rise apartment building that was four or five streets to the north. The building, an older edifice that housed tenants that normally would not live in such a prosperous neighbourhood, was generally known as the "bummy apartments".

Richard and Jean had often heard people in the neighbourhood make unkind references to the building although no one was ever able to assign any particular transgression to anyone who lived there.

Richard stood motionless, patting Margie who was cooperating by sitting silently while her master continued his staring. Richard had thought of attempting to draw the attention of the man in the window but before he could take any action, the man withdrew from the window. Richard looked down at Margie who had stood up, as if she knew that conditions had changed, and looked ready to bolt. He then turned and walked down the driveway. He took another look at the window, over his shoulder this time, and beheld an empty window. He had a fleeting thought of the so-called bummy apartments and understood any curiosity that the man in the window would have in them, the possibility of prurient interest coming to mind. He was reasonably certain that most of his neighbours likely thought, if they thought at all about the building, that all sorts of inappropriate, if not criminal activities went on within its one and two bedroom suites. They also thought about the building's future and its inevitable demolition, of which they were sure.

They continued up the street, Richard contemplating the question of whether the man in the window had a schedule for his sojourn in the window, whether or not he had a specific time of day and day of the week for his appearance in the window. By the time he arrived home, he had not developed any particular hypothesis as to the man in the window and the details of his window habit but he continued to think about it. He also wondered about his nascent fascination with the man in the window and the possibility of history repeating itself, a barely conscious deja vu.

ANOTHER DAY ON THE STREET

About a week after the day when he first glimpsed the man in the window on Belcourt Avenue, Richard decided to augment his usual route on his walk with Margie. He had decided to walk down Belcourt Avenue to survey the front of the house where that man had first appeared to him in its back window. He had seen the man in the window four out of the previous six days, including today, a frequency significant enough to motivate him to seek more evidence of his discovery, that is, if it was a discovery and not an apparition which he had managed to imagine. He briefly considered the possibility that he had imagined, or at least exaggerated the scene of the man in the window. He considered his developing fascination with the man in the window a dangerous development. For that reason he guessed, he hadn't mentioned the fact that he had succumbed to an interest in the man in the window to Jean. He suspected that she would have discouraged any further exploration of the phenomenon of a man standing in a neighbourhood window, suggesting perhaps that his retirement had had a disturbing effect on him, reminding him that he was once convinced that one of their previous homes was haunted, a family fable that was now barely remembered and hadn't been discussed in years. He did not think of mentioning that he had had such a fascination before.

As for the house of interest, he had calculated that it was halfway down the block on Belcourt, the number being 240, its backyard facing the backyard of 233 Coolbreeze. From the street, one could see the back deck to the house on Coolbreeze. Richard hadn't noticed that the Coolbreeze patio was equipped with an outdoor barbecue, even though he had practically stood in that back yard several days ago when he had walked up the driveway of 233 Coolbreeze with Margie. In view of its size, he wondered whether the people who lived there had ever thought of putting in a swimming pool, although he realized that it was a surprisingly rare landscaping accessory in the area. Richard could think of only one other home in the neighbourhood that had a pool.

When he arrived in front of the right house, or at least what he thought was the right house, he had trouble persuading Margie to calm herself long enough for Richard to conduct an appropriate reconnoitre. While he was tempted to tie Margie to the edge of the fence which belonged to the house next door, she would have gone crazy. So he decided to have the dog accompany him, up along the side of the house on 240 Belcourt Avenue to check out the back of the house, to ensure that it was the right house. He crept around the corner of the house, verified that the window on the far right side of the second floor was the likely the correct window, and was about to return to the street, his investigation complete for now, when Margie, who had her nose down in the lawn foraging for whatever scents dogs pursue, started to bark and pulled on the leash like she was about to attack. Richard turned from Margie to be suddenly accosted by a man who had just appeared on the house's patio. He appeared to be on the outer edge of middle age, a tall, thin man with a lifeless pallor and a hawkish nose. He had just stepped through the sliding door and was standing on the patio. He was holding a steel cane with one hand and was leaning on the frame of the sliding door with the other. The resulting exhortation from the man was loud, predictable and frightening.

"Hello sir, what the hell are you doing in my backyard?" he shouted, lifting his cane off the patio, looking like he was about to advance on Richard. Margie was still barking, a common display of aggression toward any strange man, Richard was not surprised. The man was apparently ready he thought to accuse Richard and Margie of trespassing, which Richard realized would be completely accurate. He stood there at the corner of the house, considering the invention of an explanation or an excuse. He was standing there acting and being guilty. He could feel a wave of anxiety coursing through his chest like an electric current.

He started to stutter like a thief about to be caught, wordlessly mumbling, a memory of being nabbed shoplifting like a hundred years ago flashing through his mind for a moment and then evaporating. It was another memory that had entered his mind and then escaped. It was like kneeling in a confessional. Then a reply came out, softly and plaintively true. He was confessing.

"I was curious, that's all." Richard explained weakly, his voice barely audible. Margie continued to bark. Richard reflexively struck Margie in the nose with his open hand and then passed her a liver treat, the usual training procedure erroneously reversed. She whimpered for a moment and then laid down. She also seemed a little frightened of the man. He was walking slowly toward the both of them, his cane dragging across the surface with a kind of strange cadence. Richard thought that it was making a sound like chains on a metal sheet. Richard thought the scene almost theatrical, theatrical and creepy. Predictably, the image only enhanced his concern. He was scared of the man advancing toward him with a cane.

The man was now standing on the edge of the patio. "Curious? You're were just curious?" The decibels of his voice had gone up a bit. He was almost yelling. "Curious about what? This is private property. This is my house. I live here, you don't. You sure don't belong here." He then thrust his chin out like he was about to make another accusation, which would have been unnecessary in the circumstances.

"I was walking Margie here over the past week or so." explained Richard. He pointed at Margie, who was still laying down in the driveway, fortified by several liver treats. She had started licking herself, a routine practice, apparently oblivious to the fear that the man still represented. Richard started to expand on his account. "I have been walking my dog on Coolbreeze. I could see into the backyards of the houses on this street. One day, over a week ago, I saw someone in the window of your house here. I saw that same someone four or five days in a row." said Richard, pointing up to the window above the man's head. He didn't dare look. He guessed that the man he had seen maybe ten minutes ago from the other street had withdrawn from the window into the house just as the man with the cane had emerged from it. "So I was curious about it, about the man in your window." Richard delayed for a moment, struggling for further explanation. "I honestly didn't know what I would do if I managed to get closer to the window and the man in it. As I said, I am just curious, too curious I guess. I'm really sorry."

The man first looked up to the window above the patio, seemed to shrug a bit, tilting a little on his cane and then returned his gaze back to Richard with a quizzical look on his face. "Just curiosity you said. I don't know why anyone would be so curious. Ordinarily, somebody might think that you might be planning something, you know like breaking into my house.", which seemed ludicrous given that no one would bring a dog to stake out a man's house for a potential robbery. He paused for a moment and then continued. "Perhaps I will just telephone the police on you and your dog here."

Another flash of anxiety went through him. "You don't have to do that. I mean, I really haven't done anything." said Richard, casually pleading. "I just wanted to make sure, you know, to confirm what I was seeing. I meant no harm, I had no plans to break into your house, no plans to steal anything. Please try to understand." It was a strange request since he couldn't understand his own behaviour himself. Whether he was aware of it or not, it was effecting his most sincere expression. He reminded himself of every single admission he had ever made about any unfortunate action he may have ever committed, including the venal sins, which this trespass surely was.

The man nodded sympathetically he thought, wishfully thinking perhaps. He then tried to stand up straight, pushing himself up on his cane. It was a near impossible task. He managed to get within ten degrees of straight, his cane almost perpendicular to the patio. He then turned over his shoulder to take another look up at the window and then looked back at Richard. Instead of any sort of accusatory stare, he surprisingly offered Richard a crooked grin. It was evident that the man had changed his mind about the entire situation. Apparently, his earnest confession about intention was persuasive enough to change the man's mind. Or so it seemed. Or so Richard wanted it to seem.

"That's my son up there." the man explained, "That's his room up there. He likes to look out the window, sometimes all day, practically every day." He hesitated for a moment and then continued, apparently certain that a further accounting was necessary in the circumstances. He thought about his explanation. He never had to account for the spectacle of his son in the window. He looked up at the window again, motioning Richard to come further onto the patio, allowing him to get a better view of his son. "His name is Andrew. He is twenty years old and he is, as you may have guessed from his habit of staring out the window, a little odd. They used to call boys like him slow, you know retarded, a term I never liked. Now he is regarded as handicapped, mentally handicapped. Doctors have always told my wife and I that the poor kid is autistic although I have never really understood what that means. As I guess you know, there are many different types and they show many different symptoms." He paused again and then added. "I should mention though, that we have only lived in this place for six months or so."

Richard nodded. He was receiving a great deal more information about the man/boy in the window than he had expected. He hadn't noticed that Margie, who would normally be straining at the leash in full throated barking, was still lying at his feet, apparently as interested in the man's story as his master. The man also took note of the dog's sudden serenity. "It looks like your dog is ready for a nap. She didn't look like that a few minutes ago." Richard felt that he owed the man a comment. He was more surprised than the man might have been. Usually, Margie didn't relax until eight o'clock in the evening when her head went down on her paws and the day was over.

"You must have a soothing effect on her. Margie usually doesn't calm down during the day, not like this, especially near a man she doesn't know." Richard offered the man a tentative smile. He acknowledged his smile with a thin grin.

Richard then asked, taking advantage of the apparent improvement in relations between the man and himself, about Andrew. He looked up at the window. Andrew was no longer there, the sight of his father talking to Richard likely enough to spook him somehow. Richard asked about Andrew's care. "Do you look after Andrew by yourself?"

The man looked up at his vacant window wistfully. "Oh no. Taking care of Andrew is difficult at times. I couldn't possibly do it myself. Even when my wife was with us, the two of us couldn't manage it." Richard nodded knowingly, as if he expected the explanation although he briefly wondered about the fate of Andrew's mother. "We have a social worker living with us. His name is Douglas, Douglas Kane. He used to work in a group home. It was the same group home where my wife and I were thinking of placing Andrew. We were lucky. Douglas started talking to the two of us and he decided to come work for us. Four or five months ago, he moved in. He has been marvellous with Andrew." With that, he started back toward to the back door, his cane scrapping across the surface of the patio.

Richard nodded and resumed his smile. He hadn't forgotten. He was still interested in Andrew in that window, specifically the purpose of his staring, the reason, if there was one. "What about Andrew's staring out the window? I am still curious about that you know."

The man, whose name he had not volunteered, had his hand on the handle to the patio door when he turned and tried to reply to Richard. He had a puzzled look on his face, almost as if he either did not have an answer to the question or did not want to provide one. They both stood and looked at each other, waiting for one of them to continue the conversation. He spoke slowly and softly. At first, Richard could barely hear him. He had to take two of the patio's four steps up to the house. With that, Margie started to stir. The man noticed Margie pulling on the leash. He motioned towards the dog and turned back toward the glass patio door. He slid the door open and was suddenly in the house, Richard's question about Andrew and his times at the window unanswered, at least for the time being. Or so he thought.

"I don't know why he stands at the window but it seems to relax him." He had looked back over his shoulder from inside the house. Richard had to step up to the surface of the patio to hear the man's last comment. He then turned and went back down the stairs to attend to Margie who had now resumed barking. His visit at 240 Belcourt Avenue was over. Richard and Margie hurried back to the front of the house and continued their walk. It was almost as if they were escaping.

PREQUEL

May 1955 And Thereafter

Four months after he entered grade one that first time, Richard, who had endured several months of sitting behind a kid named Goudreau who frequently expelled gas, was asked to leave the scholarly precincts of the St. Louis Elementary School. His parents, Rene and Frances, were informed by somebody in the office of the local school board, that their son Richard was not old enough to continue his studies until the next September, the September of 1955 that is, he was being disqualified because he had been born sixteen days into the year of 1949 and therefore was not yet six years old by the end of the year of 1954, the age requirement for entering grade one. He was therefore sixteen days short of qualifying, the decision to remove him made a few days before Christmas. Richard would return the next year, more prepared than any of his new classmates to face the wrath of Miss McCarthy, the grade one teacher. His parents never really explained their motives for attempting to enrole their son in school earlier than ordinarily permitted, his mother wanting him out of the house a possible motive. Either that, or they had plans to accelerate their son's academic career for reasons unknown.

Richard often wondered about the alternate configuration of his history had he stayed in the first grade one in which he had been enrolled. Everything would have been different: his studies, his friends, his participation in athletics. About the latter, he would have been a lot younger and a lot smaller than the boys he would have had to compete against, therefore a lot less successful at sports than he would eventually turn out to be. He thought of one of his old high school classmates who was born in late December. It had given an advantage in sports where age was a determining factor in deciding the league where you played. In any event, Richard sat out another eight months at home with mother, relieved from the anxiety of grade one, at least temporarily, a by-product being that he was remarkably calm when he entered grade one a second time. His two best friends from those days, one of whom ended up his best man at his first wedding, were in that second grade one class, a bit of fortune that followed him until he graduated high school eleven years later.

Sometime during the spring after his abortive entree in the Saint Louis school, he had again noticed, the last time a couple of months after Richard and the family moved in, another boy who would have been expelled from grade one the previous September, prematurely just like Richard. He was standing in a window on the second floor of that old clapboard house immediately behind his house. It was a house that inhabited the last street on the western edge of the old Valois Village, a final physical though pointless barrier against the suburban invasion that had started to eradicate the pastoral life that the old village had enjoyed since all the clapboard houses in the Village had been built, sometime between the advent of the twentieth century and the start of the Great War.

Richard had just finished lunch, his mother's cheese and walnut sandwich already sitting uneasily somewhere in his stomach, when he spotted the boy in the window. He was just standing there, just still as if he was impersonating a mannequin, staring out into the distance that was currently comprised of the two hundred or so homes of the McGill housing development. Before they were built more than a year ago, the distance used to provide a vista of endless acres of woods, rolling green fields, and in the deep distance, a brick making factory only visible because of two tall chimneys.

That sighting prompted the obvious memory from Richard. He just looked at the figure in the window, waiting for him to move, wondering what he was doing there. Just like any other six year old boy, he had been curious, a little frightened and yes, a little guilty with his staring. His father had berated him for staring at any neighbour, commanding him not to bother the neighbours, not mentioning that one of the neighbours was a grumpy old man named Barnes who often fought with neighbours over a variety of minor issues; things like people planting hedges too close to property lines, mothers hanging their washing out on certain days of the week and kids playing ball on the street at all hours. Aside from frequently engaging in disputes with the neighbours, old man Barnes also had a strange, almost creepy habit of sitting on the steps of his front veranda and watching the neighbourhood go by, making a lot of people quite uncomfortable. He eventually figured out that his father was cautioning him about staring at a man who made a habit about staring at everyone else.

On the other hand, when he wasn't staring at Mr. Barnes, he was looking at the boy in the window. Richard felt a little like old man Barnes. He also wondered whether old man Barnes had also noticed the boy staring in the window. Although it did not occur to Richard, while it would be possible, it would require a considerable effort for old man Barnes to himself catch the boy standing in the window, his house being two properties north, its backyard likely too far from the clapboard house to comfortably survey the boy in the window. Richard also wondered whether anyone other than himself had noticed him in the window. That first time, both of them spent maybe five minutes staring, Richard at him and him at nothing in particular. The staring could be a habit, a major fault according to his mother who often rebuked him for going into a stare at the kitchen table during meal times. Miss McCarthy must have raised her voice, if not her yardstick several times at Richard during the four months he attended that first grade one, the one he spent as an apparent imposter, reminding him to pay attention. That first time with the boy in the window, Richard did pay attention. It was curious to him, not surprisingly since he was a kid who was curious about practically everything, that the boy in the window did not seem to move, at least while Richard was looking at him, not a motion, not a twitch, not a wiggle, standing at attention, just like all the elementary school boys were to stand before they lined up and then strode two-by-two into the school after the bell rung.

His reverie was interrupted by his mother announcing dinner. He took one last look at the boy in the window. He was still there. While he had planned to question his parents about the boy in the window, specifically about the family who lived in the house with the window, he never did at the time, fifteen minutes of Howdy Doody on television, a recently purchased black and white set of which Richard's father was particularly proud, taking precedence. Richard would however return to his inquiry about the house with the boy in the window at a later date, on several occasions in fact.

STILL ANOTHER DAY
ON THE STREET

It was maybe three days after his encounter with the man who lived at 240 Belcourt, the house with the man in the second floor window. Richard and Margie had avoided Coolbreeze Street and certainly Belcourt Avenue, concerned that the temptation to catch a glimpse of the man in the window would overwhelm him or, even worse, he would encounter the old man whose son stood in the window. Richard had invested two full nights contemplating his fascination with the man in the window. Not so much the man himself, whoever he was or is, but the fascination itself. He began, unavoidably at first and then almost casually, to think of other circumstances in which obsession had taken over. He had taken Margie along alternative routes all three days, almost indifferent to the specifics, walking in straight lines so his contemplations would not result in him or Margie end up getting hit by a car. Margie was behaving surprisingly well, no barking at bearded men, other dogs, or nothing at all, no straining on the leash, as if she knew that her master had larger matters on his mind. Jean had often suggested that dogs were often perceptive regarding their master's moods, which presumably was the basis for dogs having secured the designation as man's best friend. Richard had no opinion either way, not having thought much about it.

Along the walk on the day after he had spoke to the father of the man in the window, his thoughts were predictable. He replayed the conversation, as if he was searching for evidence of something. While his interest in that encounter waned, it had managed to spark another memory. It was not as haunted as that person in the window. It was only a memory. The man in that window had been a hallowed neighbourhood relic, someone who managed to preoccupy practically every kid in the area. The man looked to be an elderly man who everyone called "Old George". No one knew how old he was or whether that was his real name. He had emerged at some point in the Village of Valois's history as a character who both fascinated and frightened every kid and some of their parents in his neighbourhood. He was a little more than a vagrant, a drifter who didn't really drift, an aimless vagabond who lived in a dilapidated shack two blocks east of Columbus Avenue, the first of the five suburban streets laid out and built by McGill Construction Limited and on which the Matthews family had lived.

"Old George" resided on the edge of the old section of Valois, one street over from Parkdale, the street on which the house with the boy in the window stood. Everybody in the neighbourhood was at least aware of "Old George", who did little but accumulate junk in the spring and summer and collect beer and pop bottles at the football games on autumn weekends at Valois Park, there being a semi-professional team playing there since the late 1940s. In the winter, "Old George" took care of the rinks at Valois Park, the latter position probably the only way he could actually make a living, in cash that he then spent playing poker in the rear of a local barber shop. Like most of the boys in the neighbourhood, Richard was interested in "Old George's" derelict shack. They had been told, by some of the older boys in the neighbourhood, that it was a one room hell, a one room domicile equipped with a stove, a table, a sink, a toilet, and a bed but no television, no radio. Neither Richard nor any of his friends had any evidence of the accuracy of that report on the details of the furnishings in "Old George's" place. However, they believed it.

They did personally investigate the property on which his shack sat, their bravery enough to support a field trip every now and then. Behind the shack were piles of mostly unidentifiable objects, the junk that most of the neighbourhood was certain would eventually be sold to all sorts of unsavoury characters, including people like the local shoe maker, whose name was Hyduk and who fought on the wrong side during the war. Other possible customers were a nameless Charlie Starkweather type who worked at the local filling station and a candy store owner named Helen who also happened to be the only female cab driver in the area. The boys, hardly connoisseurs of junk, were still savvy enough to identify discarded automotive parts, broken chairs, steel pipes and aluminum cans among the swag available to the customers of "Old George".

Still, Richard was particularly fascinated by "Old George", more so than his pals he thought, who were generally convinced that their interest was transitory at best, an interest that would evaporate with the next comic book. Sure, like pretty well everyone else in the neighbourhood, Richard was afraid of "Old George". In addition to his shack and his property, which were bad enough, he cast a frightening impression, suggesting some sort of caricature from a horror movie, like maybe one of the many actors who scared audiences wearing fake scars and a cosmetic pallor. All "Old George" needed to complete the role was a black cape and a scythe. Richard had seen "Old George" many times, the latter's work at the local rink during the winter the most obvious occasion for any sighting and always from a discrete distance. The prospect of getting any closer was a scary proposition. He was elderly thin and relatively tall although it was difficult to say since he was usually hunched over, almost stumbling when he walked. He always wore a tattered baseball cap, some remnant from a bygone era when the name Abner Doubleday was still familiar. He smoked incessantly, usually if not always sucking on cigarettes that were not purchased in retail stores, filterless handmade butts his preference, forty cents for a pack of normal cigarettes apparently too expensive for a man of such little means. Although Richard realized much later that the term applied to "Old George" was probably a trifle anachronistic, he always thought of him as a classic hobo, a vagrant who in his younger days would have been riding the proverbial rails.

When the more mature Richard thought of "Old George", which was hardly the frequent occurrence that it may have been when he was a kid, he invariably wondered about his eventual fate. Although Richard ended up living in that neighbourhood for almost fifteen years, he never did find out, never hearing even a rumour of his eventual demise. The shack came down at one point, the year Richard could not recall. He was in college when he first noticed that the shack was no longer on the corner of Donegani and Broadview. It was suddenly an empty lot, hardly a fitting testimonial to such a well known character in the community. Frances, Richard's mother, occasionally an intrepid busybody when she wanted to be, later informed him, during one of their infrequent conversations that the police had been seen at "Old George's" place several weeks past. Although a local constable named Hume often visited "Old George", the presence of stolen merchandise a constant possibility, Hume was accompanied this time by several other officers, not to mention an ambulance. Someone later theorized to Frances that such a contingent could only mean one thing: "Old George" had been found dead. The mystery, at least according to Frances and her neighbours, was how anyone would know "Old George" had died in the first place. They laughed about it.

As for Richard, he was less interested in the circumstances of the death of "Old George" than he was in the life that preceded it. He actually proposed a research project on "Old George" to one of his college instructors, a history prof named Grady. The idea, however, lasted about as long as it took Mr. Grady to laugh it off. He advised Richard that such projects were usually, if not always, limited to people or incidents of historical importance and/or interest, characteristics that were not arguably applicable to the story of "Old George".

Walking down Coolbreeze with Margie that day, he had the fleeting thought of writing the story of "Old George" as a retirement project. It sounded like a good idea for at least two minutes, at which point a black pug ambled along across the other side of the street and precipitated a spasm of barking from Margie. By the time Richard managed to establish control of Margie, any thought of "Old George" and his history was gone. And the house at 233 Coolbreeze was coming up on the left.

Almost by rote, an unexpected example of Pavlovian conditioning Richard thought, Margie stopped in front of the house at 233 Coolbreeze, waiting for her master to decide whether to check out its backyard and the house behind it. Richard stood with Margie for moment, fed her a couple of treats, and finally walked up the driveway to survey the second floor of the house at 240 Belcourt Street. And there he was, almost waiting, standing motionless in the window on the second floor, apparently staring without point, not fixed on any horizon, simply gazing. He looked like he was impersonating a statue, like someone in a wax museum. Three days ago, while he had been discussing the man in the window with his father, he hadn't taken any particular notice of the man in the window, or more accurately, the son in the window. He did not know, therefore, whether the window man had taken any notice of the conversation that was taking place below his window, which was not particularly surprising, given his normal disposition of standing still and staring.

Usually, anytime he was looking up at the window man, he wondered about the purpose of his fixation, this apparently irrational interest in a man who apparently had an irrational interest of his own, like staring from a second story window into nothingness. This day, he pondered that irrationality again, standing there with Margie sitting surprisingly calm at his feet, his absentminded and almost constant provision of liver treats to her an appropriate sedation, an adequate substitute it appeared for the canine Prozac she was taking when he and Jean first brought the dog home as a rescue from the Humane Society. For several moments of tranquility, a benefit with which he was not normally familiar when walking Margie, he become the six year old boy looking at a boy in another window, one in an old clapboard house in the old neighbourhood, more than sixty years ago. He also had enough time to realize that he had not thought about that boy in the other window for some time. He used to think about him all the time, not for decades but he used to.

Richard stood there for a while, the limit of Margie's patience beginning to fray, like her collar was able to lose its usefulness, a dangerous situation if you were trying to handle a dog like Margie. He figured she was about to break into a usual demonstration of misbehaviour, about to pull him down the street like an old woman tied to a shopping cart with a busted wheel. So he started to gently back out of the driveway of 233 Coolbreeze with Margie, trying to lead her down the block on the remainder of her scheduled walk. Margie didn't seem to want to walk in that direction, tugging him east rather than west, back over ground they had just travelled. She led Richard across the street toward the house on the corner. It had caught fire more than a year ago but had not been burned to the ground. It was, however, damaged enough for the family who had been living there to abandon the place.

Since then, there had not been any action taken to dispose of the house, an astounding circumstance for a neighbourhood that usually saw real estate properties being sold within weeks, if not days of becoming available. Richard and Jean, not to mention several of the neighbours, including in particular the old Italian couple across the street, regarded that state of affairs as a mystery, prompting all variety of possible explanations. The prevailing theory regarding the origin of the fire was that the owner of the house, who had leased it to a relative who inexplicably never returned after abandoning the house once the fire started, had arranged for an arson for the insurance money, a motive that was as predictable as it was fascinating. Neighbours were all atwitter, as observed by the elderly Italian woman, the speculation ranging from a clandestine love affair to a large gambling debt. In any event, the house remained an enigma. It was said that there was a considerable competition among local real estate agents for the listing, the commission on the property on which it stood worth more than the cost of a BMW automobile, a popular automobile in the neighbourhood. That was his last thought as he stood before the boarded up house with the flashes of burn marks all over the place.

As he continued his walk, he wondered whether the man in the window could see the burnt house on the corner or whether the man in the window saw anything at all from his perch on the second floor of 240 Belcourt, his stare apparently absolute. He was wondering that when Margie suddenly went after a pair of Huskies presumably minding their own business on the other side of the street. The dog sprang and Richard was practically pulled out of his shoes. Fortunately, he held on the leash firmly and long enough to stop her in her tracks. In doing so though, he thought she was going to break her neck, a persistent danger given Margie's penchant for occasional displays of excitability. In fact, both Richard and Jean were surprised that the crazy dog hadn't seriously injured herself with her gymnastic reactions to dogs or people who frightened her for some reason.

While concern for their dog's well being was always ubiquitous, so was their embarrassment with explaining Margie's misbehaviour to other dog walkers. While Jean was relatively relaxed in such circumstances, Richard was often paranoid, worried that any explanation would somehow fall short, increasing his embarrassment, a curious reaction because Richard generally seemed dismissive, or claimed to be dismissive, of the opinions of the neighbours. Jean often rebuked him about this apparent inconsistency in his disposition.

Heading home, he came across an abandoned cellular telephone on the street, a relatively old fashioned model that appeared to be still functional. He briefly inspected the photograph gallery, thumbing through maybe a dozen pictures, none of which attracted his interest. For a moment, he actually considered bringing the phone home for examination although he also realized that he was not familiar enough with the functions of cellphones to actually detect anything of significance. Instead, he left the phone on the top of the postal box at the end of Coolbreeze. By the time he arrived home, he had forgotten about Margie's incident with the huskies but had managed to develop another proposition about the man in the window. He had decided to walk by 233 Coolbreeze to survey the second floor window of the house at 240 Belcourt, this time in the evening, in darkness. That was his plan for the next time if he decided to continue with his interest.

ANOTHER PREQUEL, ANOTHER PERSPECTIVE

His name was Gary Vessey although he was more generally known as Butchy, or so the story went. He was born in the rustic clapboard house in which he has lived since. That was more than thirty years ago, back before the advent of the World War II, back when the rustic clapboard house was situated on a large farm, at least ten acres over which very little actual farming actually took place. The house itself was built sometime before the turn of the century, supposedly his grandfather was the builder. Back then, the Vessey home was only one of maybe five houses which would later constitute the street named Parkdale in the town of Valois. The house, which at one time did not even have a street address, now sat on the precipice of a growing suburban development that was threatening to cover the entire ten acres that the Vesseys previously owed with streets and streets of identical three bedroom houses with identical three children, carefully manicured lawns, hedges, fences and asphalt driveways. The Vessey family, Gary, aka Butchy, his wife Dorothy, and their children, three boys and two girls, had all watched with a sense of bewildered regret as the houses for their new neighbours were built, sold and inhabited in the last two months of 1953 and the first several months of 1954.

Gary Vessey was initially convinced that his world was about to come to an end, often suggesting that he was glad that both his parents were not alive to witness the extinction of the farm and an invasion of hundreds of city types. But the rest of the family was not as sure as the head of the family about the dire circumstances facing them. After all, they still lived in a house that had been in the family for decades and they still had a relatively large property, it being twice the size of the properties on which the new houses sat. Besides, Gary had never really worked the farm, nor did anyone else for that matter. He had worked for the General Electric plant in Lachine for more than twenty years. Dorothy took care of the kids and, while she did not socialize much, she seemed friendly enough. There were five children, an eighteen year old boy named Kenny who worked in a plastics company in Dorval, two teenage girls who attended the only high school in the area, a ten year old boy who went to an elementary school which was about half a mile away, and the youngest, a boy who went to the St Louis school for a couple of days but now never left the house. There was something obviously strange about him. Richard's father said the kid was plain crazy while his mother was much more charitable, often wondering why the Vesseys had not placed their youngest in an institution, the most notable being the Douglas Hospital in Verdun.

Many years later, after the Matthews boys were on their own and their parents had moved to Ottawa, the topic of the Vesseys had come up during a conversation about the old neighbourhood, a discussion that had been prompted when his mother mentioned that she had come across an obituary for a Mrs. Mary Jackson, who lived with her husband Morris and their son Douglas beside the Vesseys on Parkdale Avenue. Apparently, at least according to Richard's mother, Mary Jackson, despite having little in common with Dorothy Vessey, was close to her, happily extending to her and the family all matter of benevolence, helping her out with the kids in particular, advice regarding doctors, schools and the like. As a result, Mary Jackson was quite familiar with the Vesseys. On the other hand, the Vesseys knew virtually nothing about the Jacksons, a situation with which Mary Jackson was content. Richard's mother was told that the youngest Vessey boy, whose name was Scott, eventually ended up in some sort of group home for the mentally handicapped, apparently when Gary and Dorothy couldn't really care for him anymore. Neither Vessey nor anyone else for that matter could say specifically what was wrong with Scott. The most obvious symptom of his handicap was the fact that he never said a word although he occasionally emitted strange sounds, almost all of which verged on the alarming. Again, according to Mrs. Jackson, Dorothy had told her that Scott Vessey's favourite pursuit was simple staring, almost always out the window of his room on the second floor of the Vessey house. Richard's mother said that she wondered whether Scott was staring out the window of his group home.

⬤

It came as no surprise that his walk down memory lane about the Vessey family with his mother reminded Richard of his occasional fascination with the figure who he used to see staring out of a second floor window of their house all those years ago. As faded as it was, the memory became back real enough. After that first time he saw Scott, whose name he did not know at the time, it was only a few days after he had started school before he would notice him again. After that, he would start to frequently see him staring out that window, at least until he went back to school. When he had seen him again, he had recognized him immediately as the boy that Miss McCarthy had chastised so harshly with her ruler that first day at school but had not seen since the day after that. He remembered, he had been reading or more accurately re-reading an Adventures of Mighty Mouse comic, a copy of which had been purchased by his father for his fifth birthday.

Several months later, Richard joined Scott on the sidelines. It was after he had spent a few months in grade one, at least the first time, just after he had been told by his parents that they had been notified by the St. Louis school, or more precisely the Montreal Catholic School Commission Board, that he was not eligible to continue in grade one since he was not six years old by December 31 of that year, sixteen days short of being qualified.

So it was that his parents were informed that their son Richard's official entry into grade one would be delayed until the following September when he definitely would be six years old. His parents had been mistaken about the effect on Richard. He was hardly saddened by his banishment from grade one. He was generally unhappy about grade one. He was probably the youngest, if not the shortest boy in the class. He was seated close to the front of the class, behind that boy who smelled funny. He was within easy reach of Mrs. McCarthy's dreaded yardstick. Although she never intended to discipline Richard, he would sometimes be the accidental victim of a swing intended for another student in the class, more often than not the gas expelling kid who sat in front of him. While he had made some friends, boys named Doug and Gord came to mind, he missed his neighbourhood chums Brian and Peter who had been too young for registration for that school year. He also didn't like taking the bus to school. The trips were almost always chaotic and frightening, kids throwing things and fighting with each other, and the bus driver, a fat man named Lavigne who all the kids called "the washing machine", ceaselessly yelling at his passengers. Finally, he was reluctant to spend any time in the schoolyard. It was worse than the school bus, with the fights, always between boys in the higher grades. Then, there were the host of schoolyard games like British bulldog and cops and robbers causing the younger kids to run for cover. Richard was happy to escape, at least until next year when he, now older and physically bigger, would be better equipped to survive grade one again.

As Richard stared at the motionless Scott in the second floor window in the Vessey house during one of his early observations, he had noticed, a miracle considering that he was generally an empty headed five year old who was seldom observant, that Scott was usually wearing the same clothes he wore the first time he saw him, at school a few days previous. Although it did not occur to him at the time, and it never would occur to him for decades, it was a curious coincidence that Scott was wearing blue shorts and a red t-shirt in the first sighting and every sighting afterwards. Richard waited at the window, sitting on the radiator, staring at a boy who was staring as well, not at him but at something, the identification of which continued to remain unknown. Scott was just staring, not moving. To Richard, it was like looking at a picture, like a photograph in the newspapers his father read every day. He sat there on the radiator until his mother called him for lunch.

His mother was happy to see Richard either sitting in his room staring at Scott Vessey or playing in the backyard or on the street in front of the house. She had Richard's two younger brothers to look after, both of them fairly active and therefore quite a strain. So when Richard reported on his sighting of Scott, she reacted quite positively, thinking that she was encouraging him to make friends with Scott, his condition unknown to her at the time. She wanted to keep him as active as possible. She remembered a neighbour, a woman who had four kids at home herself, had suggested buying a television, a revolutionary new home appliance that could be a pretty good distraction. The neighbour told Frances that sometimes the kids would spend the entire day watching the screen and therefore stay out of trouble. It sounded like a good idea. When she brought up the idea of buying a television set with Rene, he told her that even with his department store discount, they still couldn't afford to buy a television, at least not then.

Still, he continued to watch Scott in his window, often checking in every day to ensure that he was still in the window.

By March of the next year, further to his mother's suggestion, if not insistence, he had reduced his Scott surveillance days to maybe three days a week, less than half the time he had invested previously. In a way, the habit was further modified when his mother ran into his friend Brian's mother Sally at Steinberg's. She invited Richard to her son's birthday party the next week. It was no surprise when Sally brought up Richard, asking about her adjustment to having her eldest back home again rather than at school. Frances was a trifle reluctant to respond to what she could have regarded as a personal question, not being friendly enough with Brian's mother Sally to confide. But she did anyway. "He was happy, relieved I think. I think he was a little scared, of school I mean. I guess any five year old would be. He never said anything to Rene or me about school but a parent could tell. All I can say is that his mood sure got better once the Commission decided that he was too young and sent him home."

Sally nodded throughout her explanation. "I think I can understand. Like most mothers I guess, I'm worried about Brian. He's my eldest too. He looks a little scared any time I mention school or grade one. I think he's thinking about it, not often mind you, but enough. I mean, he's just about to turn six years old. I don't think they think about anything but dingy toys and playing outside with Pete, your Richard and some other kids in the neighbourhood. But a couple of days ago, a school bus went by when we were both out in the yard and I mentioned it to Brian and you could see that he was bothered by it. In fact, he gripped my hand. He was definitely worried, like a lot of little kids I guess."

Frances mentioned the scene when she accompanied Richard to his first day at the St. Louis School the previous September. "Pretty well all the kids were crying, all except the ones who were repeating. Richard was crying too. He kept it up until they started to line up." Frances didn't mention Miss McCarthy and the ruler, mainly because she hadn't known about it, Richard having not told her about the incident. He had been worried that his mother might somehow blame him for Miss McCarthy's pernicious use of her ruler.

Sally reached out and touched Frances on the arm. "Well, I guess my Brian will have to face that in a few months, won't he?", referring to her son's first day at school, four months hence. "On the other hand, your boy will be a veteran in first grade. I don't expect him to be doing any crying this time."

Frances was just about to go about the rest of her business when Sally mentioned Brian's birthday party. She invited Richard and mentioned in passing that Richard's other friend Peter will likely be there as well. Frances thanked her and assured Sally that Richard would be there. "Tell your boy that they'll be quarters in the birthday cake." She did not say whether a birthday present would be required. And Frances did not think to ask.

As soon as Frances got home, she put away her groceries and then went into Kevin and Richard's room to inform him of the invitation to Brian's birthday party. Richard just happened to be sitting in his usual spot on the room's radiator, staring out at the Vessey place. He appeared motionless, as he usually did, almost transfixed, gazing into the backyards. For a moment, she thought about giving Richard those binoculars that Rene facetiously proposed that they buy for him when he first mentioned watching Scott. But Frances had taken the proposal seriously and had started to pester Rene about it. Rene finally yielded. They had intended to give him binoculars for his birthday in January but they never got around to it. Although the cost for a pair of simple 8X21 Bushnells was less than $10, the price that Rene would have paid in the sports department of his store, Frances had run out of her allowance the week before Richard's birthday. So she had asked for some extra money for groceries. After expressing some noises of complaint, Rene gave her an extra $20 and dropped the binocular plan. Still, that evening, Frances reminded her husband of the plan to buy binoculars for Richard. Rene said that, on reflection, he had decided that it was not really a good idea, explaining that possession of binoculars or a telescope, which had been an earlier suggestion, would only encourage their son to increase his staring into the Vessey yard, a habit he had almost given up anyway. Frances grudgingly agreed and that was almost the end of the discussion of the Scott phenomenon in the Matthews household.

The family's television set arrived within the week. It was large, a black and white model – there was no such thing as colour television back then – that was encased in polished wood and looked more like a piece of furniture than some sort of device. It actually fit in nicely with the stereo system they bought last year and was placed in the opposite corner of their living room. With the arrival of the television set, Richard and his two brothers were almost immediately afflicted with an addiction to daytime television, mainly cartoon shows like Tom & Jerry, Felix the Cat, Popeye the Sailor Man, Mighty Mouse, as well as Captain Kangaroo and the Mickey Mouse Club. As a result, Richard basically substituted his viewing out the window at the Vessey place with television, having limited his surveillance of Scott to weekends and occasional evenings before bedtime. It appeared that the compulsion was fading. It was a late August afternoon, a Tuesday, and the three of them, Brian, Pete and Richard, were parked in Richard's room. Richard was staring out the window, occasionally looking back over his shoulder to check his two friends going through the latter's comic books. Both Pete and Brian started to spend a lot time at Richard's house, going thorough his comics, his toys, mainly matchbox cars and toy soldiers, watching the family's television set, which was a little newer than the models that Brian and Pete's families had in their places, and enjoying his mother's cookies. During a discussion of Richard's old habit of staring into the Vessey backyard, Pete tapped him on the shoulder and made a suggestion. Brian was down on the floor playing with Richard's die-cast cars, making quiet little motor sounds as he pushed them up and down the floor. Brian probably didn't hear Pete's suggestion.

"Hey Ricky," Pete practically shouting, excited with his sudden thought. "You used to like staring at that guy Scott so much, why don't we sneak over there and take a closer look." Richard, who had turned away from the window when Pete tapped him, looked at him momentarily with a slight grimace. Brian then up to his knees, suddenly engaged in the emerging conspiracy.

"Huh" replied Richard as if he hadn't heard his friend.

Pete nodded his head and mumbled a laugh. "Yeah, we can go over there, like to get a closer look at that guy in the window, you know, that kid Scott."

"How can we do that?" asked Richard, sounding a little scared. "We can't just climb the fence and walk over there. He'll see us and tell. Besides, I don't much care anymore."

"You used to, didn't you?" responded Pete. "You still like staring at that kid, don't you? You are doing it now, aren't you?"

Richard provided his two friends with an embarrassed shrug.

Pete moved closer to Richard and the window. So did Brian. "Maybe we can go through the yard next door." said Pete, pointing to the Jackson's place.

"That's where Doug Jackson lives." Richard informed Pete and Brian. "He and his mother are always home. They'll see us or hear us." Richard then turned back toward the window. He was now staring at the Jackson place.

Then Brian got to his feet and was now standing behind his two friends, also looking out the window. "Just sneak over there. Pretend we're cutting through, like we did at the Gallaghers.", a reference to an adventure the three experienced the previous week when they went through the Gallagher's backyard to get to Windcrest Avenue, the next street over from Columbus. All three of them took the shortcut for the simple adventure of it. They were scared but excited. They were almost intoxicated when they made it into Brain's backyard, giggling like they were being tickled. Still, despite the triumph of their escapade, they were worried that the Gallaghers would somehow find out about their caper.

Richard was nervous. Like most six year olds faced with a dilemma, particularly something that could get them in some sort of trouble, he had a grip on his genitals like he had to go. Brian and Pete were comparatively calm, both of them having already shown more daring than Richard in the short time the three of them had been friends.

Pete then piped up with his own suggestion to allay Richard's fears. "We're going with you, just like we did with the Gallagher yard. It'll be okay."

Richard just sat there on the radiator for a moment and thought about Pete's proposal. He decided to go along. "Okay, when should we go?"

Both Brian and Pete were standing and already at the door to Richard's room. "Now." said Pete. It was three o'clock in the afternoon, three hours to dinner in the Matthews house, when the old man came home. They would have the time. Richard nodded like Miss McCarthy had just ordered him to the principal's office. Not that it ever happened to Richard in his abbreviated stay in grade one but he had been witness to several classmates, only the older guys and poor Scott it seemed, being sent down.

They tumbled out of Richard's room and out the house. "Going out to play." Richard called out to his mother as the three of them went down the stairs, through the kitchen, and out the backdoor. Mrs. Matthews was over the sink at the kitchen window and waved to them as they crossed their own yard towards the fence separating the Matthews' yard from the Jacksons'. Pete was leading the three of them as they walked through the Matthews' garden, carefully not to step on any of their vegetables. Sure that no one was looking, Richard having cautioned his pals that Mrs. Jackson sometimes was seen during the week managing her flower pots behind her house, they climbed the Jacksons' fence, crossed Jacksons' backyard, and hid themselves in the Jackson garage. The three of them were then looking out of the window in the rear of the Jackson's garage. They could look out at the entire Vessey backyard, which was not burdened with gardens, flowers, or even grass to any extent, the surface of their yard mainly dirt with occasional strips of grass. The yard was empty, which was surprising since, aside from Mrs. Vessey, there were five Vessey children, four of which were not standing in front of a second floor window staring. While he didn't know for certain, Richard thought that the four Vessey children were likely playing in the park, it being a sunny afternoon in August. They could not see Mrs. Vessey, who Richard's mother often said usually spent her entire day doing laundry.

"Let's just sneak across the yard to your guy's window. I don't think anyone will see us." whispered Pete. Brian and Richard both nodded. Still crouching, they left the garage and started to sneak along the wall of the Vessey house in their yard, slowly lurching toward a spot under the window on the second floor from which Scott stared. It took them maybe five minutes or so to reach the spot. They stepped back from the wall and looked up at Scott's window. As expected, he was starring out over their heads. The three explorers looked at him, not really knowing what to expect. Why were they there? What did they expect to see?

"Maybe we should try to get his attention?" suggested Pete. "Make some noise or something." The other two just shrugging, not knowing what to do. Then Richard counselled caution. "I don't know. Maybe his mother will notice if we do that." Brian and Pete nodded. They then just continued to kneel there. Being six years old, none of them were wearing watches. They didn't count or anything, they just waited. Nobody knew for how long.

Richard was looking up from his squatting position, staring at Scott, not really paying any attention, thinking about what to do next, wishing there was somebody, preferably somebody older, who could suggest their next move. He looked at Pete who looked like he had abandoned the stakeout. He had reached into his pocket, pulled out and started to examine a couple of those comic-strip wrappers that came with Bazooka bubble gum. Brian was in a sitting position, apparently lost in thought, almost hypnotized, not paying attention to anything really, maybe just wanting to forget about the Scott project and go home for some chocolate milk and cookies.

Suddenly, for the first time, Richard thought he saw Scott actually move in the window. Maybe he was just imagining it but he thought he was looking down, at the yard, not at the horizon but at somewhere or something in the yard. He almost thought he was pointing at something on the lawn.

NIGHT AFTER DAY
ON THE STREET

It was a few days after he found the abandoned cellular telephone on the street. He had come to regard the discovery as some sort of sign, unsure of the meaning. Over the next several days, he had started to take an alternate route on his walks of Margie, going by neither 233 Coolbreeze nor 240 Belcourt. His plan, as he developed it maybe a week after he was caught spying by the owner of the house at 240 Belcourt, was to walk by the Coolbreeze address during the evening, a walk without Margie who never like to be walked anytime it was dark or approximating dark. In the meantime, he had tried to put the man in the window at 240 Belcourt and his father out of his mind. But it was difficult and maybe even impossible as the thought of the man in the second floor window seemed unavoidable. He started to envision his obsession with the man in that second floor window as a possible Twilight Zone episode, back when they were shown in black and white. He could not, however, conceive of a possible ending for such an episode, that twist of narrative that made the show as popular as it was, that other dimension through which the viewers travelled. He had always regarded Rod Serling as some sort of a hero, right down to the cool way he smoked a cigarette.

It was a Wednesday evening. He told Jean that he was going for a walk, the purpose being to check out the backyard of 240 Belcourt from his usual vantage point on Coolbreeze. But it would be his first sighting of the window at night and his first sighting without the dog. He outlined his plan to Jean who acted like she was interested but he knew she was feigning curiosity as she had since the second or third time he mentioned the man in the window. He was retired she thought, maybe he had nothing better to do, although she wished he'd find something else. She had again suggested he return to writing, an interest he pursued from time to time ever since she had met him over forty years ago, back when he had the nerve, if not the ambition to present himself as a writer, a collection of short stories, some college era poetry and two unfinished novels the only evidence of his literary aspirations. But every time she brought it up, usually if not always when they were both in good moods, Richard would suddenly turn defensive, as if she was accusing him of something, like a missed opportunity. He just did not like to hear it. So she didn't suggest that he return to his literary pursuits too often. Besides, she concluded that it could be worse. After all, a strange though innocent hobby like obsessing about a man standing in a neighbourhood window wasn't exactly terrible, only weird. So she went along without comment, only the odd suggestion every now and then. She even suggested that he write about his obsession with the man in the window although she didn't use the word obsession. For a moment, he seemed to be listening.

It was nine o'clock in the evening. It was a strange feeling walking in the neighbourhood without Margie pulling him along. He had no leash in his hand, no plastic bag full of beef liver treats, no plastic bags for her poop, he was walking free. He walked around the block until he reached 233 Coolbreeze. He stood in front of the address for a moment and then started up the driveway, creeping slowly as he had noticed that lights were on in both the living room and one of the bedrooms upstairs. He stopped by the garage and looked over the fence at the house at 240 Belcourt. There did not appear to be any lights on there except, and Richard was only guessing, perhaps in the front bedroom on the second floor and the porch. He then looked up at the window in the rear of the second floor. He saw a ghost figure, little more than an outline, the only available light coming from the bedroom on the front side of the house and maybe the light from the porch. He couldn't really tell whether Andrew was standing in his window staring out into the darkness. He crept closer to the fence separating the two properties until he was standing as close as he could. He was in a crouch, looking up. Andrew would look like a shadow, barely recognizable as the man he had seen during his many walks with Margie.

He continued to look, wishing he had bought and then brought a pair of binoculars, something he had been contemplating for several weeks but was reluctant to do. The idea of standing on either Coolbreeze or Belcourt with a pair of binoculars was a little too obvious. It could precipitate one of the neighbours to call the police or, failing that, mention it to each other.

On the other hand, he thought that maybe binoculars may not be such a bad idea if he were to use them in the dark. Maybe next time he thought. He stood there looking at the window on the second floor, wondering whether he would get a better look at some point. He concluded that it was unlikely. So he stood up and started to return to the street. He was halfway down the driveway to the street when he noticed a man, a portly man about Richard's age wearing a baseball cap, standing at the end of the driveway. He hesitated for a moment, sort of nodded, and then continued to the end of the driveway onto the street. He stopped a couple of feet from the man standing there on the street.

Richard greeted the man with a curt nod. He recognized him. He lived further up on Coolbreeze toward Hawthorne. He would often see him in front of his house, a small cottage with white stucco walls and a relatively new green roof, tending to his yard or shovelling his driveway, both of which were almost always pristine. They would nod to each other, just like they did almost every day and just like they did on this night.

The man in the baseball cap returned Richard's original nod, as reluctant as it was, and started a conversation. "Evening." There was a slight pause. "Where's your dog?" He pushed his baseball cap further up on his head. He had a slight smile on his face, almost a smirk.

Richard answered. "I didn't bring her tonight. She doesn't like the dark. I feel kind of strange walking without her."

The man with the cap nodded. "I know what you mean. My old dog was the same way." He then spread his hands out and made a surprising observation. "I assume you're here to catch the show.", pointing to the house at 240 Belcourt.

"Pardon me." replied a slightly stunned Richard. He certainly did not expect anyone to become so quickly aware of his intentions. He had been certain that he was being sufficiently secretive, not that he thought that he was committing anything improper but it would still prove a little embarrassing if he were caught spying on one of his neighbours by one of his other neighbours. Still, on the other hand, he should not been surprised when one of those neighbours saw him crawling around in the backyard of 233 Coolbreeze.

The man with the baseball cap continued. He had an explanation. "Hey, don't be surprised. I may be just as curious as you are."

"Curious? Really." Richard responded, again with a stunned inflection in his voice.

The man with the baseball cap further explained. "I first saw the guy in the window on Belcourt after he and his father moved in. Just by chance mind you, just by chance. After that first time, I started seeing him in that window every time I went by, either driving, walking, or cycling. He was there every damn time, every damn time. So I become curious as to what the guy was doing up in that window. Just like you are curious."

Richard nodded, still a little anxious but calming down somewhat. "To be honest, I have to admit to being a bit surprised that somebody else is curious about him." He paused, still looking at the man in the cap with some trepidation. "By the way, the guy's name is Andrew. His father told me." Richard then placed his hands to his side in a gesture of resignation, as if he had just been caught admitting to some sort of falsehood. "And oh yeah, my name is Richard."

The man in baseball cap reached out to shake his hand. They shook hands. "Please to meet you. My name is Pat, Pat Bissell. I live up at 255." Mr. Bissell pointed up the street.

"I guess you know that I know where you live." Richard said, a slight smile surfacing on his face. "I walk by your place practically every day."

"I know, I've seen you too, practically every day." admitted Pat, chuckling softly, "I don't think I've ever walked by your place. Fact is.... fact is....I don't know where you live." The chuckle erupted into a serious laugh, like he was telling himself a joke that he thought was irresistibly humorous.

Richard returned with a prompt reply. "275 Lakeview, a block over, down near the corner with Fisher."

"Right." said Pat. He paused and moved a little closer to Richard. "Did you actually speak to his father?"

"Yeah, I spoke to him. But it was more like him speaking to me you know." Confided Richard.

"You run into him on the street?" asked Pat.

"Sort of. He ran into me in the backyard of his place." explained Richard. "He kind of caught me in his backyard."

Pat looked up and smiled. "He caught you? Caught you doing what?"

Richard returned the smile and explained. "Margie and I – Margie is my dog – sneaked into their backyard to get a closer look at Andrew. I admit it was a stupid thing to do but I got so curious that I had to do it, at least once."

"And you got caught." pointed out Pat.

"Yeah, we got caught, Margie and I." replied Richard. "To be honest, I thought he wouldn't be home. It was two o'clock in the afternoon for god's sake."

Pat frowned and observed. "I heard the guy's retired, just like the two of us." I guess Pat had assumed that Richard was retired as well, a predictable guess considering that he saw Richard and Margie walking by his house nearly every day around the same time.

"How do you know he's retired?" Richard inquired.

"Our neighbour Mrs. Guzzo told me. She damn well knows everything about the neighbourhood." said Pat, "I've lived on this street for thirty years and I'll bet she's been here for fifty. No wonder she knows everything. Hell, she's like the neighbourhood's Google."

"Good to know." answered Richard in a low voice. "Good to know."

They both stood there in silence for a moment staring at the rear of the 240 Belcourt and contemplating their next comments. Richard told his new friend Pat that Andrew's father had not formally introduced himself but had told him that he moved in six months ago, a fact that he assumed that Mrs. Guzzo had already related. In response, Pat said that the father's name was Stewart Davidson. "Did he say anything about his son?"

Richard related his information that Stewart Davidson had told him during their conversation that day behind 240 Belcourt. "He said his son was autistic and that he and a social worker named Douglas look after him."

"Autistic, that's tough." muttered Pat.

"Yeah, it's tough, real tough." replied Richard.

They both went silent again. Pat said he was heading home, something about going home to watch television with Mrs. Bissell. He tapped Richard on the shoulder and started up Coolbreeze. Richard walked in the opposite direction. The night was over.

—

Richard arrived home after a slow, solitary walk returning from 233 Coolbreeze and his conversation with Mr. Bissell. It was during the walk that the name of Scott Vessey came to him like a revelation, like something divine, like Paul on the road to or from Damacus. Now he remembered, no explanation but the mysteries of the human mind. Scott Vessey had been another man in a second floor window, the second floor of a house that stood behind his family home on Columbus Avenue in Pointe Claire, more than sixty years ago.

He discussed the night's encounter with Jean when he finally arrived home that night. She shrugged and suggested to him, for the millionth time it seemed, that he forget Andrew Davidson and his window on the second floor of the house at 240 Belcourt Avenue. Richard had ignored Jean's entreaties many times since he had started watching Andrew. But this time, having finally rediscovered the memory of Scott Vessey, he was ready to listen to Jean's guidance and forget both of them.

A DISCOVERY

It was almost a year after he had conquered his obsession problems with the man in the second floor window of a house in his neighbourhood. Although he had not thought of Andrew Davidson for that period of time, he had continued to avoid taking Margie anywhere near 240 Belcourt Avenue on their walks, walking neither on Belcourt itself nor the adjacent street Coolbreeze, the street which offered Richard the best vantage point from which to watch Andrew in his second floor window at the back of the house in which he lived. He was occasionally tempted to try walking Margie on either Coolbreeze or Belcourt, just to test himself, to determine whether he was truly cured of his man in the window compulsion. He did not, however, take on the challenge, reasoning that it may turn out to be like giving up smoking or alcohol, the often quoted "one is too many and a thousand not enough" coming to mind and warning him away. He recalled having unsuccessfully abandoned smoking half a dozen times until the habit was gone for good after he suffered two heart attacks and underwent heart surgery more than fifteen years ago. It was the same concept he thought. One swing down Coolbreeze Avenue with Margie and he could be back doing it every day. So he avoided it.

It was more then a little surprising when Richard's brother Hugh e-mailed an article that concerned the old neighbourhood. Hugh still lived outside Montreal, relatively close to the old neighbourhood. He was not in touch with him as much as he should have been so he was initially pleased but confused with the communication. The article appeared in the city section of a recent edition of the *Montreal Gazette*. His e-mail said that the article, which had been referred to him by a neighbour who was aware of where Hugh grew up, might arouse in him memories of the old neighbourhood. The message also suggested that Rene and Frances might have been interested in the news story he was forwarding, that is of course if they were still alive. The message did not mention the possible reaction or interest of their other brother Kevin. He was probably too young to be familiar with the history that the story might evoke.

He printed out the article. It was dated Monday, April 10, 2017 and written by a reporter named Gilles Tremblay.

Remains Found At Pointe Claire Building Sight

The SPVM police station for Dorval and Pointe Claire has reported that on April 8, unidentified remains were found at a building sight on a property on Parkdale Avenue in the Valois area of Pointe Claire. In an April 9 telephone interview, Officer Pierre Gagnon said that what appeared to be human bones were discovered by workers excavating the basement of a house being constructed there by Laurent Construction. Preliminary indications by police officers at the scene of the discovery are that the bones, which appear to be decades old, are of an adult. The bones have been sent to the chief medical examiner in Montreal for the further investigation.

The discovery has already attracted some local attention. The property is known for having been the site of a fire that destroyed the original dwelling almost forty years ago. The original dwelling, a picture of which hangs in the Pointe Claire library on Rue Saint Jean, was built more than one hundred years ago. It was one of the first houses constructed west of Broadview Avenue, the original boundary of Valois Village. More recently, the site, which is located at 109 Parkdale Avenue, has been vacant since the current house was sold and demolished several months ago.

Richard did not have to be prompted. He knew immediately the reason that his brother had sent him the article. The remains had been found at the Vessey place, the home of Gary "Butchy" and his wife Dorothy and their five children, one of whom habitually stood in a second floor window and stared. His name was Scott and Richard had been obsessed with him throughout some of his childhood. He was, of course, fascinated with the *Montreal Gazette* story, raising it with Jean as soon as he had read his brother's e-mail, He also telephoned Hugh that evening to thank him. Jean got a curious look on her face and had to be reminded of the location of the building site at which the remains were discovered. She did not refer to the staring Scott, presumably having forgotten about her husband's stories about him. As for Hugh, he was surprised, not expecting immediate gratitude, if any at all for passing along a little childhood nostalgia to his brother. Richard defended his predilection for memory by referring to some sort of slogan that may have appeared on a poster he had seen somewhere, i.e. "My future is in my past and my past is my present." He could not be certain whether he actually believed in the wisdom of such apparently fashionable quotations but he was enamoured with them anyway. It reminded him of university classes when some professor would say something erudite that most students could not understand but thought was "heavy" nonetheless.

Richard was practically sleepless that night, thinking about the discovery of the remains near the Vessey house. It was almost like a mystery story he had read years ago but could not remember how it ended or even began for that matter. His ruminations that night reminded him of thoughts he had had when he was a boy, when he was five and six years old and had been mesmerized by a teenage boy named Scott Vessey staring from a window on the second floor of a house that sat directly behind the backyard of his own house. Back then, when he was staring at Scott staring at what he came to realize many years later was likely nothing at all, he had been frightened but unwilling to look away. Now that he knew that the house had been destroyed by fire a few years after he, his brother Hugh and finally his parents and his youngest brother Kevin had all left the address on Columbus Avenue, the mystery that the Vessey house and its serene occupant Scott had forced on him when he was a boy became understandable. If he was still in university and still willing to pursue the literary pretensions of the pseudo-intellectual he at one time sought to be, he would call the entire episode gothic and a fantasy narrative worth pursuing. By the time sleep came that night, several hours of sporadic contemplation finally yielding results, he had decided that he would investigate the history of the Vessey house, starting with the remains that had just been found and had likely been buried in the backyard of the Vessey house.

The next day, during his morning walk with Margie, he started to formulate his plan for probing the mystery of the remains found in Valois several days ago. He would have to obtain a daily copy of the *Montreal Gazette* for any news of further developments in the case although he was skeptical as to the paper's continuing interest in the story, as intriguing as he thought it may have been. He realized that even if the paper did report on further developments regarding the remains unearthed at 109 Parkdale Avenue, it wouldn't attempt to connect it, if it could be linked, to the house that burned down almost forty years ago and to the circumstances of the fire. Richard also managed to convince himself, the result of several hours of fitful sleeplessness the previous night, that there were events that not only led to that fire but also explain it. By the time they returned home from their walk, a walk that was without incident, Margie being surprisingly tranquil that morning, he had decided that he would first discuss his plan with Jean who, despite her misgivings about his fascination with men in second floor windows, was understanding enough to offer him some realistic advice. At least, that was his intention, if not his hope that morning.

Jean was sitting in the living room doing a crossword puzzle when Richard got in the door. Margie gave her a quick bark which prompted a rebuke from Richard and some mild criticism from Jean who invariably would let her husband know that his dog training skills were sometimes lacking. Richard expressed some surprise, claiming that Margie's walk had been remarkably calm, despite two dogs, a man in a dark coat, and a cat in the window of a parked car, usual vexations for a dog with Margie's behavioural shortcomings. Jean responded with a sardonic snort and a shrug, thinking that he must have used up plenty of liver treats or Richard was fibbing about Margie's behaviour. She went back to her crossword while Margie slumped down on the carpet in front of the television. The video was on but the audio was not. Margie didn't seem to mind, she wasn't watching anyway, looking out the glass doors of the patio her preferred target. Richard immediately took up a spot beside her on the sofa. She didn't look up. Richard immediately brought up the decision he had reached on his walk with Margie, seeking her counsel, if not her agreement.

"You know, I could barely sleep last night." Richard began, "I couldn't stop thinking about that article."

Jean put down her crossword, turned toward Richard and responded predictably. "Somehow, I am not surprised. Your brother sends you an article about the discovery of some bones in the backyard behind your family's old place and I'll bet you now have a plan."

Richard moved forward to the edge of the sofa. "Yes, I do. How do you know that I have a plan?"

Jean offered up a slight smirk. "We've been married for almost forty years. I think that pretty well qualifies me to take a guess." Jean then spread her hands and nodded toward Richard, her gesture urging him to tell her about his plan.

Predictably, Richard grew animated with Jean's invitation. She had occasionally attempted to encourage Richard to return to what she had often assumed to be a long lost aspiration of his, that of a writer, an ambition he said had occasionally consumed him when he was in high school and university. She suggested that he might want to write about his plans. "Maybe but first I'd like to find about the remains – you know, who was it, how long ago were the remains placed there, what were the circumstances, you now, that kind of thing." Richard then took a quick breath and continued.

Jean acknowledged the difficulty he might face in attempting to satisfy this interest. "That might be hard. In fact, the paper may not even follow up on the remains thing. The cops might but I don't know."

Richard nodded and continued his explanation. "Well, I can always find out from the police I guess."

"You're going to bother the police!! That's a little extreme, isn't it." observed Jean, "I didn't think you were that interested."

Richard gave his head a quick shake. "To be honest, I don't know if I'm that interested. Fact is that I am more interested in the old story, the one about the fire."

Jean asked the predictable question. "Why?" She then looked at him quizzically. She was mildly interested.

"Well, the house that was right behind ours in the old neighbourhood burned down several years after we moved away. It seems strange. I'm just curious that's all." A flicker of doubt entered his mind as he heard himself justifying his interest in something which happened in his old neighbourhood after he and his family had moved away. He knew that Jean would question it. She did.

Jean sounded sympathetic, almost comforting, as if she was speaking with a child. "Well Richard, there's curiosity and then there's curiosity."

"I guess so but...." answered Richard, quietly, almost whispering.

"But you want to find out...." Jean finished his declaration and then added a final insight. ".... because of the kid in the window of that house, wasn't it? Not the fire, which happened after you moved, not the fire."

Richard just nodded.

"Geez Richard, when's the last time you actually saw the boy? Sixty years ago?" Jean didn't want to bring it up but she felt she had to, for reasons she did not quite understand herself. Curiosity about her husband's curiosity was a possibility although there was a rather significant difference in the duration of that curiosity, his having lasted more than sixty years, a history of wonder. After he didn't answer, she brought up the connection to the present, an obvious motivation for his renewed fascination with that particle of his past. "It's that guy you see in the window on Belcourt, isn't it? Without him to remind you, you might have forgotten about the kid in the other window a long time ago. Right?"

Richard nodded again, slowly. So did Jean who then offered him a cup of coffee and left the sofa for the kitchen. While she was busy in the kitchen, a clattering of dishes emitting and a short bark from Margie, he rehearsed the usual examination of his own memories. Jean was right. Sitting there waiting for Jean to bring him a cup of coffee, he wondered whether he would have had any interest in the *Montreal Gazette* story if he had not come across the guy in the window of a neighbourhood house. For reasons that he shared with many of his friends in high school and university in particular, he had realized that he actually enjoyed analyzing himself. He also wondered whether any of his old friends still pursued such analysis.

Jean brought his coffee to him and retook her seat beside Richard on the sofa. Margie had followed her into the room. "So I'm right, right?" Jean continued. "And no matter what I say, you will somehow try to find out about the bones they found on that property in your old neighbourhood. She paused, moved closer to Richard, took his left hand in both her hands, and looked into his eyes with a sympathetic gaze usually reserved for serious situations. "So I guessing, that's your plan, isn't it?"

Richard gave Jean one of his proverbial shrugs and said simply. "I guess so."

Jean moved back from Richard on the sofa, gave his hand a little pat, and smiled like she was in on a joke. It was apparent she didn't believe him, at least didn't believe him about undertaking his plan or any plan for that matter. She thought he knew that. He didn't agree. So he thought. He could be determined or so he thought. He finished his coffee. He watched his wife leave the room with a funny little smirk on her face. She often had a funny little smirk on her face.

PREQUEL YEARS LATER

It was three o'clock on an August afternoon when Richard saw Scott for the first time in what was likely years. Richard and two of his teammates from the Valois Colts, a local little league football team for which they had just completed afternoon practice, had just entered the A&P grocery store on Donegani Street, their intent to shoplift whatever they could, usually packaged cakes, candy bars and other snack items that could easily be concealed in pants pockets or, more profitably, in some sort of bag, like a knapsack or equipment bag. It was a practice that they usually referred to as "crooking sprees", a pastime of creative thievery that had become almost a compulsion among the three of them. No more than once a week, when they had little else to do, due to weather, or had grown tired of what they usually did, either swimming at the local community pool, cycling to the Dorval airport, football practice, the latter reserved for August, or just hiking through the woods near their homes, they did find themselves embarking on thievery.

When the three of them entered the store that day, they immediately noticed that there was some sort of disturbance near the front of the store, where they kept the discarded boxes that the pack boys used for groceries for customers who preferred boxes to paper bags. Reflecting on the incident later, the three realized that they could have easily taken any number of grocery items right off the shelves without any vigilant clerks noticing. But they passed up the chance, more interested, like every other person that happened to be in the store that afternoon, in rushing up to the front of the store to see what had happened. By the time they got there, there was a crowd of people standing over a kid laying on the floor quivering. His movements were more like a spasm than a quiver, like he had some sort of nervous condition, his arms and legs flailing in involuntary movement. There was a young man attempting to control him, not exactly holding him down but ensuring that he could not hurt himself or anyone else. Frightful sounds were emitting from the kid, nothing other than loud noises, nothing that could be understood, not words, just sounds.

The manager of the store, a generally disagreeable fellow named Choquette who patrolled the front of the store, watching the cashiers like they about to pocket some cash, was standing over the kid, exhorting the young man to get control of the kid on the ground, assuming, as they all did, that he was somehow responsible for the quivering kid. The young man looked up with an exasperated though plaintive look on his face. The young man was still battling the kid's swinging arms and legs as he started to explain the situation. He was almost yelling. "Can't you see he's handicapped, handicapped! He can't help it."

Manager Choquette stepped back as if someone had just spilled something on the floor. He then, in a lower and less intimating voice than he had employed thirty seconds ago, asked whether the young man could do something to control the kid, "I don't think these people want to wait for your friend here.", a sweep of his arm toward the bank of customers standing around him. Those customers looked annoyed but a little embarrassed. Everything had stopped. The cashiers, all of whom seemed to be blessed with fairly impressive bee hive hairdoes and all but one were smoking cigarettes. The cigarettes were seemingly stuck in their mouths like permanent facial features.

The exasperated expression on the young man's face was starting to change to something resembling serenity, a surprising reaction given the circumstances. It reminded Choquette of the fervent look that one of his high school teachers, a Jesuit priest named Gabriel, had used when one of his pupils was unable to answer a simpler question on a quiz testing their familiarity with Latin or ancient Greek. "He calms down after a while. Just give me time and maybe some room" the young man advised, one hand messaging the back of the kid's head, which was still swivelling like a toy soldier, and the other gesturing for the crowd to get back. Most of the gathering began to move back although several bystanders stood their ground, offering direction and editorial comment as the young man tried to control the twitching kid.

"Get control of your boy there, you have to get hold of him, get him to behave." shouted a middle aged woman wearing an out of season crochet cap and too much makeup. "He's holding up the line." she stated, an obvious though obviously inappropriate observation given the circumstances. Another woman, who looked as equally mean spirited and strident as the crochet cap and was wearing a blue sunhat, demanded that the young man immediately discipline his charge, as if the boy who was constantly spasming came equipped with a hidden switch somewhere. The young man responded by inviting the woman to take charge of the kid herself, his voice rising but still relatively calm. "Why don't you take him home now, to your home", as if he was offering the woman a cup of coffee. The young man then stood up and stepped away from the kid who was still spinning on the floor, the volume of the sounds coming out of him lower. He then invited the woman to take over care of the boy, offering him to her with a simple sweep of his arm. "Let's see if you can discipline him. I urge you to give it a try." said the young man, "Just once, in front of all of these people." The remark seemed to shock the crowd into regaining its normal composure, a group of suburban women wearing dowdy clothes going about the business of buying their groceries, their so-called orders, a term usually used by ordinary women to describe their weekly provisions. The woman recoiled, as did most of the crowd who had gathered around the kid and the young man. She turned, retook possession of her grocery cart, and returned to the line behind the cashier named Lorraine, who happened to be the youngest and most attractive of the cashiers. She faded into the anonymity of the other grocery shoppers. The rest of the crowd seemed to turn with her, slowly dispersing into smaller groups, pushing their carts back into their original lines, waiting to pay for their orders.

The scattering of the crowd coincided with the arrival of a Pointe Claire police officer who had obviously been summoned by manager Choquette. His presence, however, was unnecessary by then. The young man had finally managed to calm the kid down, his charge was now quiet, as if he had been tranquilized by the introduction of a hypodermic needle.

The kid who a few short minutes ago had been the center of a frenzy of frightening activity was now sitting up with his hands up to the police officer who was now standing almost over him.

For the first time, he was making sounds that were actually words, well at least one word, the word being "cuffs". He sat there repeating that word – "cuffs" as he continued to gesture with his hands held together at his waist. The young man, who now was standing up and had pulled the kid to his feet as well, the kid's hands still together at his waist, explained. "He wants the officer to handcuff him. Most times when the police are called when Scott here can't be handled by a worker, he expects to be handcuffed by the police. He likes it, he thinks it's fun. It's happened dozens of times."

The young man looked at the officer, whose name was Tessier, and asked him if he knew Officer Bertrand. "Officer Bertrand knows Scott, must have applied the "cuffs" on him a dozen times. Scott likes him." Scott was pointing to Officer Tessier and the handcuffs on his belt. He offered a strange little lopsided smile and repeated the word "cuffs".

Richard, who had been waiting with his two teammates in the rear of the crowd, waiting for the crowd to dissipate before continuing with their larcenous intent, stepped forward to better hear the conversation between manager Choquette, Officer Tessier, the young man and now a handicapped kid named Scott. He thought he had caught the name Scott from the edge of the crowd and was therefore pulled closer to the four now huddled in a tight circle near the front of the store which had, not surprisingly, returned to its routine. The sounds of cash registers, cashiers, grocery products rolling down conveyor belts, shopping carts being guided across linoleum floors, grocery products being packed into paper bags and cardboard boxes, customers, pack boys and other store employees all circulating around the four of them, requiring Richard to move even closer. His two teammates did not move forward with Richard, preferring to stand back and wait before the three of them could resume their plans for the afternoon, whatever remained of it. Richard said he had to find out something, whatever that meant, as his two teammates agreed.

Richard returned after spending a couple of minutes eavesdropping. Before either of his teammates could ask, Richard explained his interest. "I knew it. I knew that kid, I mean I know that kid. His name is Scott and he used to live in a house on Parkdale, just behind us."

Both of his teammates looked almost bored. "So, a retard used to live in a house in your backyard."

Richard immediately looked agitated. "Don't call him a retard. He's not retarded, he's handicapped. He's not a retard." Like most kids, if not adults, Richard had occasionally called Scott a retard, which was the supposition about him in the neighbourhood. Even his own parents used the term, which was not the derogatory term it would eventually become but still seemed wrong somehow, even to a six year old. Now that he was twelve years old, it had become even more improper, almost like a swear word. He had learned that the appropriate term for people like Scott was handicapped.

Last year, there had been a boy named George Farley enrolled at St. John's elementary for maybe a week in grade five. When kids started calling him a retard, which happened almost immediately after he showed up in September, the class teacher, a fairly virtuous man named Clark, admonished the class, telling them in a resolute tone, that the term itself was wrong but that using it was likely a sin, a transgression that could lead anyone employing the term to hell. He said that George Farley was handicapped, not retarded, and forbade his students from ever using the term. Still, most of the school's administration did not agree with Mr. Clark's more charitable attitude toward George, asking George to leave the school after a week of continually disrupting class and getting the strap from Principal Sinclair. They did not, however, call it an expulsion. They just asked his poor oppressed parents to take him home from school for good. Richard could not remember Mr. Clark ever commenting further nor did he ever see George Farley again. He had just disappeared.

It took the three teammates maybe twenty minutes to leave the A&P grocery store after the incident was over, the young man and police officer Tessier escorting Scott the handicapped kid out of the store. Although officer Tessier did not need to apply the manacles on Scott, much to the latter's disappointment Richard assumed, it took some effort to get him into the group home worker's car, some struggle and a variety of strange noises coming out of his mouth before Scott managed to yield. Manager Choquette stood at the window of the store staring until the cars carrying Scott and the young man escorting him and Officer Tessier disappeared from the parking lot. The teammates, unwilling it seemed to waste a trip to the A&P, shoplifted a half dozen Jos.Louis cakes by hiding them down the front of their shirts before one of the three, a guy named Joe Boyle, thought he saw one of the clerks working in the fruit and vegetable department eyeing them suspiciously. They hurried out of the store which was probably a more questionable activity than had they continued to stuff chocolate desert cakes into their shirts.

They had cleared the parking lot and were a couple of blocks away on Donegani when they entered the waiting room for the Strathmore train station. They were relieved when they found the waiting room empty, as it usually was in the afternoon. The three of them sat on one of the wooden benches in the waiting room and started in on their stolen Joe. Louis cakes, stuffing them into their eager mouths like they expected manager Choquette to show up any minute to reclaim them. They were finished snacking when Dennis, the third of the three teammates, who hadn't said a word since they had entered the A&P, asked Richard about Scott.

"When's the last time you saw that handicapped kid?"

Richard looked at Dennis, crumbs of Jos.Louis still clinging to the corner of his mouth, and answered almost reluctantly. He was embarrassed somehow, as if it had been been a secret. "I think it was maybe six or seven years ago. He used to stand looking out from a second floor window in the house behind ours on Parkdale. It was weird, the way he just stared from that window. I saw him almost every day, every time I looked. And then, I don't know why, he just wasn't there. The family stayed – their name was Vessey – but he didn't."

Joe, who appeared to have been listening intently, asked the obvious question, a question he didn't expect to be answered. "Did you ever find out where he went?"

"My parents thought that he was living in an institution, like the one in Baie-D'Urfe they said, or maybe in a place called a group home somewhere." Richard answered, his voice soft, almost wistful, as he were dreaming. "Nobody knows. All I know is that I haven't seen him since I was six years old." Richard then starred out the door of the waiting room, which wasn't a door at all but an entrance in the shape of a door without the door. For a moment, he thought that maybe Dennis or Joe might have known Scott but neither of them ever went to Saint Louis elementary school or any other Catholic school for that matter. It was likely that both went to Valois Park Elementary, the local Protestant school.

There was a silence as all three of the teammates started to think about going home. A commuter train went by and Joe identified it as the 3:30 pm out of Windsor Station. That meant that it was probably close to 4:00 pm. Joe said that it was time to head home. He also complained about the relatively scant haul of stolen A&P merchandise they had managed that afternoon. They all laughed and agreed to do better next time, which was likely the next day.

A PLAN BEGINS

It was two days after Richard admitted to Jean his interest in investigating the story about the human remains found in the excavation behind Vessey's old house. He had been considering possible plans for an investigation, basically the same idea repeating like a song that he could not get out of his head. So after thinking about it almost constantly for those two days, he had decided that he would approach the *Montreal Gazette* reporter who had written the April 10 story. He could wait for the paper to follow up on the story about human remains being found at a building site but there was no guarantee that they would and even if it did, it may not cover the specifics in which Richard had an interest. That led him to conclude that his best approach would be to talk to the reporter who wrote the story, maybe persuade him to share details of the situation which did not appear in the paper or, if there were no further details to share, somehow encourage him to pursue those details. After all, he thought that most reporters, this one's name was Gilles Tremblay, might be interested in investigating a story that had the mysteries this one could have. There were the identification of the remains, the duration and circumstances of their interment and basically how they got there. These could easily qualify as minor mysteries, the kind of things a reporter, particularly if Gilles Tremblay was a relatively young reporter looking for notoriety might have an interest in. He had decided. He would approach Mr. Tremblay with his request, encouraging him to take up the investigation, the results of which could, as Richard pointed out repeatedly to himself, promote the man's reputation as an investigative journalist. It could mean more stories, bigger stories, maybe promotions.

Richard was firm. He would contact Gilles Tremblay. His life could take a turn for the better.

—

After crawling through the website of the *Montreal Gazette,* he found an e-mail address for the City Desk, the section where he had determined that reporter Gilles Tremblay might have been working. He sent an e-mail to Mr. Tremblay care of the City Desk editor, somebody named Drouin, and briefly outlined his proposal. He had waited maybe three hours, after which time he had not received a response from either the City Desk or Gilles Tremblay, when he had decided to telephone Mr. Tremblay directly. He dialed the number for the City Desk and asked for Tremblay. The woman on the other end of the line wanted to know if the call was related to a current story that Mr. Tremblay was working on. Richard replied affirmatively and said that he had more information on one of the stories that Tremblay had written for the paper a couple of weeks ago, a minor prevarication but necessary he thought, part of the plan he rehearsed before he placed the call. The woman said that Tremblay was out in the field on a story and said that he could leave a message on his voice mail if he wanted. Richard asked for his cell phone number. The woman said that she was not authorized to give him the number. Richard said that he would leave a message, thanking her. He then heard the prompting signal and then left his message.

"Mr. Tremblay, my name is Richard Matthews. I was very interested in your April 10 story about the discovery of human remains at a building site in Pointe Claire. My family used to live on Columbus Avenue, one street west of Parkdale Avenue. Our backyard faced the house that you reported had been destroyed by fire more than fourty years ago, several years after my family moved to Ottawa. As you'll understand, I would like to talk to you about the finding of the remains, including the possible findings of the chief medical examiner which I hope you will report."

He then gave his telephone number and his e-mail address. As soon as he hung up, he felt a pang of nerves. Was contacting a reporter inappropriate somehow? Aside from repeating or nearly repeating the carefully crafted talking points he regularly created for his superiors in the government department for which he worked for more than thirty years, he had never spoken to a member of the press. While he used to have a high regard for the press, his interest in political news stories nearly obsessive, his enthusiasm gradually waned over the years as the media seemed, at least to him, to become more theatrical, like show business. That general perspective, as well as his occasional dealings with journalists who thought that every exchange with a government official had the potential to turn into a story of Watergate dimensions, had turned him into a reluctant witness.

In addition, after several days of wondering if Mr. Tremblay would respond to his message, he had started to think that maybe Tremblay had forgotten about the whole thing. Richard still regarded the discovery of human remains in a suburban backyard a story worth pursuing but was not sure whether Gilles Tremblay or his newspaper would agree. That anticipation or reluctance or whatever it was had almost faded when Tremblay responded to his voice mail with an e-mail message. It was eight days later. He was relieved that Tremblay chose to answer by e-mail rather than by telephone, worried that his anxiety would somehow overwhelm into confusion or silence. He preferred e-mail or facebook to actual verbal exchange. It gave him, as well as everyone else he would imagine, a chance to reasonably consider what he wanted to say without a possible case of the nerves intruding. He often wondered how much different his social life would have been had e-mails or facebook been available when he was navigating the perils of adolescence. He would often remember sneaking into the cloistered porch of their three bedroom family bungalow to ask Susan Ashworth or Beverly Mills to the weekly sock hop.

On the other hand, sometimes one could go too far and Richard was convinced that a lot of people did.

As was his habit with e-mail messages, he printed it out before reading it.

"Mr. Matthews, my apologies for taking a week to respond to your telephone message about my April 10 story concerning the human remains found in Pointe Claire. I understand your interest but doubt whether I will continue to report on the discovery. I contacted the chief medical examiner's office and was told that further investigation on the bones is not a high priority. Naturally, my editor doesn't think the story itself warrants a follow up, at least not at this time, unless you can provide me with any information that would warrant further reporting. Again, I'd like to thank you for your interest."

Richard was disappointed and relieved at the same time. At first, he thought he could consign into history the entire collection of circumstances – the newspaper article, the memory of Scott Vessey, and the possibly continuing presence of Andrew Davidson – that had occasionally but consistently bedevilled Richard since he first saw Scott in that window more than sixty years ago. That evening, after reading and rereading the e-mail from Gilles Tremblay, he started to think that maybe it would not be simple, the influence of the fixation too significant to overcome, only resist. In fact, that very evening, almost midnight, he couldn't sleep. He then found himself, having left his house alone without Margie, in front of 233 Coolbreeze looking into the backyard of 240 Belcourt Avenue. Given the hour, he should not have been surprised that Andrew Davidson was not visible in his second floor window but was surprised anyway. He stood there, at the bottom of the driveway of 233 Coolbreeze, just waiting, even though it was close to midnight and he could not have anticipated any appearance by Andrew. It was probably weeks since he last saw Andrew. Maybe longer. He had almost forgotten about him, until that was until his brother had e-mailed that damn press article. Standing there, the night closing in on him like some weird twilight shadow, he wondered whether Andrew was still on sentry duty at the window at 240 Belcourt. After standing there for a time, maybe five minutes, thinking that if anyone happened to see him standing there, they certainly would have been suspicious of something. Maybe they would have called the cops. Maybe they would have recognized him. After all, a lot of people might have seen him on the street in that exact position many times. He decided that he would be back tomorrow, with Margie, as usual.

When he arrived home, taking care to sneak into the house due to the late hour, he was surprised when Jean greeted him like it was around dinner time. She smiled, a cup of tea in her hand, explained she couldn't sleep and said she thought she would wait up for him.

She then suggested, with a knowing look and one of her patented smirks on her face, that he had been out walking by his favourite window. He agreed by nodding slowly. Margie then slowly came bounding down the stairs, yawned and settled around Jean's feet. She looked up at her, obviously wondering about what disrupted her mistress's slumber. Both Richard and Jean were relatively confident that the dog wouldn't start her customary barking at this time of night. For some reason, Margie did not bark at night. It must have been the darkness they had concluded shortly after she got her.

"It's still that article that Hugh sent you, isn't it?" Jean said, almost sympathetically. "You can't help it, can you?" Jean starting to walk into the living room. Richard followed. She sat down. He sat down. "And I see that you've started your surveillance shit of the window on Belcourt again. I thought you'd given it up". She looked at him, almost a stare, waiting for an answer.

Richard couldn't help but provide one. "So did I. But I just had to get the feeling back, you know, the drive, the magic."

Jean laughed. "The magic? Are you now calling your obsession with a guy in the window magic?"

"In a way, yeah. Why not? I've decided that to call it magic is better than calling it a compulsion, an obsession or some other dumb psychiatric term."

Jean's laughter subsided as she seemed to be evaluating her husband's most recent comment. "Talk about dumb! You can't be serious." She hesitated for a moment, searching for an appropriate comment. "I'm starting to get worried about you."

"Worried? You shouldn't be – I'm okay. I can explain." said Richard.

Big smile from Jean. "Ok, I'm here. I can wait. I can wait, at least for a while. Actually, I'm kind of curious about the kind of explanation you can come up with. I mean, magic – what the hell is that?"

Richard moved a bit in his chair and leaned forward. He began to speak, first in a whisper, the volume barely increasing. "Look, I have come to realize, like a damn bolt from the blue, ever since I got the article from Hugh, that I absolutely have to solve the mysteries starting with the Scott Vessey kid, in the second floor window. You're going to think I'm crazy – you already do I guess – but it's all connected, the guys in the windows and that damn article, all connected, it has to be."

Jean's smile faded as quickly as it had emerged. He was being serious. She wasn't sure about him five minutes ago but now she was. He was edging toward the kind of condition that he had demonstrated maybe thirty years ago when he was regularly in consultation with a psychologist named Doctor Arthur Bennett. They called it an anxiety disorder, its primary symptom being frequent panic attacks that sometimes rendered him immobile with fright. Aside from biofeeback therapy, which didn't provide much in the way of therapy, Richard was spending a lot of time gobbling Xanax or Activan like they were Chiclets, sometimes up to three a day, at which point he would flying pretty high and pretty well useless work wise. Jean remembered hearing stories about her husband acting quite strangely on airplanes or at meetings, situations bound to prompt serious panic attacks. Was this some variant of that condition, had her husband somehow developed a new madness, or had he been drinking?

So Jean was getting pretty close to being speechless now, an unusual condition for her. Should she immediately drive him to the Royal Ottawa on Carling Avenue, it being less than a kilometre. Even if that were advisable, what would any mental health professional think of Richard and the absurd story he was telling Jean. It was all too ridiculous. Either that or some sort of elaborate prank. She didn't know what to do. It was almost one o'clock in the morning. She said she was returning to bed and left him in the chair in the living room. He was just sitting there. They could talk about his crazy plan tomorrow. Jean hoped that he would forget about it, forget that he ever brought it up.

A PLAN CONTINUES

The next morning, around eight o'clock, Jean was sitting in the living room watching the CBC news channel, which was repeating the same stories endlessly, Margie was at her feet, just looking through the patio door, waiting for an opportunity to bark. Richard dragged himself down the stairs in that ratty housecoat of his, so slow and clumsy that Jean always thought of that dumb stairmaster advertisement whenever he ascended in the morning. He joined her on the sofa, flopping down, pushing the cushions into the crevices where Margie liked to hide anything small enough to fit, plastic bones, plush toys, gloves, and socks, pretty well anything that she could drag around with her teeth and stuff in the couch. Jean acknowledged Richard and asked him, with a casual grin on her face, whether he was feeling better. Richard looked at her as if he couldn't understand what she was talking about even though he certainly did. He just didn't want to talk about it, at least not then. So he employed one of his dodges, one of his methods of avoiding sensitive issues. He pretended to either not hear or understand the question. It was obvious that she was referring to his crazy rant of the previous evening. He could pretend to be a little befuddled about that discussion but he knew he couldn't keep that pretense up for very long. He had been unhinged and he knew it and so did she. So he gave her a typical excuse of someone who regretted something they did or said the previous evening. "To be honest, I'm not sure I remember what I said last night. I don't think I knew what the hell I was saying anyway. I was upset and not thinking straight." Jean just smiled. "You're sure weren't. Even Margie could have told you that."

After providing the both of them with a proverbial shrug, Richard got up, almost sliding off the sofa, and headed for the kitchen for a cup of coffee. By the time he returned with his cup of coffee and along with a peeled banana, his gesture toward the diet he had embarked upon a week ago, he once again reviewed in his own mind the harangue he had inflicted on Jean last night. The both of them sat in silence for a time. Jean then made a suggestion.

"Look, if you are so interested, and you sure seem to be, why don't you come up with something that would interest the reporter." suggested Jean. "I mean, he is a reporter and he has sort of given you an opening."

"You mean the thing about information that would lead to further reporting." replied

Richard, "I don't know if I have anything the reporter would be interested in." Jean brightened a bit. "How about the kid in the window?"

"What about the kid?" asked Richard.

Jean went serious for a moment, speaking almost in a whisper, she leaned forward and grasped both his hand in hers. "I don't know. He may have seen something all those years ago. I mean, you told me that he was always looking out that window. He could have seen something that may have had something to do with those bones they found in the backyard of the house he lived in."

Richard looked at her as if she had just spun him a fairy tale, like she was his mother and he was eight years old. "You're crazy. First of all, the house isn't there, it burned down forty years ago, and the kid, who was around my age then and would be like almost seventy by now, hasn't lived there since he was six or seven. It would be difficult to even find him, that is if he was still around. And on top of that, what makes you think he could remember anything that would have anything to do with those damn bones which, by the way, could have been buried long before he started looking out that second floor window." Richard then leaned back on the sofa, spread his arms out like he was concluding a debate, and waited for her rejoinder, which he expected would be more like an apology than anything else.

Jean quietly reminded him of a story he once told her several years ago, when Richard was discussing his one time obsession with Scott Vessey.

Richard had said he saw him many years later kicking up a fuss in a grocery store in his old neighbourhood. It was obvious, at least according to Richard at the time, that Scott was no longer living in the Vessey house on Parkdale Avenue. He hadn't been seen in the window for years, not that Richard was spending much time watching the window for Scott anyway. In fact, he would occasionally check the window, out of habit he assumed but every month or so, he would look up at the window for Scott, convinced he wouldn't see anything but worried ever so slightly that he would. It had been almost ten years between his last sighting at the Vessey house and the incident at the A&P when he last saw Scott.

Jean then made an extraordinary, if not at least an unusual suggestion. "Why not find out if Scott Vessey is alive?" She paused as her husband bowed his head and became to massage his temples with his fingers. "I know....I know, it seems like a long shot but who knows, maybe he knows something."

Richard almost gasped and went on to explain his doubts. He was dubious to say the least. "Remember. I told you the kid was handicapped, mentally handicapped. I don't know if he could even talk. I never heard him speak or know of anyone who ever heard him speak." Jean interrupted. "That may be true but you didn't lived with Scott, you don't know for certain. Besides, maybe he can communicate in some other way. You said that he went to school with you for a couple of days."

"That's right. The school had him for two days, two days before they asked the Vesseys to take him home for good." explained Richard, "But I don't remember him saying anything in particular, no words really. He just made a lot of funny noises, not words, just noises that could have been words, at least to him. He liked to throw things around, liked to rip up pieces of paper. All of it was enough to get him in trouble with Miss McCarthy, who would hit him with a yardstick although it did not have much of an effect. She would then throw him out of class. She'd tell him to go down to the principal, this fat man named Sinclair but he never got there. He would just wonder the halls until someone found him and bring him back to class. I don't think he ever got to the principal's office. Good thing too since that he was a sadistic bastard who liked to give kids the strap, even the kids in the first grade. Miss McCarthy and her ruler wasn't enough. I don't know if Sinclair's strap would have been enough to control Scott anyway."

Jean seemed mildly shocked. She had heard Richard and his brother Hugh occasionally tell stories about the almost pathological discipline that seemed to be fundamental in Catholic elementary schools back then. But she never really believed their stories, at least not all of them. Being a female who was eight years younger than her husband, she had never experienced or even heard of any classmate suffering any kind of corporal punishment, the ruler, the strap, the belt, or the electric cord, the latter a favourite of Richard's second grade teacher, Miss Decarie. They both sat there mute for a moment before Jean came up with a suggestion. "Find him and see if he knows anything or knew anything. Tell that reporter friend of yours that Scott could provide information on what happened back then. While that alone won't be enough to encourage him to write another story, you could help him to find any information that could lead to another story. Maybe he could give you advice on where to find Scott." She paused and added another observation. "I thought most reporters are curious. Maybe this one will be as well."

Richard looked at her pensively. He was already considering her suggestion, already pondering his next move. "I think that's a pretty good idea, finding Scott I mean, but I think, and I may be wrong here, that I may be able to locate Scott on my own. If I find him, and if he can actually give me some sort of clue about something, if anything, that may have happened in his backyard, then I could approach the reporter. Otherwise, with just a suggestion that some handicapped kid, who may or may not be able to tell me anything, may have seen something in the backyard of a house he lived in almost sixty years ago, any reporter, or anyone in fact, would just think I was crazy and forget about anything I had to say."

"I don't know, Richard, I don't know." Jean was reconsidering now. Jean thought that maybe her husband had a point. "Maybe you're right." she had to admit. She was being dismissive and understanding at the same time, almost like she was comforting a child who had just awaken from a dream that the child believed was not a dream. "Even if you decide to do this, to pursue this, it could turn out to be a waste of time, a big waste of time."

Richard spread his hands out, like he was surrendering. He then provided Jean with a comment that sounded almost flippant in the circumstances. It also happened to have an element of truth to it, a crucial element of truth. "Well, honey, I have a lot of time, and a lot of time you must admit that can be wasted." He gave her a small grin. She returned it. She had to acknowledge that she had often suggested to him that he had wasted most of his retirement of six years going to the gym, playing several recreational sports, having lunch with former work colleagues, walking around the block with the dog Margie, recording the presence of a figure in a second floor window of a house on a neighbourhood street, and attempting to write a book, a book which he had written and rewritten several times but never completed. "Look, I have time to waste. I might as well use the time I have to waste on something specific, like an investigation to find Scott Vessey, wherever he is." Jean smiled and nodded, as if she was in on some sort of joke. She felt that she had nothing to lose. She was convinced that the matter would be forgotten soon enough. She had surrendered.

Of course, the matter was not to be forgotten, at least not by Richard. Almost immediately after his conversation with Jean, he concluded if he was to find Scott Vessey, he would have to locate either members of the Vessey family, the names of whom, aside of course of Scott himself, were unknown to him, or the group home in which Scott Vessey could have been living, that is if he was still alive. Richard had remembered that the last time he has seen Scott was in an A&P grocery store near where he grew up. At that time, which was close to sixty years ago, he and two of his teammates on the local Pop Warner football team, had seen a mentally handicapped Scott cause a considerable furor in that grocery store. He was accompanied by a young man who was clearly his care worker, suggesting that Scott was either currently living in a group home or soon would be. In any event, that was his conclusion, the result of his contemplations regarding his memories of Scott and his much more recent thoughts of Andrew Davidson, another figure in a second floor window in his neighbourhood. Regarding the latter, he was convinced, by others in the neighbourhood who were aware of Andrew, including Mr. Bissell, with whom he had once shared observations about Andrew, that Andrew would eventually end up living in a group home himself. In any event, group homes in Scott's old neighbourhood could be a good place to start.

He thought he would continue his exchange with Gilles Tremblay, the reporter, just to let him know that he was still interested in the story. Richard thought it appropriate, and maybe, Tremblay would be able to help find Scott somehow. He was leaning over his desk in his office, the fourth of the four bedrooms in their house, his laptop sitting in front of him like an open invitation. He starred at the screen, pondering with words, and then composed his message to Mr. Tremblay of the *Montreal Gazette*.

"Mr. Tremblay, thank you for your recent e-mail. I understand your paper's reluctance to follow up on the story of the human remains found in Pointe Claire as you reported in the April 10 of the Gazette. I wish to inform you that I believe that I may be able to find information that could warrant further reporting. While I cannot assure you, or myself for that matter, that my efforts will result in anything that could illuminate the mystery of the remains, I will be in touch again if I do. Thank you again for your message."

While Richard was concerned that his message may have been too ingratiating, he transmitted it anyway. Almost immediately, he wondered if he should have referred to the impending report of the chief medical officer, the release of which Tremblay had indicated in his message was not a high priority for the paper. He also started to consider whether he should contact the chief medical officer himself. It might be inappropriate and maybe even pointless but he thought it might also be worth a try. That could be his first step in his investigation. It had been almost two weeks since the remains were discovered, sufficient time for the chief medical officer, whoever he or she might be, to complete an investigation and complete a report. The question would be whether the chief medical officer would share the results of an inquiry. While knowing the results of the inquiry might not solve or even provide a clue to whatever mysterious incident might have occurred in the backyard of the Vessey house on Parkdale Avenue those many years ago, it might help to know if there was a incident worth investigating there in the first place. Knowing what the mystery could be helpful, if not a requirement before he found Scott Vessey, that is if he were to ever find him. Besides, it seemed easier than looking for Scott, which to Richard would be quite difficult.

In the end, despite his misgivings about the entire project, he decided to proceed regardless. He was retired and actually agreed with his wife Jean that he had nothing better to do anyway. So now he had a plan, however difficult it would likely be for him to pursue. He had little, if any experience with the police or other civic officials, which was counter-intuitive since he had spent more than thirty years as a federal government official, dispensing advice on matters relevant to international trade. His first thought was to contact the local police, the obvious candidate being Officer Pierre Gagnon, the policeman who was interviewed by Gilles Tremblay for his story in the *Montreal Gazette.* Perhaps Officer Gagnon could offer him guidance as to his plan to contact the chief medical examiner for Montreal. He had no idea as to how to find the chief medical examiner for Montreal, his search of various City of Montreal websites, including the site for "Service de police de la Ville de Montreal (SPVM)", resulting in frequent frustration. He figured that Officer Gagnon would doubtless be able to help locate the chief medical examiner for him.

The next day, he drove to the SPVM station on Boulevard Saint-Jean in Pointe Claire. According to the SPVM website, the station was responsible for Pointe Claire and Dorval. The station was populated by 73 officers, of which he hoped Officer Gagnon was one of them. There was an obvious nostalgia to the trip, a historical longing that grew the closer he got to the station itself. The building in which the station was housed was across the street from John Rennie High School, where his date for his high school graduation dance had gone. It was also close to the arena where he had occasionally played hockey and the diamond where he had occasionally played baseball. It was also two blocks away from the shopping centre where Richard and his pals had pursued their crookin' sprees. He recognized the building itself. When he had lived in the area, it was the Pointe Claire city hall, a building that ceased to be so entitled when the city was amalgamated into the city of Montreal.

He was surprised to see that the entrance to the parking lot to the station was obstructed by a booth manned by an officer. He pulled up to the gate, rolled down the car window and waited for the officer to speak to him. He removed his earbuds, his shoulders hunched a bit, turned toward Richard, and asked him in French, in a voice that sounded annoyed if nothing else, hardly a surprise since the area was no longer the Anglophone enclave it had been when he had lived there fifty years ago. Richard said, in his embarrassingly simplistic French, that he wanted to see Officer Pierre Gagnon. The officer in the booth, almost immediately realizing that Richard was an blockheaded Anglo from Ontario, having glimpsed his license plate, told him, in English, that Officer Gagnon was on patrol and would not be available until the next day. He suggested that he make an appointment with the main assignment coordinator inside the station. Richard thanked the officer, the gate started to come up, and then Richard suddenly asked the officer if he knew how to contact the chief medical examiner for Montreal. The officer in the booth shrugged and then looked away. There was another car waiting for entry.

He parked his car and walked into the entrance to the station. A woman, a middle aged woman with her hair in a bun and wearing a small head set, looked up from her desk as Richard approached. A small name plate on her desk identified her as Helene Boivin.

"Puis-je vous aider, aider, Monsieur?"

In embarrassing French, he admitted that he couldn't speak French and apologized. She chuckled a bit.

"My name is Richard Matthews. I would like to arrange an appointment with Officer Pierre Gagnon." he asked.

Mme. Boivin nodded and asked. "I can do that but first, could you give me an idea as what you would like to discuss with Officer Gagnon."

Richard become a little anxious about her request. He started to feel a little reluctant about having to attempt to explain the reason to a third party for his visit to the station and Officer Gagnon. "Well, Officer Gagnon was the spokesman for the police on the recent discovery of human remains in Valois. I was curious about the story and thought Officer Gagnon could me some additional information about it."

Mme. Boivin looked a little puzzled. She looked up at Richard and asked, "Are you some sort of reporter?"

His anxiety, already circulating in him, heightened. "No, not at all." He didn't want to mention that he had been in touch with Gilles Tremblay. "Well, I used to live in that neighbourhood and knew the family that lived on that property."

Mme. Boivin then cautioned Richard against expecting too much from Officer Gagnon. "Most officers don't like to talk about their cases to anyone, especially people who have no official status."

Richard conquered his anxiety for a moment and quickly offered an observation in rebuttal. "So it's a case then?"

"Nice try, Mr. Matthews, I didn't say that." she objected.

Richard stood silently before Mme. Boivon and her desk. He realized that Officer Gagnon, even if he could arrange an appointment with him, would likely be unwilling to discuss the discovery of the remains with him. So he raised his original request. Perhaps Mme. Boivin would turn out not to be so reserved about sharing such information, if that is she had any relevant information. "Actually, all I wanted to know from him was the name of the chief medical examiner for Montreal. The article in the *Gazette* said that the bones were sent there for further investigation."

Mme. Boivin nodded almost in resignation and commented. "And you think that the medical examiner will talk to you."

"I think it's worth a try. I mean, the reporter who wrote the article for the *Gazette* said that he doesn't plan to follow up, so I figured I would." Richard issued her another casual shrug although he did sound hopefully committed, a juxtapositioning of gestures that first confused and then prompted a slight smirk from Mme. Boivin. He continued to answer her original question. "As far as to whether the medical examiner will speak to me, I realize that people in those kinds of jobs may not be willing to talk to anyone other than cops and other city employees. I don't expect that it will be like in the movies where medical examiners or coroners are often on the screen explaining causes of death."

Mme. Boivin smiled and questioned his observation. "And what makes you think that medical examiners might not want to talk to members of the public?"

"Just a guess I guess." Richard smiled back.

"That's quite a guess I guess." Mme. Boivin snickered and then turned away for a moment, reaching into a desk drawer, and coming out with a booklet. She flipped through its pages, found the one she obviously had been looking for, ran her right forefinger down that page, and then read off a name, a place and a telephone number. She then handed Richard a pen and a small piece of paper.

"You can write this down. The medical examiner is Doctor Lorraine Tessier. She is on the sixth floor of SPVM headquarters, 1441 St. Urbain Street in Montreal, Room 1252. Her number is (514) 280-0002, extension 109." Richard scribbled the information down on the piece of paper that she had provided. She then put the booklet away, looked up and wished him luck.

Richard put the paper on which he had written the information Mme. Boivin had given him in a trouser pocket. "Thanks so much for this."

"You're welcome." she replied. "I hope Doctor Tessier will talk to you."

"So do I." Richard then turned, walked out of the building, was in his car and gone out of the parking lot within minutes. He exchanged dirty looks with the booth officer on his way out. His plan now was to stop by his old home on Columbus Avenue and then take the opportunity to visit the construction site on Parkdale where the human remains had been found.

Richard turned right from the parking lot on Boulevard Saint Jean and drove straight down Saint Louis to Summerhill Avenue where he passed both his old elementary school and across from it, the church in which he attended services until he was fifteen. After that, he was finally able to avoid them without incurring the wrath of his parents, not to mention the almighty. He passed the park on Belmont where he had played baseball, football and hockey and went to the community swimming pool and then down Columbus, stopping in front of his old house. It had not changed much in the forty seven years since he had left it and the forty four years since the rest of his family had left as well. The house had had at least one new paint job, a new veranda had been installed, the two trees in the front lawn had shown spectacular growth, and the roof had been reshingled at least once. A new Lexus was parked in the driveway. Contemplating the obvious prosperity of the current owners of their old house, Richard remembered that Hugh had recently informed him that their old house was probably worth more than ten times what the old man had sold it for in 1974 and almost thirty times what he paid for it twenty years before that.

He sat in his car for maybe ten minutes, took a couple of photographs, and drove down toward Donegani where he turned left and left again to find himself in front of the site of the old Vessey house on Parkdale. There were two relatively new houses of modern design situated on either side of the previous Vessey property, which was now just a large fenced hole in the ground, bordered by the cement walls of a cellar for a new house. There was a large sign with a rendering of the finished building standing in front of the property. It showed two residences with entrances at each end of the entire structure, two floors, two garages, two small balconies jutting out from the second floor. Richard parked the car across the street, got out, and walked to the edge of the fence. There were maybe five men working on the site. Staring through the fence, he saw no indication whatsoever that something unusual had been found there in recent memory. He tried to imagine the Vessey house, realizing that he was much more familiar with the rear of the place than he had been with the front, trying to recall the latter, even its address having disappeared from his mind. There may have been a small lamp to the right of the front door, above the street number that he could not remember. He found himself clenching and unclenching his fists trying to remember.

There was a man parking his car across the street. He was an older man wearing a tan suede jacket, brown corduroy trousers, a maroon sweater and a peak cap. He crossed the street and before he knew it, he was beside Richard, having joined him in gazing through the lattice of the fence.

Pointing to the building illustration on the sign in front of the property, the man spoke in a casual, friendly tone. "They all seem to turn out the same, don't they. All the local architects seem to like the same designs."

Richard nodded. "Yeah, it's the same where I live. The old houses come down and these mansions that all look the same go up."

The older man turned and look at him. "Where's that?"

"Ottawa now but I used to live on Columbus a long time ago." answered Richard. "I just went by the old place to take a look."

"It's still there I suspect." commented the older man.

"Yes, it is." Richard replied. They then just stood there for a time before Richard asked the older man if he remembered the Vessey family.

"No, I don't but the people from whom we bought our place told us that they were living here across the street when the Vessey place burned down."

"It was in the late 70s, wasn't it?" mused Richard.

The older man answered. "Yes, as far as I know, it was in the late 70's." Richard then asked if the house was rebuilt. The older man provided further information. "No, the Vesseys didn't rebuild. I understand that they just sold the property and moved away. A family named Caplan from Montreal West bought the lot and then built a house, nothing too ostentatious mind you but nicer than the place the Vesseys had lived in. I understand that the new house was about the same size as the old place. In other words, no one dug up the backyard. The Caplans then sold the place and the property on which it sat when their youngest daughter moved out. Somebody then knocks down the Caplan house and starts to build the house on the sight. And then a couple of weeks ago, somebody finds some bones out back, the police show up, and the story ends up in the paper." Richard snorted a bit and asked facetiously. "I know, I read the article in the *Gazette*. I was disappointed that the Vessey family wasn't mentioned in the article."

The older man smiled like he was in on the joke, if it had been a joke. Both of them went back to staring through the fence as if they expected one of the men working on the site to offer them a guided tour. The older man then turned toward Richard and remarked. "You know, according to some of our older neighbours, the Vessey family apparently was quite a story for a time, a long time ago. Apparently, local people talked about them for years."

"Really. What do you mean?" asked Richard.

"There was something strange about one of their kids, some sort of handicap. And something about his mother too. To be honest, I never really got the whole story." Richard immediately knew that the older man was talking about Scott Vessey, the boy he had last seen in a grocery store.

"I knew that kid when I was a kid myself. His name was Scott. I was in grade one with him a long time ago. But he left school after a couple of days. Most of the time, I used to see him in the window on the second floor of his house starring into his backyard. After a few years, I didn't see him in the window anymore and then years later, I saw him again. It was obvious to me that he wasn't living at home with the Vesseys anymore. But that too was a long time ago."

The older man listened with interest. "Mmm, you know much more than I do about the Vesseys. All I have is second or even third hand innuendo and gossip. You actually knew the family." Richard shook his head. "I didn't really know the family. I knew who they were but I don't remember if I ever spoke to them." Both of them were again plunged into a short silence in which a memory of the last time he saw Scott at his window flashed through Richard's memory, that time he and his two friends, Brian and Pete sneaked into the Vesseys' backyard to explore. Richard then continued the discussion about the Vesseys. "You mentioned the mother? What about her?"

The older man offered a shrug. "I'm not sure. I just remember people mentioning that something had happened with the mother."

THE CHIEF MEDICAL EXAMINER

The next day, having returned to Ottawa after completing his tour of the old neighbourhood, Richard planned to drive to Montreal again to visit the chief medical examiner of the SPVM. He had told Jean of the information he had gathered from his visit to the old neighbourhood, particularly reporting on the discussion he had held with the older man who was living across the street from the address that the Vessey family used to inhabit. Jean had pretended to be enthused about Richard's report. She could not help but be mildly pleased that Richard had found some substance to a fixation with which he may have suffered for decades and which had recently been rejuvenated with his walks around the block with Margie. On the other hand, however, she was worried that his new found enthusiasm for the quest of whatever mystery was behind Scott Vessey might lead Richard into more pointless pursuits. Besides, and more importantly, she remained unconvinced that all Richard's efforts would ever lead into something that would satisfy those ambitions he had harboured for decades. Quite frankly, she sometimes thought that her husband would eventually fall over the edge into some psychiatric abyss if he kept following his search much longer, the end of which she was convinced would be absolute zero. Certainly, he had been particularly encouraged by the article in the *Montreal Gazette* and that conversation with the older man from Richard's old neighbourhood. Now, he was about to return to Montreal for more encouragement. There was nothing she could do now but continue to listen to his reports of his detective work.

He had telephoned the number for Doctor Lorraine Tessier he had been given by Mme Boivin of the SPVM station in Pointe Claire. It was 10:30 in the moring, the day after he had visited his old home and the old Vessey place in Pointe Claire. She answered the telephone on the second ring, She answered in French but immediately switched when Richard greeted her in English. "Hello, Doctor Tessier. My name is Richard Matthews and I would like to speak to you. I have an interest in one of your investigations, the human remains found out in Pointe Claire a couple of weeks ago. I read in the *Gazette* that your office would be examining the bones. I know that it may not be proper but I would really appreciate it if I could meet with you to discuss any findings your office has made on the case."

Doctor Tessier's response was stiff, almost robotic, a clear demonstration of bureaucratic grooming. She also sounded older, probably close to retirement age, a woman who was probably stern and tough minded. It was not going to be easy he thought to persuade the doctor to discuss her office's findings, that is if it had made any. "You want to discuss findings in one of our cases." she stated, it sounding more like an accusation than a question. "You were right in stating that it may not be proper. The fact is that it would not be proper."

He should have been and was prepared to respond to Doctor Tessier's reluctance, which of course he had anticipated. He had decided that he would fabricate advice that he would say had been given to him by *Montreal Gazette* Gilles Tremblay. He thought that Tremblay had sort of implied it anyway. Now on the telephone, Richard delivered the falsehood in his most charming voice, a facility which he had been told was particularly well received by older women. "I realize that it may be against the rules but Mr. Tremblay, the reporter who wrote the story about the discovery of the remains in the *Gazette*, told me that since the bones are so obviously quite old, it was very unlikely that the police will want investigate further. If that's the case, then what harm would it do if you could share the findings with me."

There was a disquieting silence on the other end of the line, as Richard assumed Doctor Tessier was either formulating a way of expressing her outrage or pondering his request. Richard honestly had no idea. The telephone receiver felt heavy in his hands, like he was about to drop it. Then, unexpectedly, there was her voice on the line. "Gilles Tremblay of the *Gazette*? I don't think I know him. I don't think I have ever dealt with him." There was a pause and then she surprisingly asked. "He actually told you that?"

That caught Richard by surprise. He casually agreed with Doctor Tessier, having already hopefully concluded that the good doctor would never consult with Mr. Tremblay, now pleased that at least she didn't know the reporter. Again, there was a pause on the line, Richard thinking that she was considering his request. It was less than a minute before she go on the line again although Richard figured that he must have waited almost five minutes. Her voice was low, tentative, almost as if she was talking to herself, like she was relating a confidence to him. "What do you want to know, exactly?" Richard exhaled and then answered her in a correspondingly low voice. "Well, Doctor, anything you can tell me." She paused again, pondering his request. Although Richard did not expect her to ask, she posed another question. "Why do you want to know? It just seems curious to me that anyone would want to know about the remains anyway. Is it just curiosity? Did you used to live on the property?"

It was the opportunity that Richard could have been hoping for but could not have expected. It was a perfect invitation. "Well, to be honest, it is curiosity although it is probably more than that. It is more like fascination."

"You're going to have to explain that to me. Fascination? What does that mean?" This time, the tone of her voice was verging on annoyance again. He thought that he had better start explaining himself quickly. "Well Doctor, to be honest, my family used to live on the next street from the property where the bones were found. In fact, the property was practically in our backyard. So when I read the story in the *Gazette* a couple of weeks ago, I had to know more. Just had to. You understand, don't you?", the last phrase more like a pleading than an explanation.

"I have come across such curiosity sometimes – sorry, fascination – but it was usually from relatives, not neighbours." she said, seemingly more pensive than annoyed he thought. She then asked another question. He was relieved. She was still interested. "How long ago did you live there?"

"Almost fifty years ago." he replied. Doctor Tessier was obviously impressed enough because she invited him to meet her in her office at 10 o'clock the next morning. Richard almost dropped the telephone receiver. Such was his surprise, even shock. Tomorrow morning it was. He told Jean. In addition to surprise, she was impressed but still a little concerned.

The address of SPVM headquarters in Montreal was 1441 Saint Urbain Street. It was two blocks west of St. Laurent Boulevard, one block east of Place des Arts and one block south of Sherbrooke Street. Richard was generally familiar with the area, having enjoyed many weekends with Jean at the Hyatt Regency on Jeanne-Mance over the last couple of years. He found a parking lot on Clark Street, parked the car and walked up to the nine floor building at 1441 Saint Urbain. It was a spectacularly plain building with maybe a dozen police patrol cars parked in front of it, officers coming and going at a casual pace. He was not surprised to see that the building, which was entirely devoted to the SPVM, had a general entrance and three secure entrances with electronic gates protecting the inhabitants and visitors from each other. On the left was an entrance for police, the centre was for people having official business with the police while the entrance on the right was for members of the public. All three entrances featured desks behind which sat SPVM officers. The entire scene reminded Richard of the immigration gates at airports in Europe, particularly the ones in Paris, where he occasionally visited on business.

He went to line up for the desk on the right, the one reserved for the general public. In front of Richard was an elderly man with a service dog, a younger woman who was wearing a bright blue sweater over distressed jeans and zippered black boots, and a large middle aged woman carrying two grocery bags. All three of them spoke french to the officer sitting behind the security desk. When his turn came, he announced in English that he had 10 a.m. appointment with Doctor Lorraine Tessier, the chief medical examiner. The officer, whose name badge was unreadable, nodded, picked up the telephone, spoke for maybe two minutes and then pushed the sign-in book and a pen toward him. He printed his name, signed and then walked between two glass security barriers towards the elevators. He got in the elevators with two policemen, a man who could have been a lawyer, and the large woman with the grocery bags.

He got off on the sixth floor and headed for Room 1252. It was on the left and about halfway down, the only office it seemed on that side of the sixth floor. Her name and title was announced on a black metal door with an engraved brass plaque. It reminded Richard of one of the Ministers' offices to which he had been summoned when he was working in the government. The door was open a crack. He knocked on the door, it opened about half way and he saw Doctor Lorraine Tessier sitting behind a large desk correcting some sort of document. Her desk was neatly arranged, two pens on the right side of what looked like an expensive blotter, a small desk lamp, a telephone to her left, and a pile of papers in front of the blotter. Behind her was a suitably large screen which could have been a television monitor but was actually a radiology screen for reading x-rays. He identified himself and stepped cautiously into the room. She looked up and invited him in, which was sort of redundant since he was by then already in the room. There were two leather chairs at angles facing the doctor's desk. The rest of the room was dominated by a large table that accommodated eight chairs, six of which sat horizontally and one at each end. As well as Doctor Tessier's framed professional certificates, there were several hotel quality paintings on the walls.

The doctor waved Richard into the chair to the right. "Hello, Doctor, I'm Richard Matthews, I spoke to you yesterday."

"Yes, I know." said the doctor, "What can I do for you?"

Richard sat straight up in the chair and leaned partway toward the doctor, as if he was about confide a secret to her, which in a way he was. "I would like anything you can tell about the remains, like how the person died, how long the bones were there, their gender – anything that you can tell me."

The doctor picked up a file folder from her desk and opened it. "I have the report here. We completed it about a week ago and sent it to the fourth floor."

"The fourth floor?" commented Richard.

The doctor nodded. "Police detective investigation section though I suspect that they will give it a quick read, realize that any foul play was likely committed decades ago and then close the file. That's what I would do." she explained. "In summary, we found that the bones are that of the skeleton of a woman probably in her thirties who was buried on that property a long time ago, having probably been murdered, our best guess being maybe sixty or seventy years ago."

"What? Murdered?" exclaimed Richard, excited and mystified at the same time.

"Yes, Mr. Matthews, murdered." confirmed Doctor Tessier. "She had a broken neck. It looks like the poor women was probably strangled. Obvious foul play."

"Could it have been some sort of accident?" asked Richard, the inquiry almost a reflex, like he thought he was supposed to ask. "Is it possible? Could she have hung herself or something?"

"No. I've seen my share of suicides by hanging and I can assure you that this definitely wasn't a hanging." Doctor Tessier asserted with a pronounced aura of authority Richard then inquired about her office's estimate of the age of the bones. It seemed evident to him that such an incident would not have escaped the attention of his parents or their friends in the old neighbourhood if it happened back when the family lived there. It must have happened before his family moved into the new housing development on Columbus Avenue in 1954. That would mean that the poor woman's remains would be at least sixty five years old. Richard asked about the estimate anyway. "We estimated the age based on the rate of disintegration of the bones. It is not very precise but it is the best we can do in the circumstances."

Richard then asked about his own estimate. "Could the bones be more than sixty five year old?"

Doctor Tessier nodded warily. "Possibly, quite possibly." she said.

It now appeared that their interview was over. Richard has received what he came for.

A VISIT TO THE LIBRARY

Richard left Doctor Tessier's office and exited SPVM headquarters by eleven o'clock in the morning. He had planned to spend a little time in downtown Montreal before starting on the drive home but rethought the plan as he was drove westward on Sherbrooke Street.

Almost immediately after he had concluded his meeting with the doctor, he started to consider or reconsider his next move. He had initially thought that he would scour local newspapers, principally the *Montreal Gazette* or the long defunct *Lakeshore News* for any mention of a woman who went missing from a Pointe Claire residence sometime in the late 1940s or early 1950s. He had spent some part before his visit with Doctor Tessier searching the internet for newspaper archives and other sources of information on missing persons in the Pointe Claire area. The more he thought about it, the more he realized that his get together with the doctor was really not that helpful. It confirmed that the remains, which were already reported as being human, were in fact that of a women in her late twenties or early thirties, and that she had been murdered. But the facts in which Richard was the most interested remained elusive, specifically the identity of the woman whose bones were found in the backyard of the old Vessey place and the circumstances of her death, including who may have killed her.

By the time he had reached Atwater Street on his drive west on Sherbrooke, he had decided that instead of spending anytime window shopping on Ste Catherine Street in downtown Montreal, which was his original plan, he would drop by the Valois Branch of the Pointe Claire Library on his way home. He had invested more than an hour researching the website of the library the previous afternoon. He had looked through the on-line newspaper archives, the *Montreal Gazette* only, local news being at a minimum. The available information was fairly scant, headlines only, and limited to the last several years, back to 2015. In other words, the newspaper information was useless. There was little historical information or so it seemed, his ability to access it restrained by his lack of computer savvy. In his internet wanderings, which he recalled used to be called "surfing the net", a profoundly old fashioned term, he came across a history of Valois, the Pointe Claire village. The history, which was sixteen page recitation of facts on the village of Valois, was posted on Wikipedia by a guy named Phil. It was an interesting read to him, touching on all sorts of familar people and places that accompanied him over the seventeen years he lived in the family house on Columbus Avenue. Unfortunately, there was no mention of the Vessey family or any missing person who could have ended up buried in the Vessey backyard. Richard did find out, however, that he never did live in the village of Valois, Columbus Avenue being two blocks outside the western boundary of the village, meaning that the family lived in Pointe Claire rather than Valois, which was strange since almost everything he did, every sports team he played on, and every place he went when he was a kid was in Valois per se. Regardless, he did spend an enjoyable twenty minutes re-acquainting himself with Valois. Strangely, the posting did not make any reference to the housing development into which his family moved in 1954 which was not formally situated in Valois but did mention his Pop Warner football team, the Valois Colts for whom Richard played fullback in 1961.

By the time he passed the manicured grounds of the Loyola Campus of Concordia University, on which was also his alma mater Loyola High School and which was on the opposite side of Sherbrooke Street near the Montreal West train station, Richard had decided that he would visit the Valois Branch of the Pointe Claire Library. He thought that maybe someone working there, a librarian, a researcher, maybe even a lingering customer could give him some information on the mystery of the human remains recently found on the old Vessey property. He had to admit, however, that it was more a matter of nostalgia than anything productive.

After his recent visit to Columbus Avenue and the former Vessey property on Parkdale, not to mention his discussion with the older man who lived across the street, he suddenly had an ambition for his own history, as well as his interest in the circumstances of the human remains. He knew the address of the library. It was on Prince Edward Avenue, north of Belmont Avenue and one block east of Valois Bay Avenue, one of two main thoroughfares in Valois, a street which ran from the train tracks in the south and Saint Louis Avenue in the north. The library's website included a photograph of the library building. He thought he recognized it. It might have been an old school or an old church. On the other hand, he doubted that his memory of the building was accurate. After all, it was almost sixty years ago.

He arrived in front of the Valois Branch of the Pointe Claire Library a little after two o'clock in the afternoon. He had intended to stop in for lunch at the Green Hornet Tavern, at one time a famous watering hole on the Lakeshore Road. But it no longer existed. It had been known as the "Bug" before it was demolished two years ago. It was well known to particularly every local kid who was underage and had fifty cents for four drafts and a tip. According to the bartender at Kelly's Pub, a place on Donegani Road where he did eat lunch that day, decent fish and chips, the property on which the "Bug" had sat was still empty, some sort of real estate dispute preventing any development. Richard also asked the bartender about Marilyn's Lounge, another local watering hole that he remembered with some fascination although he had never frequented it. It too was gone, replaced by lakefront condominiums. Richard had always imagined that the atmosphere in the Marilyn's Lounge was reminiscent of a Las Vegas nightclub where Frank Sinatra imitators sang into smokey darkness and women with geometrically impossible hairdos struggled with cocktail dresses that didn't fit right and escorts who didn't behave right. It was a memory that was curious not only because it was virtually imaginary but also because just down the Lakeshore Road was an actual nightclub that fit that description. It was called the Edgewater and Richard had been there a number of times, always in the company of a potentially promiscuous girl named Allison who pretended to be his steady as long as he kept buying her cocktails. Both the girlfriend and the club in which he had bought her drinks were also consigned to barely retained memories, lost to history.

Richard had almost forgotten his original purpose when he arrived at the library in Valois. He had noted, as he had the previous day when visiting his old street, that while there had been obvious changes, any modifications were hardly fundamental. Facing Belmont Street and around Prince Edward Avenue, there still was the huge park with the three baseball diamonds, swimming pool, and clubhouse, the two churches but now four schools, a new school for children of kindergarten age having been added, when he could not tell. He parked the car on Prince Edward Avenue directly in front of the library, disembarked and walked up the eight stone steps to the two large wooden doors of the library. The place looked like the church it may have at one time been. He pushed on the wooden doors and found himself in the foyer, a narrow room that ran the width of the library. There were wooden benches on either side of the arch entrance to the main room. There were several wall boards available for notices hanging above the benches, a listing of upcoming library events being the chief announcements. Richard entered the library proper and walked up the central alley between reading tables and chairs on either side. The books were arranged in shelves against the walls. There was a second floor of books, accessible by an elevator and a staircase just inside the entrance to the main room. There was a long counter at the north end of the room behind which three library personnel were working at computer monitors. Richard imagined that it had likely been the altar if the building had remained a church, however long ago that had been. He also noticed that there were at least one other person working in the library, a middle aged woman struggling to place books she took from a cart back on the shelves. On the left side of the counter was a younger looking man who could have been interring at the library for the summer, an impression that was not at all consistent with the fact that it was not the summer and the man was wearing a three piece suit that could have been worn by his father. On the other side of the counter, the right side, was a woman who looked like a caricature of a Holocaust survivor, hideously untidy hair hanging over a face that featured a mass of aged wrinkles, lips adorned with a slash of bright red lipstick, and eyes that seemed as blank as blindness.

Then seated in the middle behind the counter was an older woman. Richard stood before her at the counter and introduced himself. She responded by identifying herself as Miss Millie Thomas, "head librarian", emphasizing both her title and her job title, which frightened Richard, a momentarily stab of anxiety across the chest. It might have reminded Richard of someone that might have scared him at some point in the past. She had stood up to shake his hand, a tall, thin woman who looked to be almost retirement age, her silver hair below her shoulders, unusually long for someone her age and in her position. She did not seem at all as stern as he might have thought she might be, the cliched impression of the appearance of an almost retired librarian obvious. His initial flash of fear had completely dissipated, her unexpected appearance enough to comfort him. He wondered long after this encounter with Miss Thomas whether there was a psychological condition known as "fear of librarians", a state that one of his college friends used to insist actually existed, the reference related to someone named Abigail Wills who presided over the Vincent Massey library at Loyola College. That woman looked like she could have been played the mother in "Psycho".

Miss Ellie Thomas further comforted Richard when she asked, in the most solicitous manner, his purpose in visiting her library. "What can I do for you, deary?", a curious introduction given that Richard was probably Miss Ellie Thomas's senior by several years.

Richard was momentarily taken aback, a little dumbfounded. He had not expected such a kind approach. "Well, I was hoping that your library was holding back copies of the *Lakeshore News*." She looked at him as if he didn't understand his request. "Do you have copies of the *Lakeshore News?*" he asked, then offered an explanation. "You see, I'm looking for articles that might have appeared in the *Lakeshore News* in the early 50s?"

"The *Lakeshore News?* From the 1950s?" asked Miss Thomas, her sweet voice up a few octaves. "You're asking me a question that I've not often heard."

"I know, maybe you have never heard of the *Lakeshore News*." Richard suggested. Miss Thomas laughed gently. "Of course I have. The *Lakeshore News* was a charming little weekly for the West Island here that started publication maybe sixty years ago or so. It had a relatively small circulation although it did get larger in its latter years. It was renamed the *West Island Chronicle* some time ago and that newspaper went out of business three years ago. I knew two of the old editors of the *Lakeshore News,* one who used to work at the *Montreal Star* when it was still publishing and another who used to work at the *Record* in Sherbrooke. We used to receive the paper when the library was over on Summerhill Avenue.

"We achieved the old copies if that's what you're looking for, but they're all on microfilm. It will take a lot of effort to go through all that and to be honest, I don't how far our holdings go back." Richard was immediately disappointed. He would no doubt have to come back to the library another day if he would be forced to go through a pile of microfilm rolls. Still, he was pleased.

Richard smiled and bowed his head a bit. "I can't tell you how relieved I am, Miss Thomas. I must have spent hours looking on-line for anything on the *Lakeshore News* without any success whatsoever." Richard looked up for a moment, just to make sure that Miss Thomas was still listening. It was an old habit, born of what he thought was a sight inferiority complex. "But I never found anything on on-line, nothing. Fact is that I was beginning to think that maybe the paper never existed."

Miss Thomas looked at Richard with a kind, motherly smile on her face. "Don't worry, deary, the paper did exist. I would be happy to show you our microfilm library."

"How far back do you think they might go back, the microfilm archives I mean?" asked Richard.

"Well, I think the *Lakeshore News* was first published in the fifties. I not sure how far back the archives go." Richard's spirits, which had been approaching elation, then went darker. He would probably need information about local news of the early fifties or the late forties, principally because he was of the idea that the human remains that had been discovered in the backyard of the old Vessey place had been placed there in those years. But Miss Thomas then produced for him a miracle by posing a question that may have been hanging over their conversation since it began. "But why are you so interested in the *Lakeshore News*? What exactly are you looking for? Maybe I can help."

Richard then told his story about the discovery of the human remains in the backyard of the Vessey house on Parkdale Avenue, a street that Miss Thomas should have immediately recognized, it being less than a kilometre west of the library. Miss Thomas was definitely interested in the narrative, listening with apparently rapt attention, so much so that she leaned over, placed her hand on his arm, and asked him to repeat the story for her colleague, the Holocaust surviving Mrs. Wurst, motioning her over with a beckoning gesture.

"Mary, listen to this gentleman's story. I think you will be interested and maybe you can help him." Miss Thomas said, "Didn't you live on Parkdale Avenue at one time?"

Mrs. Mary Wurst came over. He could not have noticed it at first with her being stationed behind the counter but she came over haltingly, the assistance of a walker the cause. "Yes, when we first came here, back in the late forties, 1948 I think. We lived on the street for maybe thirty years. My husband, his name was Morris, and I raised our three children there. There, we moved to the Lakeside Heights area and then to the Gardens about six years ago."

Richard tried to look a little bored, almost disinterested, trying to hide his surprise. He then asked where the Gardens were, just for the sake of the conversation. He knew where the Heights were, having had a number of elementary school classmates who lived there. Miss Thomas answered for Mrs. Wurst. "That Somervale Gardens, deary. It's a nice apartment building over on Lakeshore Road, down by the lake." She smiled. Mrs. Wurst nodded.

But Richard saw his opportunity and he took advantage. Mrs. Wurst lived on same street as did the Vesseys and possibly at the right time. He asked Mrs. Wurst if she remembered the Vessey family. She looked momentarily puzzled, maybe a little scared, like it was an interrogation rather than a question. She stood there as if she were crafting an answer in her head. After a short delay, she finally answered, in a disjointed voice that suggested that she was trying to remember rather than just remembering. "Yes, the Vessey family. I think I remember them. They lived in this older, sort of dilapidated house close to the Donegani Avenue end of Parkdale.

I didn't know them, hardly ever saw them, don't think I ever spoke with them. People on the street thought they were strange."

Richard immediately asked the reason for that particular opinion on the Vesseys. "Well, don't get me wrong, Mr., Mr......"

"His name is Matthews, Richard Matthews, Mary." added Miss Thomas, helpfully. "His family used to live on Columbus, right across the back fence from the Vesseys."

Mrs. Wurst brightened up a bit and continued with her historical commentary. "Well Mr. Matthews, I remember that people on Parkdale often said that the Vesseys didn't talk much with their neighbours, didn't mix with anyone. I think they must have had five or six children. One of the kids, a boy I think, was backward, supposedly simple, poor soul was retarded you know."

Richard interrupted. "Retarded?"

Mrs. Wurst's face took on a more serious expression, like she was attempting to concentrate. "Yes, sorry, that's the term we used in those days. The boy was handicapped, mentally handicapped. The neighbours hardly ever saw him but everyone seemed to know who he was. I remember hearing that he was enrolled in school but he made so much trouble that they asked him to leave after a couple of days there. Years later, the family sent him away, where nobody seemed to know."

"Did you know his name, Mrs. Wurst?" asked Richard. "Stephen, something like that?" answered Mrs. Wurst. "Scott." suggested Richard.

Mrs. Wurst nodded and agreed."Yes, it could have been Scott, probably was."

"What about their other kids? I assume that they have several kids." asked Richard.

"I think they had four other kids. Two of them went to local schools. On the other hand, the story was that truant officers occasionally called on the Vessey house about the two kids who didn't go to school. It didn't seem to do much good. There were rumours that Mrs. Vessey used to show up at the door with her husband's shotgun. Even the police were afraid of them. They didn't like going over there."

"What about the kids who went to school?" Predictably, Richard had to ask. Mrs. Wurst just shrugged with a slight smile on her wrinkled face. An answer wasn't really expected. She didn't really know. Richard then came up with another question, the answers to which he realized he might need for his further investigations. "Do you know any of the Vessey kids' names or the names of the Vessey parents for that matter?" Mrs. Wurst offered Richard another dainty shrug. She didn't know.

All three of them, Richard, Miss Thomas, and Mrs. Wurst then stood there at the counter looking at each other for what seemed like that interminable moment, each ruminating about the reminiscences just revealed by Mrs. Wurst. Richard was about to extended his gratitude and say goodbye to the two ladies when he made one last inquiry of Mrs. Wurst, a perfunctory one to which he again did not expect an answer.

"Is there anything else either of you two ladies can tell me?" asked Richard, casually. Mrs. Wurst looked at Miss Thomas and then at Richard with a confused look on her face. Mrs. Wurst was then inspired enough to volunteer an answer. "Some people in the neighbourhood used to think that Mr. Vessey had two wives. But nobody knew where the first wife went, that is if he actually had a first wife, or why or when she left. Nobody knew either of them for that matter. Fact is that I never heard anyone who knew either of the women, or even spoke to either of them."

Again, there was a quiet moment among the three of them. After Richard considered an appropriate interval for sake of courtesy, he thanked the two ladies and left the Valois Branch of the Pointe Claire Library on Prince Edwards Avenue. He didn't think he would need the microfilm archives of the *Lakeshore News* or the *West Island Chronicle*. He would be looking for members of the Vessey family, particularly Scott Vessey, the only Vessey for whom he knew his or her Christian name. At least, he had some clue as to where to look for him.

SEARCHING FOR VESSEY

Richard wasn't home from Montreal and Pointe Claire for more than twenty minutes before he had provided Jean with a detailed account of the day's meetings. She was frankly surprised with his progress although she had doubts about the eventual conclusion of his investigation. However, she still supposed, as the sympathetic spouse mindful of possible post-retirement madness, that his behaviour was relatively innocent and hardly worth any further concern. She had come to that conclusion despite her continuing apprehension regarding her husband's initial preoccupation with the boy in the window on Belcourt Street and then its possible connection to the mystery of the human remains found in the property in the backyard of his former family home. The coincidence, if that's what it was, was just too convenient a connection. It was almost as if there was something magical going on.

She had discussed her husband's recent fixations with her friend Carol a number of times. She too was married to a retiree although her observations about his post-retirement behaviour was much less fascinating. Her husband, who also had been a government bureaucrat of longstanding duration, had developed the daily habit of reading four or five daily newspapers and watching news shows on television, all of which seemed to cover the same events from different perspectives, some of which could prompt him into rages that lasted until dinner time. After dinner, both of them would watch television until she went to bed, after which he would continue his television watching until eleven o'clock, at which time he would watch porn on the computer for half an hour or so and then try to get some sleep, a luxury that seemed to elude him more often than not. Sometimes, he sought slumber through medication, sometimes he would

110

go back to the computer. Five or six hours of troubled sleep was his normal allotment, perhaps a cause for concern, a triple bypass several years ago always in the back of Carol's mind.

Compared to her friend Jean's apprehension about her husband Richard, Carol should not have been particularly worried. She was just bored, a condition that she had managed to successfully remedy with cooking, gardening, reading and lunching with her friends, none of these activities involving her husband. She did appear to be quite interested in discussing Jean's misgivings about her husband's fascinations even though Jean herself often appeared less interested. In this context, she sometimes downplayed her concerns by suggesting that at least Richard wasn't having an affair, a laughable possibility she said, or doing something else worrisome, like drinking, doing drugs or porn addiction, bad habits that they both claimed were quite common among men their husbands' age. After discussing her husband's peculiar pursuits with Jean several times, Carol concluded that she thought Richard just might be depressed, a condition fairly common among retired men she claimed, and was responding with actions rather than other more traditional methods, like the bad habits that Carol had just enumerated. She then advised Jean to just forget about her husband's particular idiosyncrasy, concluding her counsel by pointing out that at least her husband was staying out of her hair, a benefit for any wife she claimed. Carol then laughed. Jean didn't think her comment was particularly humorous although she might have if she was married to Carol's husband.

Jean told Carol that she had been quite surprised, if not impressed with Richard's efforts to make as much progress as he had in unravelling whatever mysteries were and had bedevilled him about the faces in the windows, both now and sixty years ago, both here and there, and how the discovery of human remains behind the old house that held that window might have figured into them. Carol, who was a school teacher and therefore was expected to be generally grounded about people's behaviour, said that she wouldn't be either surprised if Richard was substituting his intense interest in work with an intense interest in something akin to work, like for example this project. Jean appeared to ponder Carol's comment and then laughed, sardonically suggesting that she had wished her husband would direct his intense interest or obsession into something a little more useful, like home repairs or housework.

Jean then asked Carol, suddenly serious. "Well, what should I do about it?", not sure that she actually expected an answer.

Carol offered a semi-shrug and a slight smile. "Nothing. I wouldn't do anything." "Seriously?" Jean replied, almost theatrically indignant, her arms spread out. "You are suggesting I do nothing?"

Carol nodded firmly. "Look, Jean, I'm not a professional therapist or anything. I'm just a teacher, which may not qualify me to analyze the behaviour of husbands. At any rate, I think he will either find something out, which I kind of doubt or he won't. But sooner or later, no matter what, he's gotta get tired and give the whole thing up."

Jean looked at her with a concerned expression on her face. "So you're telling me not to worry."

Carol smiled and nodded sympathetically. "Yes, I am." She then added some explanation. "From what you told me, Richard doesn't seem to be doing anything that should worry you, right?"

Jean returned Carol's nod. "Right, he isn't, at least so far."

Carol then concluded her dissertation about Richard and his obsession with a final scrap of advice. "Well, until he does, I would try to forget about it." She then got up from the sofa, where the both of them had been sitting, and headed for the kitchen. "More tea?"

The next day, Richard seemed to spend the entire afternoon roaming all over the internet presumably looking for information that would support the next move in his investigation of the mystery in which he had been and continued to be embroiled. Jean interrupted his research by announcing dinner. Richard was relieved, his labours having become pointless over the past half hour or so, the same websites, the same links, and accordingly the same information seemingly appearing continually. He had found all he was going to find, at least until he was inspired otherwise. As soon as he sat down in the living room, their usual venue for dining unless they had guests, Jean asked about his activities that afternoon. Richard seemed willing to discuss them, which was somewhat surprising given his customary reluctance to share the status of his investigation.

"I've been searching the internet for information on housing available to the mentally handicapped in the old neighbourhood, basically Pointe Claire and maybe the rest of the West Island area." explained Richard. He had been leaning forward and then fell back on the sofa, pleased with his own explanation, feeling for a moment like he had managed to survive one of those indomitable government meetings during which certain senior managers liked to find fault with their subordinates. Or so it seemed. He was awoken out of his daydream when Jean brought his supper out to him and asked him to turn the television news on, the public broadcast channel preferred, and returned to the kitchen for her dinner plate. Once she sat down beside Richard on the sofa, she turned to him and asked about the reasons for his hunt for information on housing for the intellectually handicapped. Richard smiled and explained his optimism. "I have to find Scott Vessey if I can. He is the only key left to possibly unlocking the mystery of what may have happened in the backyard of his family's place on Parkdale, sixty years ago or so. He's the only one who could possibly tell me anything."

Jean then asked, "Can't you try to find some other member of the family? From what you've told me, there were the parents and four or five children."

"That's true but I wouldn't know where to look. That older man I spoke with on Parkdale a couple of days ago thought that the Vesseys moved away after their house burned down in the late 70s. He didn't know where they went and to be honest, I would not know where to even begin to look." Richard explained.

And Jean helpfully interjected. "And Scott Vessey?"

Richard nodded and expanded on his reasoning for his search for Scott Vessey. "Well, I have an idea as to where he might be – in a group home, probably in the same neighbourhood in which he grew up. Remember, I saw Scott when I was a teenager and I was pretty sure then that he was in the care of a group home. So, if he is still alive, and I have no reason to think that he isn't, he should still be in a group home, probably somewhere in Valois or on the West Island."

Both Jean and Richard finished their dinners without any further discussion of the planned search for Scott Vessey. While Jean was concentrating on a television news story, Richard began to plan his next day's endeavours. He had determined that the most likely source of information on group homes in the preferred area would be the West Island Association for the Intellectually Handicapped (WIAIH) which, as providence would have it, was headquartered in the old Valois Post Office, a two story stone Edwardian edifice that was completed in 1915. It was located on Donegani Avenue in Valois.

It was a curious discovery. Richard remembered that a local civic organization had purchased the building after the Post Office was moved to a much larger building further east on Donegan sometime in the late 50s. The organization used the building to establish several small enterprises at which handicapped adults were employed. Richard had remembered being aware of that fact, having frequently seen handicapped people coming and in out of the old Post Office, the building situated near places with which Richard and his childhood pals were familiar, like the snack bar in Johnson's Drug and the train station across the street. The story was that handicapped people were engaged in minor manufacturing like assembling small toys. Richard's father occasionally complained that the organization's leaders may not have been paying the workers, suggesting that some of its members were keeping money that was intended to pay the people assembling the toys. Richard later concluded that his father had likely fabricated the story about the misdirected money because he didn't like the man who ran the organization, a fat, disagreeable man named Ashworth who lived two streets over from the Matthews on Michigan Avenue. In addition, he later had been told, by someone he could not recall, that Richard's father had attempted to join Mr. Ashworth's organization but had been told that one had to belong to the United Church to join. Richard didn't believe the story. The Matthews were Catholic.

After dinner, Richard told Jean that he may have to take another trip to Pointe Claire/Valois, likely the following Monday, his purpose to visit a group home in the area that might have Scott Vessey as a resident. He had invested considerable time and effort on the internet in researching the location of local group homes without much success. He had then telephoned the head office for WIAIH in the old Post Office building and had been told, by a woman who introduced herself as the administrator of the office, that while she could provide him with a list of group homes on the West Island, she did not have any information on the residents themselves, some of whom she said may have resided at an institution that had been located in Baie-D'urfe, another West Island community further west. It had basically been a branch of Montreal's Douglas Hospital, one of the earliest such facilities in Montreal, if not in Quebec. It had been regarded, at least in Richard's memory, as an asylum, a place of harrowing potential. He had been there once, to serve mass for an uncle of one of his classmates, a Catholic priest. He had been frightened by the experience. The Baie-D'urfe facility, about which he knew little, if not anything, had been closed decades ago and its patients moved to local group homes or in with their families, the consequence of a policy of returning the mentally ill and the mentally challenged to the community, where presumably the government could wash its hands of them. Or so thought Richard's parents, particularly his mother who did not consider institutions as uncomfortable or malevolent as was commonly believed.

He had asked the administrator to e-mail him the list which was divided between public and private long term residences. Fortunately, it included telephone numbers. He decided that he would spend the next morning telephoning the group homes on the list looking for a resident named Scott Vessey. Jean seemed a trifle comforted by her husband's report and his plan. However strange the entire enterprise still seemed to her, she thought that her husband's latest plan was sensible, if not logical in the circumstances. She had to admit. He was getting closer.

FINDING VESSEY

The next day, Richard started making his telephone calls to the group homes on the list that the WIAIH administrator had e-mailed him the previous afternoon. He had decided that he would introduce himself as a relative, a first cousin on Scott's mother's side named Richard Matthews, the use of his own name a cautionary move in the event that somewhere someone would ask for identification. The first group home on the list was a place called the Playfield House, which provided accommodation to ten residents in individual bedrooms but was currently housing only eight when he called, a fact related to him during his call. The voice of the person who answered the telephone was barely audible, background noise supplied by people who seemed to be howling about something or other overcoming whatever it was he intended to say. He decided that he had no other choice but to hang up the telephone and try again later, which he did.

He next dialed the number of the Manoir Beaconsfield, which was obviously located in Beaconsfield, another suburban community located west of Pointe Claire. Richard immediately recalled the summer he spent caddying at the Beaconsfield Golf Club, a private course for golfers prosperous enough to pay an annual membership fee of $5,000, an enormous amount back in 1964. He remembered it as a generally onerous job in which he carried a heavy bag full of expensive golf clubs for four hours for $2.00, a complimentary soda at the eleventh hole refreshment stand, and a gratuity of a quarter. It amounted to a basic hourly wage of little more than 50 cents at a time when the minimum government mandated wage was 85 cents an hour. Sometimes, not every often, Richard managed to carry golf bags for two clients during one day. It was called doubles, a feat that would net him almost five dollars, enough to prompt his mother to ask for money for groceries, not that she ever meant it. Some of his fellow caddies, older guys who seemed to spend most of their time at the caddyshack playing cards, would invariably carry doubles; singles apparently not worth their time. It was an admirable ambition and one that he never achieved, not even once during those three months he invested during the summer of 1964 at the Beaconsfield Golf Club. That was the only summer he spent caddying, his job the next summer packing groceries at the A&P, his pay a princely $1.10 an hour, the recently increased minimum wage.

The voice on the other end of the line at the Manoir Beaconsfield sounded almost elegant. Richard immediately assumed that she was a member of the officer staff as opposed to one of the care givers, whom he had begun to notice would always sound harried, like they were about to collapse from fatigue or confusion or both. He introduced himself and said, as he had planned, that he was the first cousin of a man named Scott Vessey who may be a resident of the Manoir Beaconsfield. She then asked a question for which he had not rehearsed an answer. "Why do you think he is one of our residents? Do you not know where he lives?" she asked, delicately, as if she was speaking to a child.

Richard was momentarily silent, searching for a response that did not sound like an invented excuse. He decided on a barely modified version of the truth. "He could be one of your residents. I mean, I'm not sure at all but I have some evidence I guess you would call it. While I have not seen him for many, many years, maybe fifty or sixty years. I do know where he and his family used to live. I also know that Scott might have come to live in a group home when he was a teenager. So I am starting with group homes near where he used to live."

"And where was that?" asked the woman on the telephone. Her voice reminded Richard of a woman named Rosemary, who was the secretary to one of his first government bosses, a man named Stewart Campbell, a World War II vet he much admired.

"He lived in Valois at one time and may still live somewhere on the West Island." replied Richard. "So I thought it possible that he could end up at your home."

The woman then come to an obvious conclusion. "And you are calling every group home on the West Island?"

"Yes, I am." admitted Richard, as if he revealing some sort of secret. "So, is Scott Vessey one of the residents at your home?"

The woman immediately answered, with a sarcastic tone. "No, we have nine residents and not one of them is named Scott Vessey." She then added an answer to a question he might have been considering asking in any event. "And I don't think the home has ever had a resident named Scott Vessey."

He suddenly had a thought. The idea that Scott Vessey might have passed away had never occurred to him before. It was possible after all. He and Richard were around the same age and well, he might not have been in perfect heath, living in group homes or institutions or wherever.

"How long has the group home been there?" asked Richard. The woman on the telephone answered by repeating the question. "How long have we been here? We have been here for ten years." The woman then completed their conversation by suggesting that he try the other group homes on his list, a list that she asked him to share with her. He then read off the eleven group homes that the WIAIH official had e-mailed him. The women noted that the Valois headquarters also provided space for eight residents, suggesting that Richard add the Valois House to the list. She gave him the telephone number. Richard then thanked her and rang off.

Although Richard was tempted to contact the recently added Valois House next, he chose to continue with the list, switching to the public residences as rendered in the e-mail. It was a place called Bayview, a residence that was located on Lakeshore Road in Pointe Claire, less than a kilometre away and below the tracks from the train station in Valois and just up from Lake Saint Louis. Perhaps not surprisingly, the telephone was answered by a man who seemed decidedly disinterested in assisting Richard with his inquiry. The representative of Bayview almost barked in greeting him and then followed with a terse demand. "What exactly do you want, sir?"

Taken aback somewhat by his ill-mannered tone, Richard nervously asked if a Scott Vessey was a resident of Bayview.

"Who?" replied the unidentified Bayview representative.

Richard repeated his inquiry, calmly as he could, still worried about getting any type of answer. "Scott Vessey, does he live at Bayview?"

There was a muffled silence on the line, like the Bayview representative had his hand over the receiver and was speaking to someone. "There's nobody here by that name – Vessey."

Richard sought confirmation. "Are you sure?"

The Bayview representative answered, now understandably annoyed, giving Richard a curt confirmation. He then hung up. Richard was left wondering whether the Bayview representative was telling him the truth, his honesty obviously affected by his irritating manner during their conversation. Richard then hung up himself.

The next home on his list was called Maison Herron, a private facility located in Dorval, another West Island suburb immediately east of Pointe Claire. Richard was quite familiar with Dorval, not only because of the airport, where he spent the summer of 1970 working at its gift shop, but back before high school, he and his pals would take their bicycles to the airport in the summers where they would spend their days watching the airplanes. They would occasionally shoplift model soldiers from the gift shop where Richard would work years later, and spending their allowances and whatever they could lift from their mothers' purses on chocolate bars and sodas.

Before dialing the number for the Maison Herron, Richard looked at the address that had been provided by WIAIH administrator, which happened to be Herron Avenue, and thought whether the large old building located just below the highway near the Pinecrest train station was now a group home. He dialed and the telephone was answered by a young man who mumbled his greeting, making it difficult to identify the language in which the greeting was being given, neither English nor French being discernible. Richard suspected that the kid on the telephone was from Jamaica or somewhere in the Caribbean. He asked for Scott Vessey, thinking that a direct request to speak to Scott Vessey would be more likely to get a direct response than if Richard asked if Scott Vessey was a resident. Again, he received a reply but he couldn't decipher it. He asked for Scott

Vessey a second time and, after a brief delay, another voice, a woman's voice this time, came on the telephone. For the third time, Richard asked if he could speak to Scott Vessey. The woman told Richard that he had a wrong number. Richard apologized and hung up.

Again, he switched from a private to a public group home on the list. The next public home on the list was another location in the suburb of Dorval, this one identified as Centre d'hébergement Dorval, its address on a street named de la Présentation, east of the airport, closer to Lachine than Pointe Claire, in a location with which Richard was not familiar. He had looked it up on Google where he discovered that it was a large, relatively modern looking building which housed at least fifty residents with various handicaps, both physical and intellectual, or so the sign in front of the building in the internet photograph claimed. He telephoned the main number without delay. Again, he chose to ask for Scott Vessey directly rather than inquire about his possible presence in the facility. A man had answered the telephone, seemingly bored, not surprising since it was after four o'clock in the afternoon and Richard's call could easily have been the last of four or five dozen the man had to endure that day. But the man wasn't rude, which was surprising. He introduced himself as Pierre Langlois and then informed Richard that the Centre did not have anyone named Vessey on its list but seemed genuinely interested in Richard's plight, if indeed his request was more than just a passing interest. Sensing that he now had an opportunity for some desperately needed assistance in finding Scott Vessey, he went on to explain, in accordance with his already developed script, that he was Scott Vessey's first cousin.

The man on the telephone sighed sympathetically and repeated Richard's family relationship back to Scott Vessey. "First cousin you said?"

"Yes, on my mother's side." For some reason, Richard then felt that he had to explain a relationship that was obvious on its face. "Yes, my mother is his mother's sister. But neither has seen each other for a long time."

"Why now? Does your mother want to see Scott now?" asked Mr. Langlois. Fortunately, Richard had a cover story for that question as well. "No, she passed away months ago. But before she died, she made me promise that I try and find her nephew Scott. Apparently, she had been thinking about her sister, who she hadn't seen for a long time, and then started thinking about Scott, who she hadn't seen since he was a baby. She wanted to see if I could find him. And she knew that he could have been living in a group home somewhere on the West Island. We lived near Scott's family in Pointe Claire." As a fiction, it wasn't particularly compelling but it was better than nothing. He thought about sharing the truth with him but he wasn't sure that anyone would believe him. He thought about the real reason that he was searching for Scott Vessey. He wasn't sure that he could actually explain that. What was it anyway? Curiosity, a post-retirement hobby? Something to do?

"I see." observed Mr. Langlois. "Sorry but I have to tell you but Scott Vessey is not one of our residents." Then he had a question, which demonstrated a surprising interest in Richard's quest. Maybe Mr. Langlois was more bored than Richard thought he was. "Since your and Scott's family lived in Pointe Claire, maybe you should try the Valois group home. It is called the Omega Group Home and it is in the same building as the WIAIH headquarters in Valois." Richard immediately thought of the old Post Office building. He could have walked by the place where Scott Vessey was living dozen of times when he was still living in Valois, that is if Scott was actually living in the Omega Group Home.

"Yes, I spoke to them. An administrator there gave me the list of group homes in the entire West Island. But I didn't know that there was a group home next door." said Richard, surprised that he had overlooked a group home so close to the last known address for Scott Vessey, even though he didn't know about it.

Mr. Langlois then continued with some advice. "I suggest you telephone the WIAIH, tell them that you are looking for a resident in the Omega Group Home. It houses maybe a dozen people. Maybe he's been living there." Richard chuckled and remarked. "That would be a miracle. I mean, I moved out of that neighbourhood maybe fifty years ago."

"Maybe so." said Mr. Langlois. "But he could still be there. He's around your age, isn't he?" A lucky guess. "As I am told, the home has been been around since the early 60s. So maybe you should try to contact them. I know the guy in charge over there. His name is Steve Boileau. Look, I'll give you his number." Richard agreed and took the telephone number. He thanked him. He then heard Pierre Langlois wish him luck.

Richard sat near the telephone, holding the receiver. He was contemplating the irony of possibly living near Scott Vessey, at least for maybe a few years when the Matthews family still lived in the area, on Columbus Avenue, and Scott Vessey was residing at the Omega Group Home several blocks away on Donegani.

He hoped that a telephone call to the Omega Group Home would be his last in the series of telephone calls to group homes. He thought that maybe he was being overly optimistic but there were indications that he was on the right track, by fortune of course but by fortune nonetheless. It was a stroke of luck. He dialed the telephone number that Pierre Langlois had given him and asked for Steve Boileau who, as he was informed by the man who answered the telephone, the supervisor of the home and one of its owners. The man answering the telephone told Richard that Mr. Boileau was on holiday and therefore was not available. Then, the man on the telephone suggested that Richard might want to speak to someone else, recommending a case worker named Leonard who, at least according to the man on the telephone, was the longest serving of the dozen individuals on staff at the Omega Group Home. Richard then asked if he was available. He was.

"Hello, my name is Leonard." said the voice on the telephone. "I am told that you want to talk to Steve Boileau. Maybe I can help you." The man sounded almost elderly, a gravelly voice that seemed to require some effort. Still, Leonard sounded calmly cheerful, almost therapeutic, the outcome of countless encounters no doubt with people whose behaviour was usually unpredictable and sometimes dangerous.

Richard almost cheerfully replied. "Well, thanks so much, Leonard. I hate to bother you but I'm looking for someone that might be a resident there. My name is Richard Matthews and I am looking for someone who I haven't seen for a long time, a cousin of mine. His name is Scott Vessey. He used to live in this neighourhood, right there in Valois, a few blocks west on Parkdale. He is mentally handicapped and is probably about 65 years old now. My mother, who recently passed away, had wanted me to look for her nephew, my cousin, and I've been telephoning the group homes on the West Island looking for him."

Leonard cleared his throat and observed. "And you've finally gotten around to our place." Richard agreed. "Yeah, you could say that. Funny thing though. I could have started here at Omega but I didn't know it was a group home. I just thought this place was the head office of WIAIH and that it didn't house anybody." For a moment, a memory of the mentally handicapped people working in the old Post Office flashed across his mind. He wondered if all of them ended up living in the residence, that is when it become a residence.

There was a dead silence on the telephone, as if Leonard was contemplating doubts about his story, a possibility that frightened Richard in a shallow sort of way. But the line came alive again when Leonard started to mutter something that Richard he could not hear at first. "I'm sorry to have to tell you this, but we had a resident named Scott Vessey for years. In fact, I understand that he was one of our first residents. He was placed in here from some institution, maybe even the Douglas Hospital downtown in Verdun." Richard recognized the name of the place, he had been there. "Anyway, I'm sorry that Scott is no longer with us.", there was another significant pause, "We lost him several years ago."

"Lost him, what do you mean?" asked Richard. "He passed away five or six years ago, just slipped away one night. We thought he had a fever but it was worse than that. Anyway, I'm sorry to have to tell you this." answered Leonard.

Richard was elated at the same time as he was shocked. He had found Scott Vessey there but he wasn't there. He had to know more of the picture. "So I guess you contacted his family.", realizing that his fiction about being Scott's first cousin might come up in discussing Scott Vessey's death. Leonard replied to Richard. "No, we didn't, we couldn't. We tried but we just couldn't find them. They had moved from Valois a long time ago, probably out of province. Maybe you know where they are." Now Richard was faced with extending his prevarications about his relationship to Scott Vessey. If Scott had been his cousin, then he should have some idea as to where his mother's sister lived. So he made up another story. "My mother, my mother who passed away months ago, told me that her sister and her family moved to the West Coast maybe fifty years ago."

Leonard finished the thought. "And they left Scott behind.?"

"I guess so. I think that Scott was in care long before they moved away from Valois. In fact, the last time I saw Scott, he was not at home anymore and I suppose his family had moved away." He was referring to the only honest thing he had said about Scott, aside from his name of course, a reference to the incident to the grocery store more than fifty years ago. Richard then asked after Scott's final resting place, almost on reflex. His search looked to be at an end.

"Well, we buried him in Lakeview, in a cemetery out at the end of Donegani here in Pointe Claire. Omega has a section of burial plots out there." Leonard explained. "I'll give you directions if you like."

"Okay," replied Richard, the sound of resignation palpable. Leonard recognized and tried to ameliorate the tone. "If you're interested, I think we still have a small box full of his stuff – you know, things he left behind, things from his room in our home here, mementos if you will. I don't know why we kept the stuff. I mean, it's been so long."

Richard was suddenly interested again, a recovery from his resignation. "Mementos?" he observed hopefully. Leonard explained. "Yes, mainly pictures, he was very interested in pictures, you know snapshots. He used to carry some around with him all the time but they never stayed in good shape. They were always being folded up and crumbled. I remember the staff always looking for ways to keep the pictures in good shape. We put scotch tape on them, put them in plastic sleeves, that kind of thing, just to protect them. Finally, his last worker started laminating them."

He thought he could imagine Leonard shaking his head over the telephone line. He went on. "It didn't work. They would last a while and then they would end up under his bed or in the garage. One time, he actually peed on a bunch of pictures that we were keeping in this plastic bin in his room. He only did it that once. Never did it again. Like all the residents here, there is never any explanation for strange behaviour. In fact, when we chastised him for peeing all over his pictures, he thought it was funny."

Richard commiserated. "That must be tough." He then asked. "So did you do anything about it in the end?"

Leonard answered in an apologetic manner, as if he had no choice. "Well, we just made him more pictures." Then he offered Richard a barely audible laugh, like he was embarrassed about a response that could be regarded as somewhat feeble.

Again there was a silence, neither Leonard nor Richard saying a word, like there was nothing else on which to comment. Then, Leonard came up with one more thing, ". As I say, I think we still have some of Scott's things, mainly his pictures. I don't why we kept them. We thought that maybe one of the other residents would be interested in them. I remember that a couple of others were jealous of his pictures, tried to take them from his room. I think they're still in storage. You can have them all if you want."

Richard's mood turned again. Leonard was now offering to give him a clue, probably the only clue left for him in his lengthy search for the truth, if indeed there was truth to be had. He immediately agreed to take possession of Scott's pictures, telling him that he could be in Valois tomorrow to pick them up. Leonard told him that he was working the day shift tomorrow and that Richard could drop by pretty well any time to pick up the pictures. Richard may have seemed a little too enthusiastic in accepting Leonard's offer, thinking that it may have sounded a little too zealous. But his concern was misplaced. Leonard didn't even sound surprised. He just said that he was looking forward to seeing him the next day and said goodbye, adding that he was certain that Richard knew the way. Richard agreed.

SCOTT'S PICTURES

As was his habit, which may have grown tiresome to her, Richard briefed Jean on his conversation with Leonard of Omega Group Home, reporting on the disclosure of Scott Vessey's passing, the information on his demise the apparent finale of telephone conversations with representatives of several group homes. Jean was pleased, if not relieved to be told that Richard seemed to be on the verge of the end of the road that was Scott Vessey. She was not as surprised as she should have been that her husband was still pursuing the mystery of the human remains on the Vessey property through the pictures left in the estate of Scott Vessey even though it seemed that it had been as close to being resolved as it could be. He said that he would be going back to Pointe Claire, to the Omega Group Home to meet with a man named Leonard the next day. Jean was certain that the pictures that once belonged to Scott Vessey and that were now the residue of his estate would be the final piece of the puzzle that her husband had been pursuing.

The next morning, after a short discussion during which Jean provided him with a gentle warning not to expect anything significant from Scott's pictures, Richard started out on another trip to Pointe Claire. It was a curious development. Here he was visiting his old home, a place in which he hadn't lived in almost fifty years, for the third time in the last several days after basically disregarding it since he left it. He arrived at the Omega Group Home on Donegani Road in less than two hours. As he had supposed, the group home was a relatively modern looking building attached to the rear of WIAIH headquarters which was located in the old Post Office. It was a large building, large enough it seemed to provide accommodation to the dozen residents that Pierre Langlois of the Centre d'hébergement Dorval said were housed in the Omega House. He could have entered the Omega House by its front door, which was located on Valois Bay Avenue, on the corner immediately west of the WIAIH, but chose, for reasons of curiosity, if nothing else, to walk up the steps of the WIAIH headquarters to announce himself and his intention. A woman, who sat behind a large desk with a gold coloured plaque identifying her as Marie France Cousineau, greeted him with a thin smile.

Richard explained that he was here to pick something up from an Omega staff member named Leonard, all the while looking all over the place as if he was trying to remember whether there was anything familiar in the lobby he had just entered. He had forgotten whether he had ever been in the room, either when it was still the original Post Office or when it was a local civic organization that was employing handicapped people who he had seen coming in and out of the building when he was a kid.

"This is WIAIH headquarters. You didn't have to report here. You can go directly to the Omega, it just around the corner." advised Mme Cousineau. Richard smiled and quietly replied "I know. I'm just curious." Mme Cousineau just stared at him and commented. "Curious? Curious about what?" Richard then went on to explain that he lived in the neighbourhood and must must have passed the building dozens of times when he was a kid. Richard then apologized, turned around, left the building, turned right and then right again to arrive at the front door of the Omega Group Home. There was a tall thin man wearing a backwards baseball cap standing by the door smoking a cigarette. He offered Richard a cigarette and then asked him if he wanted to buy a lighter which he aggressively thrust towards him like a weapon. Richard declined both offers which prompted the tall thin man to say something that was unintelligible but likely profane. Though he wasn't frightened, Richard was still relieved when one of the group home workers, a young woman blessed with violet hair and an impressive tattoo of a blue lizard on her neck, appeared and gently directed the tall thin man away from the entrance. She called the man Sam and assured Richard that he was not as harmful as he appeared to be, his bark worse than his bite an obvious metaphor. She then led the tall thin man away, both of them disappearing into the house without a further word.

There then appeared at the door an older man, silver hair, well wrinkled face, a kindly smile that would not have seemed out of place on a shopping mall Santa Claus. This had to be Leonard who was introducing himself before Richard had come to that conclusion.

"Good morning, I'm Leonard. I'm glad to meet you." he greeted him with a nod, a grin, and a reassuring voice, then offering Richard his family name – Chapman – and one of those left handed, backhanded shakes that seemed usually applicable to hipsters and people with injured limbs. Richard returned the salutation and then was ushered into the foyer of the Omega Group Home. "I'm glad you made it before lunch." said Leonard, "It can get pretty busy here with a dozen people around the dining room table. Sometimes, it gets so hectic that we have to serve lunch in shifts, you know when there are visitors."

Richard assured Leonard, "Well, I think I'll be gone by lunch." Leonard smiled. "Okay, but you can stay for lunch if you want."

"Thanks but I promised to get home by the early afternoon." said Richard, a white lie to cover his plan to do a little shopping and maybe have lunch in the Fairview Shopping Centre in Pointe Claire.

Leonard started to escort him toward the basement stairs where Richard assumed the home kept their storage. It was a large basement with three bedrooms, a washroom, a makeshift office, and a storage room. Richard then noticed that Leonard had a ring of keys secured to his belt. It almost immediately reminded Richard of several janitors with whom he was at one time or another familiar, a man named Bill who worked in an apartment building in which Richard and his first wife lived back in the early 70s, a man named Jimmy with whom Richard worked on a summer job in a Pointe Claire factory, and a couple of other fellows whose names he could not recall. Leonard went to the storage room, a key already out and opened the door. Richard stood at the door to the room as he watched Leonard begin to move cardboard boxes around. It did not take him long to locate a comparatively small box, identified as "Scott V" by a faded black magic marker written across one of the flaps. Leonard pulled it out and pushed it across the floor toward Richard.

"Well, here it is." announced Leonard. He then asked. "Will you be taking the box with you or do you want to look through it here?"

Richard knelt down and start to look through the box, too excited to resist. The box was, as Leonard advertised, almost entirely awash in photographs, possibly hundreds of them, most the standard size of 4" X 6" although some were a little larger at 5" X 7" while others were the size of index cards at 3" X 5". Some were also laminated, an innovation that Scott's last worker, a younger man named Andre who, according to Leonard, was responsible for Scott's care over the past two years of his life, had introduced. The other significant fact of the photographs was their subject matter. The photographs almost entirely pictured scenes from movies, many of them from the 1980s, the explanation being, at least according to Leonard, that the late 1970s and the 1980s, aside from acquainting the world to bouffant hair and highly stylized fashions, also introduced the videocassette recorder, which allowed for VCR tapes of movies and television programs to be played and replayed innumerable times. So it was, said Leonard, that the group home then had a new therapeutic mechanism with which to entertain its residents, such entertainment at times a superior remedy to calm misbehaving residents. Scott became a regular, if not obsessive enthusiast of movie viewing. In addition, he started to ask for pictures from the many movies he had seen, mainly scenes and characters from them. He then started carrying the pictures, clutching them like some sort of prized artifacts, almost religious relics, requiring the protection that ultimately led Andre to the lamination process. Richard, who was a devotee of motion pictures himself, recognized the scenes from many of the movies from which Scott had received pictures. These included such cinematic classics from the period as "Back to the Future", "Superman", "Ghostbusters", "Ferris Bueller's Day Off", "Stand By Me", "Big", "A Christmas Story" and dozens of others. No wonder that Scott Vessey was regarded as the doyen of film appreciation in the Omega Group Home, even by the staff.

After investing maybe five minutes looking through Scott's box, he decided to bring Scott's box with him. His cursory study of maybe four or five dozen of Scott's pictures revealed nothing that could somehow assist him in his pursuit of the mystery. Richard folded the flaps to Scott's box, picked up the box, and started out of the storage room. Leonard walked with him, up the stairs, out the door and then down to his car in the parking lot. "I hope Scott's pictures are of some use to you." He then paused for a moment and then asked. "Why did you want these pictures anyway?" Richard shrugged and provided the pithiest of answers.

"Clues, just clues." Leonard watched Richard open his car's trunk, place Scott's box there and then close the trunk. Leonard opened the driver's side car door for Richard who got in and then rolled down his window. "I hope Scott's box will bring you closer to whatever it is that you are looking for." Richard nodded, touched his hand through the open car window, started the car and slowly backed it out of its parking spot, put the car in drive and turned on to Valois Bay Avenue.

As planned, Richard stopped by the Fairview Shopping Centre, managed to purchase a fashionable t-shirt at Zara, picked up a copy of the *Montreal Gazette* and then had lunch at the Keg. He was on the road again by 2:30 in the afternoon and was home by 5:00. He took Scott's box out of the car's trunk and carried it into the house. Jean greeted him with a wave and asked if the box was Scott's. He nodded and put the box in the dining room. He told Jean that he intended to explore the box and its pictures after dinner. Jean, who was curious, asked if he wanted some help. Richard accepted her offer.

Over dinner, Richard explained that Scott's pictures seemed to consist almost entirely of pictures of scenes from movies that were made in the 1980s. He told Jean that Leonard had told him that Scott had likely viewed most of these movies countless times, adding somewhat facetiously that he could quote entire scenes from some of these movies, having committed such scenes to a memory that seemed almost infallible when it came to movies that he had favoured. Jean told her husband that it might be almost enjoyable, if not fascinating to examine Scott's pictures but asked about his objective.

"What exactly am I looking for? Is there something in one of those pictures that could help you to solve this mystery of yours?" she asked with certain incredulity, not having any idea as to what her husband was looking for.

Richard offered a quiet chuckle. "To be honest, I don't know but there might be something in one of those pictures that might be a clue. I don't know what but those pictures are the only possible clues that I have left."

Jean nodded and agreed to take up the examination of Scott's pictures. Richard lifted the box up onto the dinner room table and the two of them started to divide up the pictures to examine them.

—

They both started to look through the pictures. It did not take either Jean or Richard long to realize that not only were Scott's snapshots of scenes recognizable from certain movies from the 1980s but there were a multitude of duplicates, the same scenes pictured in many photographs. Jean asked Richard about the duplicates, as if he could provide some sort of explanation, which he couldn't. He reminded her that Scott was mentally handicapped, a condition that usually resulted in the demonstration of strange, if not bizarre idiosyncrasies, things like an enchantment, if not an obsession with duplicate photographs. But there was no explanation whatever.

Jean and Richard had been looking through Scott's pictures for maybe ten minutes when Jean came across a photograph that did not seem to belong to any movie, the main evidence being the fact that Scott himself was in the picture, standing with presumably another resident. Though surprised, Richard had the presence of mind to ask Jean to put that particular photograph aside, reasoning almost immediately that there could be clues in any such photographs. Within another ten minutes, Jean and Richard had located another half dozen such pictures, Scott in a couple of Halloween costumes, a ghost and a Batman, Scott sitting near a Christmas tree, and Scott in group shots with a number of whom Richard assumed were fellow group home residents.

After a half an hour or so, the two of them had a pile of maybe three dozen photographs that did not depict a scene from some movie or another, or at least not a scene that they could recognize as being from a movie.

Jean and Richard looked through them carefully. Jean pulled one of them from the batch they had already placed in the separate pile and pushed it across the table to Richard. It was a fairly clear black and white 2" X 3" wallet size photograph of an empty patch of grass on which stood a crude wooden cross that was maybe a foot high. On the back of the photograph was written three barely legible words, "Mother" and a date "May 1953".

Richard thought for a time of taking the photograph to the police. He concluded, however, that even if he could adequately explain the background to his discovery of the photograph, they would think him eccentric, if not crazy. He also doubted that they would be in the least bit interested in a possible murder more than sixty years old, even though the remains had been found fairly recently. Not that he had any evidence, but he was fairly certain that the police, who he thought were basically indolent, were looking forward to closing the book on the case. Besides, hadn't Chief Medical Examiner Tessier told him that she had reached the same conclusion about the likely interest, or lack thereof of the police in the case of the remains of who he had now thought was Scott Vessey's mother.

THE INTERPRETATION

Richard barely had his hand on the picture of the cross on the patch of grass when he jumped to a conclusion that was almost astonishing to Jean. It reminded him of an idea for a full fledged ghost story or a possible episode of the old "Twilight Zone" series. Richard exclaimed, with a burst of enthusiasm that Jean had not heard since he first told her about the discovery of the human remains in the backyard of the Vessey place, that the photograph was a picture of a crude memorial, a wooden cross marking the final resting place of Scott's mother, the mother that seemed to have disappeared without a trace sometime in the '50s. Jean immediately challenged Richard's hypothesis, asking with a skeptical edge to her voice for its basis.

Richard offered an almost diabolical look on his face, leaned across the dining room table and began to explain. "Look, I honestly think it could be the mother, Scott's mother, the first Vessey wife."

Jean almost rolled her eyes. "I know you want to solve this thing, whatever you think this thing is, but what facts have you got now that you didn't have before we found the photograph? I mean, its an old black and white photograph of a wooden cross with "Mother" and a date written on the back. What does it mean? What could it mean? Does it mean anything?"

The volume of Richard's voice came down, usually meaning that her husband was about to get serious, not that he wasn't being serious already. He was almost whispering, as if he was about to issue a confidence. He had moved closer to her, almost on the same side of table now. He began to summarize his findings, a recitation with which Jean was becoming quite familiar

"I've finally put it together. First of all, there's this handicapped boy constantly in the window of the house behind our place back when I was a kid. Of course, I'm curious, if not fascinated, if not obsessed. The boy's name is Scott Vessey and he is staring out of that window every single day I remember. One day many years later, a couple of my boyhood pals and I decide to sneak over to his house to spy on him. He sees us and all he does is point down to the backyard. Then, decades later, I read in the *Montreal Gazette* that human remains are found in that backyard. As you know, I was then addicted. I found out that the remains were of a woman and that she had likely been murdered. I was then told by an old librarian named Mrs. Wurst as well as an older man who lived on Parkdale Avenue that it was quite possible that the first Mrs. Vessey, who was probably Scott's mother, disappeared and was then replaced by another Mrs. Vessey, the one who lived there when I lived there although I have to admit that I never really saw her. And now, now that we have a photograph showing what looks like a grave marker and that is dated around the time that Scott's mother may have disappeared." Richard paused for a moment and looked at Jean with a certain concentrated sincerity. "And you know what I think." Richard hesitated for another moment and then continued with his story. "I think that Scott Vessey's mother was murdered because she gave birth to Scott, who turned out to be handicapped. It was like, you know, divine retribution or something like that. So thought whoever killed her. Don't forget, the Vessey family was kind of strange." Having reached his conclusion, Richard leaned back in his chair and folded his arms across his chest. His presentation was over.

Jean almost looked up toward the ceiling, eyebrows having gone up as well, grinned and offered a review. "That's quite a story. Not saying I believe it but it is a fascinating tale. And besides me, who do you intend to inform, the MUC police, the *Montreal Gazette*, that medical examiner, those two librarians." Richard could have added the Omega Group Home to the list. He really didn't know what to say. He just shrugged and acknowledged his uncertainty. "I don't know, I really don't know." He honestly had not thought about the next step. He wasn't sure that there was a next step. He was just pleased, triumphant and relieved that he had solved a mystery that had bedevilled him for so long.

THE OTHER MYSTERY

In the days following the conclusion of Richard's search for the true history of the human remains found in the backyard on which Scott Vessey would constantly gaze decades ago from a second floor window, his thoughts would occasionally drift to the mystery he had constructed of another man staring out of a second floor window in his neighbourhood, the one on Belcourt Avenue. Jean accused him of false confidence, his cracking of the Vessey case having provided him with an unreasonable amount of self-assurance when it came to solving mysteries of men who stare out of second floor windows. Richard did not know and never did come to a conclusion regarding whether there was any further action that he could take now that he had arrived at an apparent settlement of the question regarding the human remains and their relationship to Scott Vessey's position in that second floor window. Over those few days, Jean would frequently advise him to abandon the entire undertaking, suggesting that perhaps he might consider turning his search into a novel, implying that he transform his apprehension about a future project by writing about the previous project. One evening, during one of their many discussions about the issue with Jean, Richard finally agreed to start writing. He promised to begin by assembling notes about his experiences pursuing the mystery of the human remains found on the Vessey property. Jean said that she was willing to assist him in substantiating his memories by filling in the blanks, assuring Richard that she had heard him talking about his efforts often enough to help him.

The next morning, after a restless night of formulating plans about a potential book concerning his pursuit of the Vessey mystery, he announced to Jean that he had decided to turn the detective abilities he had developed in investigating that mystery into considering whether the enigma of the

Davidson boy staring out of the second floor window at 240 Belcourt Avenue was worth investigating further. Jean was speechless, shocked that her husband was talking about moving from one mystery, which he had apparently just solved, to another mystery, which may not have been a mystery at all. After almost spitting a mouth full of coffee down her nightgown and falling off her chair at their kitchen island, she suggested that her husband was losing his mind, asking him directly if he somehow had gone crazy over night. Richard was taken aback somewhat, shrugging wearily, as if he hadn't heard what Jean had just said. He felt like returning to sleep. He already had gone through this, hadn't he? Didn't his quest of the Vessey mystery already provide Jean with a previous example of his investigative abilities? While Richard had been aware of Jean's doubts regarding his Vessey project from the moment he had received news from his brother of the discovery of the human remains, he had convinced himself that while Jean was skeptical of his plan, at times seriously skeptical, she had not taken any action or expressed any reservations that would suggest to Richard that he should discontinue his pursuit of the Vessey mystery. Both sat in silence for a few moments that morning, an incredulous expression on his face and an astonished expression on hers.

Finally, Jean broke the silence and provided a further comment, more a question actually than an observation. "What exactly is the mystery of the Davidson kid? I mean, what would do you hope to discover? You already have an idea as to the reason for his standing at that window, you already know? It is obvious, isn't it? The Davidson son is mentally handicapped, just like the Vessey boy all those years ago. So what are you hoping to find out, whether the poor kid is autistic, schizophrenic, or has some other psychiatric condition? And, why the hell do you want to know that anyway? Curiosity? It doesn't make any sense." Jean then sat back on her chair, arms folded, and attempted to stare her husband into sense.

Richard finally raised his head, reached for a cup of coffee with a slight tremble in his hand and attempted to take a gulp of coffee. He successfully managed a small swig although a trickle of coffee rolled out of the corner of his mouth. He looked at Jean and leaned toward her. He looked slightly apologetic, like he wasn't expecting Jean to react the way she had, which maybe he should have. Despite an encroaching doubt, which had crept up on him like a flash of fever, he bravely outlined the basis for his plan into an investigation of Andrew Davidson. "I know you probably don't see it but there is a connection between the Vessey mystery and the mystery of Andrew Davidson." Jean looked up at him like he had just spilled his entire cup of coffee on his shirt as opposed to only the corner of his mouth. "What connection, aside of course from the fact that they both are or were mentally handicapped and liked to stare out second floor windows?" Richard looked almost smug, as if he had been holding a secret. "Their mothers, the connection, or should I say the similarity is their mothers. Not directly of course but the fact that both simply disappeared at some point without an explanation." Richard seemed pleased about his explanation but Jean cut him short. "So what, Richard. Think about it. Are you going to look into every situation in which a mentally handicapped man or boy who likes to look out second floor windows has or had a mother who is no longer around?"

She then picked up her chair and moved to his side of the kitchen island. They were seated a foot apart from each other. "Do you realize how crazy that sounds? Are you feeling alright?" She then had an inspiration, serious inspiration. "Look, I know you got a lot out of your research, your investigation of Scott Vessey – it gave you some purpose. You were.... you know...animated....determined...ambitious. You had a purpose, almost like you were back at work." Richard's face sank, as if he had just been presented with an elusive truth, an open secret. He agreed with her although it seemed like something that he would rather not face.

He had the gym, the recreational sports, even the occasional writing, the latter aspiration something that he was avoiding while he was spending his time detecting. He sat in silence. Jean then continued her observations. "Look, why don't you write about your pursuit of the Vessey mystery. It is a good story, maybe a great story. It would make a good book. Why don't you write it and forget about this other stuff."

Richard looked pensive at first. He then nodded as if he was acknowledging that he had just lost the debate. "Maybe you're right." he said, finally submitting to the unassailable logic of Mrs. Matthews, who had an excellent record over the years of showing Mr. Matthews the error of his ways. "I'm going to try to forget the whole thing."

Jean smiled wryly and added another comment. "Don't forget it, just write about it." Richard chuckled a bit and nodded his head again.

—

It was later that day, after appearing to surrender to Jean's rational persuasions, that he began to make notes of his journey into the mystery of Scott Vessey. He had completed maybe a full page describing his first sighting of him when he realized, not surprisingly when he thought about it later, that he had little, if any interest in dropping the idea of pursuing another mystery, the enigma of Andrew Davidson, another man who stood in a second floor window of a local house, this located in the neighbourhood, at 240 Belcourt Avenue. He knew that he would have to keep his detective work secret this time, Jean's opposition to another investigative diversion obvious and inviolate. His reread the page of notes that he had completed regarding the mystery that began with his initial sighting of Scott Vessey, when Richard was five years old and the Matthews family had recently moved into a new house on Columbus Avenue. It had been early in the evening in the summer, maybe a week since the family had moved in, when he saw Scott Vessey, a kid about his age, standing stock still in the south window on the second floor of that clapboard house on Parkdale Avenue just beyond the Matthews backyard. He remembered that he stood there in the window of his own bedroom, a bedroom he shared with his younger brother Kevin, for maybe five minutes, watching the kid in the window until Richard turned away, wondering until he fell asleep what the kid was looking at, if anything. He also remembered the first time he had seen Andrew Davidson. He wasn't a kid and he wasn't wearing a shirt, he thought.

Like he thought he had when he had decided to pursue the mystery of Scott Vessey, he started to develop a plan. He had to have one. For that, he needed a starting point. It came to him like an intuition, no explanation, just a thought that did not require too much in the way of mental exertion. He would be looking for Andrew Davidson's mother, the woman that seemed to disappear, gone from her husband Stewart, gone from her son, gone from every memory it seemed, no one in the neighbourhood aside from maybe her former or maybe even her current husband, a group that included the omnipotent Mrs. Guzzo seemed to know anything about her. She was a mystery and, for Richard Matthews, the mystery. He had somehow managed to convince himself, he would later come to regard the process as something akin to a religious conversion, that he was now compelled to solve the mystery of Andrew Davidson and his mother. He didn't know why. It was just blind faith.

Richard's experience with the development of a plan to solve the mystery of the human remains discovered on the property on which the Vessey family once lived was only instructive. It did not provide a blueprint for finding anyone, least of all someone's lost mother. His search for the secret of the Scott Vessey's mother was prompted by the reported clue of the discovery of her remains. In the case of Andrew Davidson, there were no clues, only facts which Richard had conjured into a mystery: he was mentally handicapped, a primary symptom of which was the custom of staring out of a window on the second floor of his house, and the evident fact that his mother's fate, if not her location was unknown. Richard thought about his predicament, if that was what it was, intermittently for several hours that evening before slipping into slumber. He identified several possible ways of finding Andrew Davidson's mother, none of which were likely to yield quick, if any results. There were of course several on-line resources available. There was of course the internet itself which would prove useless, not only because Davidson was a maddeningly common name but also because of he did not know her Christian name. Further, he did not know the mother's maiden name, which she may have reclaimed after abandoning or being abandoned by her husband, the father of Andrew Davidson. The fact was he didn't know his Christian name either. The same reasoning also applied to on-line conveniences like Facebook, Twitter and Instagram, all of which Richard sometimes regarded as a conspiracy against anyone over a certain age. Other possible research sources, like birth certificates, marriage certificates, and deeds to the houses in which the Davidson family may have lived were limited by the same lack of knowledge of personal details. Besides, such information could be confidential.

Richard would first have to find starting points, such basic information as the name of Andrew's father, his mother, the places where the family may have lived. In order to ensure his clandestine pursuit of the Andrew Davidson mystery, he obviously could not ask Jean for any such information. That was unfortunate because he thought that she would know more about the neighourhood and the people in it than he would. He could have asked Mr. Davidson himself. After all, he had already been acquainted with him, that day he and Margie were caught trespassing in the backyard of 240 Belcourt Avenue. He could not, however, think of a pretext for approaching him a second time without appearing to be totally inappropriate, if not a lunatic. That left only one source, the neighbourhood know-in-all, Mrs. Anna Guzzo. He should not have a problem approaching her.

Richard got his opportunity to interview Mrs. Guzzo the next afternoon, just after lunch when she and her husband Sam were both taking coffee at a table which sat under the trellis in the driveway of their house. This was Richard's first sighting of her since he had put her under surveillance the day before yesterday. In the meantime, further to his wife Jean's recommendation, if not her insistence, Richard had been attempting to assemble a chronicle of his investigation of the remains of Scott Vessey's mother. That project was not going very well, his enthusiasm for his current undertaking interfering with his previous one, past facts combining with possible future facts into a tentative and confusing narrative, prompting Richard to question his memory of events. Similarly, he had recently made note of the fact that he had begun to forget all kinds of things, dates, names, events, his memory loss not specific to any category of memory. Like most people he supposed, or so he had been told or thought he had been told, things that he would be trying to retain, would eventually come to him moments, if not hours, if on days after the moment of the initial memory loss. On the other hand, long term memories of any significance, the name of his fifth grade teacher, his first hockey coach, the first phonographic record he ever purchased, his first shopping lifting event, the first time he got drunk, the loss of his virginity, his first wedding, these events all appeared in his memory like they had been recorded in some sort of local historical account. So it came as a relief when his opportunity to engage Anna and maybe Sam presented itself that afternoon. He could forget about trying to record his pursuit of the mystery of Scott Vessey and his mother. He was embarking on a new mystery.

He stood looking out the front door of his house at Anna and Sam drinking their coffee and attempted to formulate his approach. It did not take him long to arrive at an approach. He would just refer to his recent exchange with Mr. Davidson, neglecting to mention of course that their conversation had been prompted by the fact that he and Margie had been caught trespassing on the man's property. On the other hand, based on what he knew about her disposition, which was universally known, admitting to being inquisitive about someone in the neighbourhood would be entirely acceptable to Anna Guzzo. He just knew that she would be more than happy to provide him with any information, fact, allegation, gossip, rumour, or innuendo, about anybody in the neighbourhood, including Mr. Davidson and his son. Still, before he started up the Guzzo driveway, which he initiated with an introductory wave, he realized that since the Davidsons had only lived on Belcourt Avenue for six months, he probably wasn't about to get much in the way of information on them. That was his expectation.

He greeted Anna and Sam. "Hi, how are you both? Nice day"

Anna immediately spoke up, in that loud, theatrical voice by which she was known by the neighbours. She and Sam both gestured to Richard, inviting him to sit down at the plastic garden table underneath the trellis. She greeted Richard with an offer of coffee and pastry. "Care for some coffee, Richard? It's the real thing, Americano. And we have some cannolis for you too." Richard smiled and sat down across from Anna. Sam raised his hand toward Richard like he waving. As usual, Anna almost immediately offered the most recent neighbourhood gossip. He had heard it before, from Jean two days before. Anna of course was able to offer a good deal more in the way of detail.

"You know about Mrs. Rydell.", a reference to an old woman who lived alone next door to the Matthews. "They took the poor woman to the hospital the night before last after falling down some stairs. "This much Richard already knew, at least according to Jean. "Jack Sullivan was talking to Bob Rydell about his mother. He said that she's still unconscious, some sort of coma. He said that it's not looking too good for the poor old lady. I think they may have to sell the house if she doesn't get any better." Richard nodded, taking it in from Anna while watching Sam pour coffee into a cup emblazoned with an Italian flag. He was a trifle surprised that Anna would take Jack Sullivan at his word, Jack Sullivan being the weirdo who lived across the street with his unemployed son. Richard didn't think much of Bob Rydell, a retired police officer who was disliked by practically everyone in the neighbourhood. Although he had to admit to himself that Bob was a devoted son, a role that Richard thought was related more to her eventual estate than any feelings for his mother.

Richard was reaching for a cannoli as Anna handed him a napkin, another dinner accessory decorated by an Italian flag, this time embroidered. Richard asked about the new house, a natural progression in the conversation. "Are you looking forward to that house coming down and being replaced by two monster places?"

Anna started to laugh, that loud, almost operatic laughter drifting across the table. "I hope not but I'm pretty sure that if poor old Mrs. Rydell passes, the boys will be putting up the sign to sell that place before that the old lady is in the ground."

Sam raised his hand like he was attempting to silence his wife. "Anna, Anna, come on, you can't dislike those boys that much. They're really not so bad."

Anna responded by making some sort of dismissive noise, "Blah, blah. They're not nice, never were, even when they were kids. They're just like their father – you didn't know him, Richard, but he was a mean guy, nobody liked him. I don't know how Phyllis could stay with the guy all these years. Fact was, and I know it was a terrible thing to say, but his death was an answer to his wife's prayers."

"That's a terrible thing to say, Anna." observed Sam who then patted her hand.

Richard didn't say a thing. He never met Mr. Rydell although he was not particularly enamoured with Mrs. Rydell who didn't seem to like anyone, the arrival of Margie the dog not helpful in that regard. Not that it mattered much since Mrs. Rydell was in her early nineties when they adopted Margie and seldom came in contact with the dog. As for the elder, long deceased Rydell, both Richard, Jean and the Guzzos as well disliked him by reputation only. The son was a police officer. Richard wondered whether Mr. Rydell had also been a police officer.

In view of Anna's inappropriate comments on the Rydells, Richard knew that he did not demonstrate any sort of reluctance whatsoever about raising the subject of the Davidsons. He knew that all he had to do was bring them up and she would fill in the blanks, of which there were many. She nodded, looked thoughtful for a moment, leaned forward and started her hearsay about the Davidsons. "You mean the man and his son who live on Belcourt? Sure, I know who they are but don't know much about them. I don't think anybody does.'

Richard tried to encourage her. He didn't want to tell her that he had spoken to the elder Davdson. He just gave her a hint of his familiarity with the Davidsons. "I understand the son May be a little handicapped. He seems to spend a lot of time standing in a back window of the house on the second floor. I've seen him there from Coolbreeze, walking Margie. It was a little strange."

Anna nodded again decisively, as if she had an explanation for his comment. "Gladys Nevin lives right across the street. You know that they only moved in there six months ago, don't you?"

"Yes, I think I heard that." answered Richard, not volunteering how he possessed that information. He was ready with an explanation, his wife Jean the alleged source.

Anna then exhaled casually, took a sip of coffee and began to pass along whatever hearsay she had managed to gather from Gladys Nevin, a neighbour of whom Richard had never heard. "According to Gladys, Mr. Davidson, his first name is Stewart by the way, and his son Andrew, are both pretty odd people as far as she could see. Gladys seldom sees them leaving the house, ever. She told me that she sometimes sees their groceries being delivered. And, like you said, she's pretty sure that the son is handicapped, likes to stare out the window in the back of the house, on the second floor."

Richard agreed. "Yes, as I said, I've seen him staring out that window many times, practically every time I have passed by their back yard." He continued to omit mentioning his conversation with Stewart Davidson. He was kind of embarrassed, not only about the trespassing incident but also because he had not mentioned it earlier. "You said that your friend seldom sees them leaving the house. I assume that they do leave the house sometimes."

Anna nodded vigorously, her white hair almost shaking. "Yes, yes. Gladys said that every Sunday morning, the father leaves the house, wearing some sort of military uniform." Anna paused and gestured with her hand, anticipating her objection. "I know, I know. He couldn't be in the military. He's almost my age for goodness sake and I don't think they would have him anyway." She then laughed, almost a funny little squeal it was, "Gladys thinks he is most likely a member of the Salvation Army, especially since he is only seen wearing the uniform on Sundays." It was obvious that the fact that Stewart Davidson was a member of Salvation Army was about all that Richard was going to get out of his consultation with Anna. He sat there, waiting for an opportunity to finalize their discussion. "Salvation Army? I guess Gladys wasn't surprised." remarked Richard. Anna nodded, a silly smile on her face. With that, Anna finished off her coffee and patted Sam's arm again. Sam looked like he was ready to take a nap.

ANOTHER PLAN BEGINS

By the time Richard walked across the street from the Guzzos, he had decided that the only serviceable avenue available to him in his search for Stewart Davidson's wife and Andrew Davidson's mother would be through her husband. He had briefly considered, as he sat there having coffee with the Guzzos, somehow employing Andrew to obtain clues as to the location of his mother. He had no idea as to how he would manage it although the eventual discovery of the photograph of the presumed final resting place of Scott Vessey's mother suggested that it was possible that somehow Andrew could provide a clue. He discounted the idea as a first option, as almost an absurdity. He could not see himself gaining access to Andrew, could not see himself talking with Andrew, could not see asking him about the whereabouts of his mother, even if he knew or even cared. It just was not possible.

That left only one other alternative. He would have to follow Stewart Davidson, stake him out, like a damn private investigator. At one time during the Scott Vessey search, he actually considered hiring a private investigator, a possibility that he rejected after calling a number of investigators, interviewing several of them and concluding that they were either not interested in the mystery of Scott Vessey or were interested but had not demonstrated any kind of ability to solve any mystery. They also had terrible wardrobes and ridiculously high fees. One of the latter, a self advertised private detective named Josh Schumacher, actually quoted a price of $1,000. an hour, suggesting that the man was a top flight lawyer as opposed to a badly dressed security consultant, a job title that hardly seemed consistent with his overall appearance and disposition. Besides the quality of the local security consultants, there was the matter of the fees, money that he would have a helluva time hiding from Jean.

Besides the matter of money, there was the issue of time. If the only option Richard had was to hire himself as a private investigator, it would require a considerable amount of time. Since he was retired, he had the time, the only problem being that he would have to excuse the time spent on his surveillance activities from Jean. Therefore, he would have to limit his time following Mr. Davidson. That meant first determining his schedule and only following him when he wasn't in the house, which was much of the time as far as he knew. He started to think that extensive viewing of television police dramas might come into handy in considering appropriate surveillance techniques. He started to wonder about Stewart Davidson's powers of observation. Would he notice Richard following him? How close? How far? He started to have doubts, thinking that maybe it wasn't such a good idea although he realized, almost immediately after that one instant in which that doubt occurred to him, that he had no other option. He would begin the stake-out tomorrow.

That first day, he had walked Margie a little earlier in the morning than usual, intending to locate a place near 240 Belcourt Avenue from which he could observe Mr. Davidson without being seen by neither him nor any of his neighbours. He had hoped that first morning that he had not left the house yet although he was fairly certain that he had not, Gladys Nevin's observation that he seldom left the house being the sole evidence. He and Margie went up Lakeview, turned south on Hawthorne and then down Belcourt, the Davidson house being on the north side of the street just about in the middle of the block. For some strange canine reason, any reason in the circumstances would seem strange he thought, Margie did not want to turn east on Belcourt, halting her walk by backing up on her hind legs and refusing to budge. She started to bark as well, prompting Richard to start feeding her treats, requiring a half dozen before she calmed down, stopped her barking and continuing down Belcourt. They reached the Davidson residence within a few minutes, stopping and staring at the house. They took in details that he had basically overlooked the times he had passed by, consumed almost entirely with the rear of the house.

He looked carefully at the place, studying it. Jean might have suggested that the house had not been well kept, anything less complimentary she would avoid saying. The house had two stories, a large picture window on the first floor and two small windows on the second, a patchy front lawn with a single tree stuck in the middle, a crumbling asphalt driveway from the street to a garage that looked to be close to falling down on the 1960s Plymouth automobile it was housing, his everyday mode of transport a rust coloured Ford pickup, and a small portico over the front door. Fortunately, the house across the street, the address being 239 Belcourt, was blessed with a fairly substantial hedge dividing the front from the back lawn. It looked pretty good for his purpose of surveillance although he would have to ensure that he could hide in the backyard behind the hedge, escape detection and still have an unobstructed view of the Davidson place. He would have to return to properly reconnoitre, without the dog.

After lunch with Jean, spending time discussing her friend Anne's propensity for curious men, her partners over the years, there were at least three of them of whom Richard was aware, and her passive aggressive tendencies toward them. Jean was generally critical of her selection of male companionship, often expressing confusion as to the reasons for her dumb choices. She said that she had recently made the acquaintance of her most recent and current mate, a man who sold real estate and regularly wore business suits that were too tight. When Richard asked whether that relationship had a chance of lasting, Jean offered up a curious smile and a shrug. She did comment however. "He seems nice. Maybe we should have them over for dinner sometime." Richard offered his own shrug in return, his reluctance almost obvious. He was feeling impatient. He could not wait to get out the door to inspect that potential hiding place across the street from the Davidson place. It was slated to become a duck blind for Richard, where the elder Davidson was the damn duck.

It did not take Richard long to return to 239 Belcourt Avenue. It was early in the afternoon. It was apparent that there was nobody home. He scanned the immediate area. It seemed there was nobody home anywhere else. He crept around the hedge into the backyard of the house across the street from 240 Belcourt Avenue and looked through it. It was close to being perfect for the purpose he sought. He could easily keep tabs on Stewart Davidson without being seen. He decided to initiate his surveillance at 8 o'clock the next morning, reckoning that his target, long retired he understood, would not be leaving the house before then. He took Margie for a quick walk before setting out for the gym, his excuse to Jean for the hours he would spend watching the Davidson house. Just to ensure that the excuse was credible, he put his gym bag into the car, got in and drove away, parking a couple blocks away from Belcourt on Hawthorne and then walking to his stake-out location. He took a brief look around, didn't see anybody, and was soon crouched down in the backyard behind the hedge at 239 Belcourt. He saw a lawn chair by the patio behind the house. He crept over, quietly picked up the chair and was soon comfortably sitting behind the hedge. All he needed was a book and a cup of coffee. He was to rectify those shortcomings in the days to come.

It would be a charitable observation to suggest that his surveillance of Stewart Davidson was much of a success. In fact, it was little more than an abject failure. He invested almost two weeks at attempting to chart Davidson's daily activities. He knew that Davidson was a member of the Salvation Army, his rank unknown to Gladys Nevin who had told Anna Guzzo about his membership in the army in the first place. He had started his stake-out auspiciously enough, confident that he would have Davidson's patterns down relatively quickly. From there, he was planning to develop some sort of theory as to the fate of his son Andrew's mother, the woman who apparently had disappeared without much of a trace years ago. All of his expectations and theories on the consequences of his monitoring of Stewart Davidson were based on his extensive experience watching detective dramas on television. If he had told anyone, particularly Jean, they might well have been less than impressed. He did not consider that possibility until he had spent almost two weeks watching the house at 240 Belcourt Avenue.

The first day he sat on the lawn chair and watched. He soon realized how unbearably tedious the activity of surveillance actually was. He just sat there on the chair staring across the street, almost paralyzed by the idleness. He recalled that he had felt himself almost drifting into slumber, barely able to stay awake. Suffice to say he had to concentrate hard to stay on the task, the task being to monitor Stewart Davidson's activities. Around ten o'clock that first morning, the man he assumed to be the social worker to whom Davidson had referred during their conversation in their backyard, he had called him Douglas, arrived at the front door of 240 Belcourt. Richard, thinking that he was suddenly prescient about surveillance procedure, realized that Douglas was there to look after Andrew while his father presumably went out. He also realized that he should not have left the car two blocks away. If Stewart Davidson left the house and went anywhere, unless of course it was by foot, he would need the car. He then would have to immediately leave to pick up the car and hope that his target had not have driven off before he returned to follow him. That first day, Richard had arrived several doors west of Davidson's place in his car just as Stewart Davidson was getting into his rust coloured Ford pickup.

He recalled that Davidson was wearing a cheap, weather beaten straw hat that had been pulled low on his forehead, suggesting that he was attempting to affect some sort of disguise. Richard had just turned off the car when Davidson started the pickup, he put it in gear, turned right onto Belcourt and drove east. Richard was behind him, maybe four car lengths, a discrete tail he thought. He was on the main street of Richmond Road within minutes. It was evident that he would be following the rust coloured Ford downtown. The two of them drove east on Wellington, north on Elgin, then Sussex, then into the Byward market area, first east on Waller and then onto George Street where he saw the rust coloured Ford pickup come to rest in a parking spot across from a Salvation Army building, in front of which was a group of vagrants, unmistakable street people loitering about, smoking, talking to each other, many sitting there staring at the tall apartment building across the street. Richard waited, motor running until he saw Davidson get out of the car, walk across the street and enter the Salvation Army Homeless Shelter. He wasn't wearing his uniform. Richard assumed that he only wore the uniform for formal events, although he was not sure about the scheduling of the formal events. He noticed that Mr. Davidson had not gone near a parking machine.

Richard was fortunate enough to find a parking place around the corner on Cumberland Street. He put a loonie into the machine, received a parking stub, and put it on the dashboard of his car. He went around the corner to the shelter, slipped past several of the street people without giving up any spare change, ignored a man sitting behind a desk who said something to him that he never heard, and found himself on the edge of a large room where lunch was being served to a large number of people with trays in hand, table and benches awaiting. The room resembled something that could have easily passed for a prison canteen. In the front of the room, behind a line of serving trays, were several volunteers serving lunch. One of them, wearing a wedge cap instead of the straw hat, was Stewart Davidson, doing his Christian duty. He was not wearing a Salvation Army cap nor was he wearing any vestige of a uniform.

Richard had stepped into the room, immediately noticing that he was attracting suspicions from several luncheon diners. He left the place immediately, quickly enough to once again avoid the man sitting behind the desk but not the street people who asked for spare change a second time. His surveillance for the day was over. That second day was a Thursday he recalled, he had spent the entire morning ensuring that Stewart Davidson didn't leave the house, which he didn't. The next day, he decided to switch to the afternoon, telling Jean that he was taking a yoga class. Again, he only saw Stewart the once, returning early in the afternoon, presumably from his lunch time volunteering. He did not stake Stewart out on the weekend, regular dates with Jean making any time monitoring Stewart's activities inconvenient. By the next week, he was back at his regular stand, fortified with a thermos of coffee and a couple of magazines. He saw the social worker Douglas show up every now and then, sometimes leading to Stewart leaving the house and sometimes not. When Douglas would stay late after dinner, he would follow Stewart to his stint at the Salvation Army Homeless Shelter. Sometimes, he assumed he already knew where he was going. He then wouldn't bother and simply go home. Within less than a week, he had predictably grown tired of the enterprise. It was inevitable since he had not made any progress whatsoever as to the ultimate objective of finding Andrew Davidson's mother. He just knew that something strange had happened to her, just like it had to another handicapped individual's mother almost seventy years ago.

He had started having trouble sleeping, contemplating the lack of progress he had made regarding his project. At moments during those interruptions of slumber, he was almost prepared to abandon the entire idea. Following Stewart Davidson during the day, either in the morning or the afternoon, had only yielded his service at the Salvation Army Homeless Shelter on George Street. He could not recall the exact moment but he came to the conclusion sometime in the dark one of those nights. He had to investigate Stewart's activities in the evening. It was the obvious decision. In addition, it might be less difficult to follow Stewart Davidson in the evening rather than during the day. He would not have to hide his car on a street other than Belcourt Avenue since, during the evening, there were more cars on the street and therefore it was would be easier to conceal his car among those many other cars on the street. He would start following him in the evening the next Monday. He was convinced that it was the only choice he had left. He did not know it would have lead to anything substantial, not knowing precisely what that meant.

THE ANONYMOUS MEET

It was a Tuesday when Richard decided to initiate his evening surveillance of Stewart Davidson. He was sitting in his car, three houses up from Davidson's place at 240 Belcourt, when Davidson appeared in his driveway to get into his rust coloured Ford pickup. Richard started his car as he watched the pickup back out of the driveway and head east toward Hawthorne Street. He pulled out and was in pursuit, three or four car lengths behind. He had been following Davidson for two weeks and was still wondering whether Davidson recognized his car, a twelve year old pedestrian black Honda Civic which was beginning to fall apart. Within several minutes, he was on Carling Avenue heading toward Bronson Avenue. They both went north on Bronson until they hit Somerset Avenue, at which point Richard had to stop at a red light while Davidson's Ford continued through on the yellow. He was, however, able to see the Ford turn right somewhere between Somerset and Laurier, most likely at an old building that once housed a high school called Holy Conception, there was only one street between Somerset and the next significant cross street, Laurier, and he never turned right at that street.

Once the light changed, Richard drove straight down to the old Holy Conception building and turned into the parking lot. The lot was fairly crowded for a building that Richard had assumed had been closed and abandoned years ago. There were maybe three dozen cars sitting in the lot. The back entrance was open. Richard parked his car, got out and walked into the building. He checked the lobby notice listing the building occupants. There were only two: a cleaning supply company and a local office of the Ottawa Area Chapter of Alcoholics Anonymous. The local office was listed as being on the first floor, Room 100. He went down the hall, past what likely were at one time the offices of the principal and administrative services. Both were now just empty rooms without doors. On the other side of the hall was Room 100, a small sign announcing it as the site of that evening's meeting of the Alcoholic Anonymous. He peered into the room. Maybe three dozen chairs in three rows had been set up behind a small podium equipped with a microphone. There was a long table on which had been laid several coffee urns, another offering tea, dozens of plastic cups, and several boxes of donuts. More than two dozen attendees, mostly men but four or five women were loitering about, most of them were smoking. Richard immediately thought that the city must have give the meeting some sort of dispensation from its strict no smoking regulations. For a moment, the occasional dispensation from the "no meat on Friday" rules that used to apply to observant Roman Catholics occurred to him for some reason. He was also reminded of the way local taverns used to look when smoking was not only permitted but encouraged, so much smoke that one could barely see across the room. He took a quick look around but could not spot Stewart Davidson. He was sure, however, that he was here somewhere.

He was contemplating such memories when an haggard older man in an equally haggard "Harris Tweed" jacket, a pair of old jeans and untied sneakers approached him several steps inside the room.

"First time? Are you here to join our group?" the older man asked.

Richard was momentarily befuddled by the question. He certainly did not expect to witness an AA meeting nor did he expect to be asked to join. He quickly realized, however, that it would be an almost ideal way of starting a relationship with Stewart Davidson, an opportunity that he could ill afford to ignore. It was not only ideal, it was almost perfect. So he replied to Mr. "Harris Tweed". "I'm thinking about it, thinking seriously."

"Are you seriously thinking about stopping drinking?" Mr. "Harris Tweed" helpfully asked. "We can help you."

It would be a simple masquerade of pretending to be an alcoholic, acting like a former drunk. Actually, he reasoned, he had been close to being an alcoholic, many years ago, back in his late teens and early twenties, when a regular ingestion of alcohol and drugs had plunged him into a chasm of frequent, almost constant inebriation, in one form or another, for several years. Like some of his friends at the time, it was almost a requirement, a passage from one frame of mind to another. Anyway, it would not be too difficult. He answered. "Yes, I'm serious. And I understand – no, more like I heard – that your group can be make it easier to stop."

Mr. "Harris Tweed" nodded and made a suggestion. "Look, why don't you join us this evening. You can just sit and listen. You won't have to share anything. You won't have to talk. Just see if you're comfortable and then decide." Talk about a lucky break thought Richard, he suddenly knew where Stewart Davidson would be maybe one day a week.

Richard wasn't really listening carefully to Mr. "Harris Tweed" who might have noticed his lack of attention and repeated his invitation. "So, does that sound alright, just sitting and listening? Will you be staying tonight?" He had placed his hand on his arm. Richard turned away from the room and faced Mr. "Harris Tweed". "Yeah, I think I will, if that's okay..... for tonight." Mr. "Harris Tweed" offered Richard a creepy little smile, as if he was about to let Richard in on some sort of confidence, and agreed. "Yes, that would be fine. Go ahead, take a chair and help yourself to a coffee and a treat, if you wish. And if you want to join, just see me after the meeting and I can take your particulars." And with that assurance, he turned away and started to greet a couple of people who had just arrived. He briefly wondered about whether he would be asked to accept one of the people in the room as his sponsor, if the organization still provided new members with someone to help them with the rough times. He also wondered whether he looked spent enough to qualify as an alcoholic, hopefully recovering or not. He pondered those questions before selecting a seat.

Richard chose a chair in the back row and took a sweeping look around the room. He counted 29 people in the room, including the eight in line for coffee and donuts, and was able to locate Stewart Davidson, as he knew he would. He was seated in the middle of the front row, maybe five feet from the empty podium. He looked relaxed, as if he was a definite and likely long term AA member, slouching down in his chair. He was seated between a ridiculously thin middle age woman with a face overwhelmed with wrinkles and a young man with a lopsided Mohawk haircut. The woman was pulling on a cigarette like she needed oxygen, a mark that could have been a nicotine stain on her left cheek. The young man looked uncomfortable, a strange expression given his hair style. Over the next five minutes or so, Richard studied Stewart's face. He had realized that he had never really examined Stewart's face, his previous opportunities obscured and distracted by the situations such as a straw hat and a situation, like that one time when Stewart had caught Richard and Margie trespassing. He looked like an AA veteran who deservedly belonged in the front row. He obviously would have to find a way to engage Stewart in a conversation, suddenly his longer term ambition to become friendly enough with him to obtain some usual information. Again, he reflected on his good fortune.

The room slowly grew silent as Mr. "Harris Tweed" made his way to the front of the room and the podium. He stood behind the podium, adjusted the microphone and opened the meeting. He had a nervous, quivering voice that sounded well suited to the room and the occasion. He introduced himself as Tim, alcoholic. He said that there were three potential new members taking in the meeting this evening and expressed the hope that they would join the group. He then informed the meeting that this particular chapter would meet every Tuesday in this room for the next six months, explaining that a new lease had recently been signed. He then announced that the chapter would be holding a picnic for members and immediate families in two weeks, on a Saturday in the Vincent Massey park. He assumed that alcohol would not be served. He again pondered two more imponderables, whether most members actually attended such events and whether most of them, or in fact any of them had families. Having concluded his administrative announcements, Tim then asked if anybody wanted to share. A short, somewhat pudgy man raised his hand and stood up. Three or four other individuals had put up their hands but had not stood up. The room had turned quiet, the only sounds the adjustment of chairs, the lighting of cigarettes, sporadic coughs and throat clearing.

Richard was mildly surprised that Tim had permitted the pudgy man to share. He could tell from the vibe in the room that the pudgy guy was not a popular choice. The man seated besides Richard whispered that he could hear eyes rolling. But Tim allowed the pudgy guy to proceed, reluctantly it appeared. "My name is Jack and I am an alcoholic." The powerhouse commentator sitting beside Richard again whispered something under his breath. "An alcoholic and a pain in the ass." Jack continued with his testimony. "I haven't had a drink of alcohol in two years but if you put a drink in front of me right now, I would have an awful time resisting the temptation of taking that drink. But I can promise you, because of the help I have received from you people at the many meetings I have attended, I can resist that drink." Tim, looking somewhat perturbed, suddenly interrupted Jack's presentation, "Jack, as inspiring as it is, we have heard you say the same thing three meetings in a row now. I think we should give someone else a chance." Tim smiled and did not need to continue his commentary. Surprisingly, Jack the pudgy guy immediately sat down and Tim pointed at another attendee, an older man who stood up slowly, unsteady on his feet and a little stooped in his stance. He had to place a hand on the shoulder of the man sitting in the chair in front of him to stand. "My name is Walter and I have been an alcoholic for as long as I can remember. Every day is a struggle, every day is a fight. And I know it will be a struggle maybe for the rest of my days. Two days ago, as I was watching something on the television, a commercial came on advertising whisky. I suddenly wanted a drink in the worst way, just one drink and I would be happy. I was craving a drink so bad that I asked Doris, that's my wife, to lock me in our bedroom." A series of quiet twitters briefly rolled across the room. "She didn't lock him in the bedroom. She just laughed, told me to turn off the television and do something else, like go outside and mow the grass." That remark prompted louder twitters, if not outright laughter. "Well, I did go out and mow the grass. By the time I finished with the lawn, my urge for that drink had gone, thank God." There was a pause while Walter looked down, contemplating his next remark. "You know, I thought about that drink for a couple of days. But that's all I did – think." Then he sat down, nods and general words of acknowledgement filled the room. Tim added his own gesture of acceptance and then went on to point at a woman in the first room, a couple of chairs over from Stewart Davidson who Richard had been watching the whole time with some interest.

The woman, who was relatively young and attractive in a hard living sort of way, looked around the room almost dismissively. Unlike the previous speakers, she looked completely self-assured, confident of herself. "My name is Lucy and I am a damn alcoholic." Tim immediately interrupted. "Lucy, no profanity please." Again, there was some quiet laughter. "Please continue."

Lucy started again. "My name is Lucy and I am an alcoholic. Every day, I'm know. Every night, I'm know. On some days, on some nights, it is so difficult that I come close to giving up. And then, well then, I remember my pledge to myself and to every person in this room. The other day, one of my old girlfriends, a girlfriend who maybe should be standing here with me, invited me to a club. I wanted to go but I couldn't. I was worried that I would want to have a drink. Maybe years from now, after I have been to enough of these meetings, when I have seen enough of your faces, I won't have to be afraid to go into a club with any of my friends." She then sat down, much of the meeting offering her discrete applause.

Lucy was followed by two older men who both looked like they had recently spent a good deal of time in rehabilitation, quite recently it seemed, their appearance disconsolate enough to suggest recent hospitalization. Their faces were furrowed, skin tone gaunt and pallid, they looked emaciated, as if they were about to be embalmed for their own visitations. One could not help but notice that both were blessed with rotting teeth and unfortunate dye jobs, maroon and dirty green prominent. Both members mumbled their way through their presentations, both sounding more like inexplicable confessions than anything inspirational. Each sat down with little reaction from their audience, most of the members looking at each other in clear relief.

The two recovering addicts, if indeed that is what they were, were followed by a much younger man who, unlike his two unfortunate predecessors, looked to be relatively healthy and hardly worthy of any suggestion of any kind of addiction. He stood straight up, his posture unusually proper for the crowd, and began his sharing comments. "My name is Frank and I am an alcoholic. As I am sure some of you have noticed, I am relatively new to this group, this being my third meeting. Like all of you, I am determined to stop drinking and never to drink again. But I know that I am and will continue to be an alcoholic. I can never forget that, even if I do not drink and do not want to drink. I am here tonight to remind himself and all of you that I must remain steadfast with this ambition. Like all of you I assume, I have had many difficult moments, and I will continue to have them. But as time goes on, it will become easier to overcome. This is my hope and my promise, a hope and a promise I will repeat at every meeting we have." Frank then sat down and a scattering of clapping followed him.

The man seated besides Richard whispered that he could hear eyes rolling. Tim quickly arose and announced a short break, after which the meeting would be enlightened by a talk from Dr. Pym, a local doctor who specialized in addictions and the author of a popular book entitled "The Struggle for Sobriety", a tome that had been and continued to be recommended by the Ottawa Area Chapter of Alcoholics Anonymous to its members. According to Tim, Dr. Pym's talk would concern the management of sobriety in the workplace.

There was a reserved rush to the coffee and pastry table, which had been refilled while the meeting was listening to several of its members bare their souls, so to speak. Richard saw Stewart Davidson line up for coffee. Richard stood behind him in the line, waiting for a chance to reacquaint himself with Andrew's father. He soon got his opportunity, slowly sidling to him as they were both pouring coffee. "Mr. Davidson" ventured Richard, a tentative approach, not certain as to the man's possible response. After all, the only previous occasion on which they interacted was hardly favourable to the renewal of cordiality. In response, Davidson turned to face Richard. "Yes." He regarded Richard with a curious look on his face. "Quite a coincidence, wouldn't you say? I've never seen you here before, have I?" Richard nodded and admitted that it was his first time. "First time, eh. I remember my first meeting. You don't have to be nervous." He paused for a moment and then stuck out his hand. "Say, you never did give me your name, did you?" Richard stood there, blank faced, wondering if Davidson was somehow on to him, like he knew that Richard wasn't an alcoholic and that Richard's visit to the meeting was a ruse.

He shook Davidson's hand and introduced myself. "Richard Matthews. Oh, and my dog's name is Margie." Davidson nodded and continued to be sociable. "So what do you think so far, you know, about the meeting?"

Richard chuckled a bit and shrugged his shoulders. "I don't know yet." He hesitated for a moment. "I just hope that I don't have to share just yet. I have a few more meetings before I have to do that." Davidson returned the shrug and offered an observation. "Don't worry about that. You just get up at a meeting and say whatever's on your mind, no matter how dumb it seems. I mean, you heard the people tonight, didn't you?. It's kind of, you know, kind of...." A word almost immediately occurred to Richard. He didn't know why. It just did. "Kind of cathartic?" Davidson smiled "Yes, cathartic. Maybe they should start using that word in the literature." The both of them toasted each other with their Styrofoam coffee cups and headed back to their seats. "Sure, why not?" Richard nodded again and immediately planned to engage Davidson again after the meeting. He found his seat in the back row. He briefly thought of moving up to sit near Davidson, maybe one seat behind him, the closest vacant seat he saw. That would have been too obvious, so he stayed put where he had been. As soon as he sat down in his previous seat, he noticed that a seat two over from Davidson had been vacated, whoever had been sitting there earlier in the meeting had thought better of it. Again, moving would have been even more obvious. So he didn't move. Davidson gave him a surprised look, as if he was wondering if Richard was intentionally trying to avoid him.

After the break, Tim introduced Dr. John Pym who spoke for fifteen minutes about his book "The Struggle for Sobriety". As informative as the good doctor was, Richard thought that advice on how to navigate the difficulties facing the recovering alcoholic at work may have been lost on people who may not have had jobs, an observation that Richard thought may have applied to half the members present at the meeting. Dr. Pym received decent enough applause, led by an enthusiastic Tim who took a few questions and stayed to take in the rest of the meeting, taking a seat in the last row.

The rest of the second half of the meeting was about as melodramatic as a television show repeat. Six more members stood up to share and those six more members inspired the meeting to ennui with similar declarations. One claimed to be frequently on the edge of a nervous breakdown without a net, another said that he continually made lists of things that bothered him enough to provoke him to drink while at least three others spoke about the origins of their drinking. All attested to being alcoholics without embarrassment, in quiet, even tones that sounded familiar to everyone in the room. Richard watched Stewart Davidson throughout the latter half of the meeting. The man seemed bored, holding on to his coffee cup, which he refilled twice to avoid falling asleep. Tim thanked each one of them with a certain reverence. Richard began to regard the meeting as being reminiscent of some sort of religious group, something like the Catholic Sodality instituted in his high school, a group that regularly met to discuss and plan activities to develop the Catholic way of life, an objective that no one Richard knew, including students who belonged to the group, really understood. On the other hand, Alcoholics Anonymous had an easily understood objective, that alcoholics recover from their disease by sharing their experiences.

After the six members had finished sharing and receiving the thanks of Mr. Lamb, the latter concluded the meeting and reminded everyone of next Tuesday's meeting. Richard caught up to Davidson before he exited the building and got into the parking lot. He asked if he wanted a lift home. "No, I drove over myself but thanks anyway." He then made a suggestion. "Hey, since we're neighbours, if you intend to attend next week's meeting, maybe we can drive over together. It would be convenient." Richard came up with a big grin. "Sure, I'll pick you up. Next Tuesday, right?" Davidson gave him a hearty shake of the hand and headed out into the parking lot. This was his opportunity Richard thought, to get friendly or friendlier with Davidson, to establish a relationship through which he could eventually acquire information about Andrew and his mother.

SUBSEQUENT MEETINGS

From the initial AA meeting on that Tuesday in which he came across Stewart Davidson, Richard had taken Margie around the block, ensuring that they went past the house at 240 Belcourt Avenue every day, hoping that he and the dog would accidentally come across Davidson. On the Saturday, Davidson was opening his front door when the two of them just happened by, the first time in four chances that he and Margie were able to casually attract Davidson. Richard gave him a wave and Margie provided a quick bark. Davidson closed his car door and returned the wave. "Hey, Richard, how's the dog? You're not headed to the backyard, are you?" He smiled, took a couple of steps towards him and stopped halfway to the street. "Yeah, and don't worry, I think Andrew is standing at the window. Doug is up there with him." Despite his surprise that Davidson was being so blunt, Richard returned with his own grin and response. "Oh, I'm sure of that." Davidson turned and then went back to open his car door and shouted "See you Tuesday." Margie started to bark again. "Pick you up around 7:30 on Tuesday night." Richard then walked ahead to continue their walk, a little disappointed that he had not had the time to take advantage of the opening that Davidson had given him. He would not miss the next opportunity that Davidson would give him. He had until Tuesday to remember that. Richard continued to walk Margie around the block past 240 Belcourt Avenue but did not run into Davidson again in the next three days, leaving Tuesday evening as next opportunity for a chat with Davidson.

Since he had managed to locate Davidson at the meeting in the Holy Conception building on Bronson Avenue, he was straining to restrain himself from telling Jean about his discovery. He thought that he could tell her. There was nothing stopping him. He was no longer compelled to invent excuses for his daily and sometimes nightly surveillance of Davidson. As for the AA meetings, he had told Jean that he had started playing squash with an old opponent at Carleton University every Tuesday. He was disappointed in a way. She would have been impressed by his detective work. On the other hand, he would also have to explain the reason for his surveillance of Davidson in the first place, which would inevitably lead to his wife questioning his sanity. So he didn't say a word.

Richard arrived at the Davidson residence at 7:30 on the next Tuesday evening. He went up to the front door and knocked. Douglas the care worker answered the door. Davidson was right behind him. "Hi Richard, right on time." It would be a twenty minute ride to the meeting, which would give him enough time to bring up his son Andrew and attempt to get some information on him, information that could lead to the identity of Stewart Davidson's wife and Andrew Davidson's mother. Davidson left the house, saying goodbye to Douglas and a loud goodbye to Andrew who presumably was standing at a window on the second floor. Douglas mumbled an adieu and he heard nothing from the second floor.

Davidson and Richard got into the car and left for the meeting. Richard started a personal conversation almost immediately, hoping to spark something about Andrew's mother. He knew that it was not likely, at least at this point but he felt he had to get friendly with Davidson. It was the only way to get closer to the truth, that is if there was any truth to his suspicions that there was something peculiar about the history of the Davidson family, the history of the Vessey family echoing in his mind like a daydream. "I meant to ask you the other night." said Richard, maybe a minute or so after they started downtown, "How long have been going to the meetings?" Davidson looked over at Richard with an impish smile. "Seems like forever." answered Davidson, the impish smile still on his face. Richard nodded and asked him about the effectiveness of AA. Davidson answered in an even, almost folksy voice. "Well, I'm pretty well clean now but I still go to the meetings. Why, who knows, probably only out of habit I think." Richard thought about his last comment for a moment. "You didn't look like you were enjoying yourself." Richard observed. Davidson almost offered up a short snort, almost a snigger. "I guess you noticed." Richard was going to point out that practically everyone else in the room noticed as well but didn't bother. They drove in silence for a while.

Richard should have expected Davidson's next comment. "How about you? What made you go to your first meeting?" Richard briefly wondered whether he had told anyone beside Tim that it had been his first meeting. He had told Tim, Mr. "Harris Tweed" as he was first approached at the meeting, that he was interested in sitting in on a meeting, having been undecided on whether he wanted to join, stating with a certain amount of certainty that he wanted to stop drinking period, neglecting to tell anyone that it was all an act, that he did not have a drinking problem. He had rehearsed a cover story and proceeded to provide it to Davidson. Richard started in on his narrative, a mixture of fact and fiction. "I used to have a problem with booze when I was in my teens and early twenties. In fact, my mother, who wasn't big on therapy or anything like therapy, even sent me to a psychiatrist. I went once." Davidson commented, "but that was what, fifty years ago? I'm thinking about your current situation?" Richard nodded. He had just turned onto Bronson Avenue. The Holy Conception building and the AA meeting was now a couple of minutes away. "Well, after I retired a few years ago, I started drinking like a bastard. There didn't seem to be anything else to do. Now I want to stop." With that admission, Richard turned into the parking lot. As Davidson got out of the car, he exhorted Richard. "You might as well join tonight, right?"

There seemed to be a better turnout for this meeting, maybe a dozen or more members, a fourth row of chairs now available. Davidson and Richard sat together this time, Davidson looking a little uncomfortable as if Richard was intruding. They both picked up coffees, Richard took a carrot muffin. Tim introduced the first speaker, a middle age man who was dressed prosperously but was cursed with the bloated, beet red face of the long time drinker. He stepped behind the podium and the microphone. "My name is Larry and I am an alcoholic. All you have to do is take a look at my face to know that." There were guffaws all around. It appeared that Larry was a well known member and perhaps a frequent speaker who shared his problems in countless meetings. "I managed, with the help of this organization, to stop drinking five years ago. It's been tough and still is tough, no matter how much time has gone by. You can call it anything you want, alcoholism, addiction, dependence, habit, craving, whatever. It is still a tough thing to overcome but you can overcome it. There are mornings, afternoons and evenings when I wished I was still drinking, the relief from the difficulties of real life that can come with a drink, even knowing that it can bring with it much greater difficulties if you allow it to go too far. That was the way it was with me and it may be that way with many of you. If it is, I urge you to remember that as difficult as it is, the other choice is even worse."

After that bit of sermonizing, Larry sat down and returned to his seat. Tim got up and introduced the second speaker, a young man who looked like he had just got out of bed and might well have been still half asleep. He managed to stand up without assistance and begin his statement. "My name is Malcolm and I sure as hell am an alcoholic." There was a scattering of nervous laughter in the crowd, prompting a dirty look from Tim and an unidentified gesture of discouragement. "As some of you may have noticed, I'm new at this, not at the drinking but the no drinking part. I joined this group because I was serious about not drinking, ever. But it is hard, sometimes too hard to stand. I sit at home a lot all by myself in my dungheap of an apartment, trying to figure out how I ended up here, telling people with problems like mine that I have problems like they do." Malcolm, the dungheap dweller, was suddenly making a lot of sense. People were listening to him, nodding their heads, even Davidson seemed to be listening, although it was hard to gauge him, even though he was sitting right next to him. Malcolm continued his sermon, into which his "sharing" was seemingly being transformed. "Well, it has been damn tough. Sometimes, I sulk, sometimes I get mad, sometimes I am so sad that I actually cry, something that I don't like to admit, even to a bunch of people who may find themselves doing some crying themselves sometimes, and something I haven't done since I was twelve years old. But don't worry, I'm not going to cry today." Malcolm offered up a smile and a lot of people listening to him smiled as well. Tim led the quiet, almost respective applause. Davidson gave Richard a big nod and joined the group in clapping.

Richard did not pay much attention to the next two speakers although the general subject of the third speaker surely prompted his interest. The speaker, a middle aged man who looked comparatively presentable, spoke extensively about the effect of not only his drinking but of the decision to stop drinking and join AA and how that decision was still having an effect on his family, particularly his wife. He admitted with a certain hesitancy, the inflection of his voice changing, his head drifting up and down with his comments, that his wife had finally left him years before because of his drinking but was thinking of coming back to him now that he had joined AA. Tim interrupted him to compliment him, an unusual move for such proceedings. While the man continued with his testimony, Richard was watching Davidson's reactions to the middle age man's comments. He thought that perhaps Davidson could have had a similar experience, a wife leaving him because of her husband's drinking and maybe a reconciliation with him now that he was attending AA meetings. He doubted the latter situation but the former was possible. It would be a conversation opener.

During the break, Richard naturally joined Davidson who was attending the coffee and donut table, pretending to look over the donuts, pouring himself a cup of coffee and casually standing by Davidson, waiting for an opportunity to engage. He opened by exaggerating the effect that his phantom drinking had on his own marriage, all of which was the ultimate exaggeration in itself, it being entirely fictional. He had previously tried to recall whether any drinking, or the use of any other substance for that matter, had caused any problem for his relationship with his first wife. Richard and his first wife, a university student who had little patience for the kind of foolishness usually precipitated by his drinking and drug taking, were only married for two years, long enough for her to conclude that Richard was a drunken loser who would never amount to anything, which ironically was an accurate prognostication for the next seven or eight years, until he met Jean.

"That last speaker reminds me of me." said Richard, thinking that an extremely minor witticism would be enough to provoke a response from Davidson. "How's that?" asked Davidson as he slipped a donut into his mouth. He seemed mildly interested, enough to at least ask Richard to explain himself. "My wife almost left me four or five times, at least. Coming to AA is my last chance, last of the many she has given me. If I were to stop going, well that would be it." Richard paused, giving Davidson time to perhaps reflect on the previous speaker's comments and maybe even comment himself. Davidson turned to him and laughed softly, almost to himself. Richard felt he was close to an admission, maybe an acknowledgement that he too faced the same problem at one time or another. "I think I know what that man has been going through." But before Davidson could elucidate further, Tim announced the break was over and called the second half of the meeting to order. They went back to their seats. As disappointed as he was, Richard would be sure to keep his last remark in mind when he drove him home.

Like the previous meeting, the latter half of the meeting was more or less uneventful. Richard was worried that Davidson would take a cab home when Richard was delayed because Tim asked him at the close of the meeting if he intended to become a member of AA. Richard said that he would, agreeing to formally join before next week's meeting. He was relieved when he came across Davidson waiting for him in the lobby of the building. They were on their way home when Richard raised the effect, the fictional effect mind you that his phantom drinking had had on his marriage. Davidson sort of hesitated for a moment, as if he was prepared to ignore the entire subject, but relented. He inhaled and exhaled. He turned and looked at Richard. "I know exactly what you mean." he said, "The only difference between you and I was that my wife didn't stay around long enough to see me join AA." Richard then asked an innocent question about his membership. "How long have you been coming to the meetings?" Davidson replied with a kind of world weary inflection. "I've been to a lot of meetings although I have to admit that they always seem the same." Richard did not look surprised. He wasn't. "Shit, just as I thought, I pretty well thought you were a veteran." A Davidson nod and a comment. "Why do you say that?" A slow shrug and an explanation.

"Well, in the two meetings I've been to, you looked reluctant, almost dismissive, like you were incredibly bored." Davidson started to snicker, like he knew Richard was going to say something like that. "Well, I am bored but what the hell, I've been going for so long, I can't imagine not going."

They rode in silence for a while. Davidson was staring out the windshield, perhaps reflecting on his decade's worth of confession, retroactive regret, and now boredem. "Does it still do you any good?" asked Richard. "I'm assuming that it used to do you some good, right?" Davidson sighed. "Well, I'm still not drinking, am I! I still don't know, after all this time, whether fact that I've been going to these damn meetings for so many years, I just don't know. But I just can't take the chance." Davidson paused and then added a quick footnote. "Besides, I like the coffee, especially the coffee served by this chapter." He then laughed, like he had just come up with a particularly memorable witticism. Davidson then abruptly changed the focus of their discussion from himself to Richard. "So you've been to two meetings. What do you think?" Richard hunched over the wheel of the car for a moment, like he was considering his passenger's question. "I believe that the organization, the other members, these meetings could help people like me, like us. If I can stop drinking by going to these meetings once a week, then why not?" Davidson nodded and remarked. "Right out of the AA manual, so to speak. And what do you think about the speakers, the members that you have heard share the last two weeks?" A casual grimace came over his face as Richard answered. "It may help, I guess."

Richard dropped Davidson off at his place without pursuing the matter of the possible effect of AA on their lives any further. It was getting a little personal and this was with a man he hardly knew, even though they had recently participated in a gathering in which strangers revealed intensely private thoughts and feelings. He had simply thought better of troubling him further, at least until the next Tuesday meeting. He did not want to spook him. He even decided that he would not walk Margie by 240 Belcourt until he felt a little more comfortable in questioning him about his personal life.

ANOTHER MEETING'S CONVERSATION

He kept the promise he had made to himself after last week's AA meeting, not once walking Margie down Belcourt Avenue. Richard had suggested to Davidson that he would again pick him up for the next week's meeting as he was dropping him after last week's meeting. So on the next Tuesday evening, he was waiting in the driveway at 240 Belcourt Avenue at 7:30. Davidson was at his door waiting. Richard didn't have to get out of the car. Davidson got into the car with a pensive look on his face, as if he had been deliberating as to whether greeting Richard was appropriate somehow. He sat in his seat without a word, not returning Richard's salutation. They were in motion for a good five minutes before Richard asked him if anything was amiss. Davidson emitted a sigh, almost a groan. "I had trouble with Andrew all day. I had to call Douglas to come in early to deal with him." Richard was mildly surprised that Davidson would be so forthcoming about Andrew, at least at this point in their relationship. He prodded Davidson for further information, asking him for details. Again surprisingly, Davidson gave him some, most of which he could have guessed. "Well, he gets a little uncontrollable at times, unruly. He starts yelling, throwing things, trying to leave the house, which definitely would not be a good idea. I'd have to call the cops."

Almost immediately, Richard thought of that incident many years ago with Scott Vessey acting up in a grocery store in his old neighbourhood. He then thought of Andrew in the window and asked Davidson about it. "So he wasn't in the window." Stewart wearily smiled and shook his head. "No, no, when he's standing in his window, he's no problem at all.

When he's staring out that window, looking for god knows who or what, he is calm, almost tranquil." Richard took the opportunity for another question, a question that had been percolating in his head since he first saw Andrew in that window some months before. What was he looking at? Again, Davidson smiled and shook his head. "I don't really know. I've never really knew. Sometimes, I think it's something. Sometimes, I think it's someone. I don't know." As much as he wanted to ask another question, he dropped the interrogation. It didn't matter anyway.

They were turning into the parking lot to the Holy Conception building on Bronson Avenue. Richard's next question was filed away for the next time, the next opportunity, if there was one.

As soon as Richard walked into the meeting room, Tim greeted him and immediately brought up the matter of him formally joining AA. Richard acknowledged Tim and joined him at the podium where he was presented with and signed a membership form. Tim then shook his hand and waved him into the meeting proper. He also presented Richard with a membership card which he tucked somewhat reluctantly into his wallet. The meeting was filling up, people filing in, most with remarkably cheerful expressions on their faces, oblivious it seemed to the gravity of the purpose of the meeting. There was a general murmur of voices and scattered laughter. Richard got himself a coffee, no pastry this time and was fortunate enough to claim a seat beside Davidson who had been talking to a woman behind him, a woman who was wearing a loose t-shirt, a pair of well worn yoga pants and a wrinkled face on which makeup had been haphazardly applied. In fact, the woman looked like she was in the process of recovering from an addiction not to alcohol but to cosmetics. Davidson abruptly ended his conversation with the made up woman and sat down, whispering to Richard, "Thanks for interrupting, I was getting a little tired of listening to that woman's craziness. For some reason, she often tries to talk to me. I think she wants me to be her sponsor, not the sponsor she has now." It was strange as Richard could not recall seeing the woman at the two meetings he had attended.

The two of them sat in silence as Tim opened the meeting with a customary greeting and an announcement of several items of interest, all of which Richard immediately forgot. He was surprised, if not stunned when Davidson's makeup woman stood up to initiate the evening's proceedings. "My name is Allison and I'm an alcoholic. I have been coming to these meetings for almost a year. I'm making progress but I still wish the meetings were held every day. Ask my sponsor who must be sick of my voice by now." She looked at the woman sitting beside her, an older version of herself it seemed. The older woman smiled, nodded and gripped her hand for a moment. "It's difficult to face everyday knowing that you could stumble at any moment, at any time, during any day or night, even if you're not thinking about drinking, even if you haven't seen a drink or you haven't been near anybody who's having or has had a drink. It's just damn hard." Half the meeting's audience looked intent, the other half looked disinterested, almost bored, no surprise there because most of them had heard this before, all of it reinforcing the message of every meeting. Allison, whose mascara had started to run down her cheeks like tears, went on to depress herself and some of the people listening to her with stories of the burden that drinking and trying to stop drinking had placed and continued to place on her and her family, explaining, as many of those who share often did, that her drinking destroyed her family, relating the sad story of losing her husband and her children and her hope of recovering them as well as herself. She finished her commentary with a flourish, introducing a show of tears to the play.

Those people in the meeting who had not joined Allison in weeping were staring at each other in silence. Tim almost seemed overcome as well, a curious reaction for a person who must have heard every sob story imaginable, dabbing his eyes with a light blue handkerchief. Three of the next four speakers took up the same theme; the consequences of their drinking, the consequence of their efforts to forsake drinking and the consequences of their efforts to recover from drinking were all on display, with emphasis on their families or what was left of them. Davidson listened to two of those next speakers with an unusual level of intensity, at least for him. Both men spoke of the woeful effect their drinking had had on their families, particularly on the damage on their wives, both of which had left them some time ago. Richard watched his body language and the expression on his face, both indicating that he recognized that the stories, as maudlin as they seemed, were having an impression. He hung his head for a moment, it had almost fallen in his hands, and he had an occasional grim look on his face. Richard thought that he was seriously lost in either memory, contemplation or both. He was ready to enter the confessional he hoped.

At the break, Richard immediately decided to take advantage of his impression of Davidson's musing. He made straight for Davidson in the coffee line, gently touching his arm with his hand as he was pouring his coffee. "Hey, you seemed to be actually listening tonight. Anything interesting?" he said to Davidson who slowly turned to him. Davidson nodded and moved closer to almost whisper his reply. "All that talk about the effect on marriage was pretty familiar. It reminded me of Elaine." It was the first time Davidson had used her name. Richard had to confirm. "Elaine, your ex?" Davidson almost bowed. "Yes, I haven't see her for more than ten years but it still bothers me, me and I assume Andrew, that is if he knew." Richard was close to another significant step in unravelling whatever mystery he believed was apparent. After exchanging several meaningless comments about the attendance at the night's meeting, a cliched conversation they had at all three of the meetings they had attended together, they returned to their seats.

As with the two previous meetings, the second part of the third meeting was predictably forgettable, the attendees were bored and restless. On the drive home, Richard was bold enough to ask Davidson about his ex-wife, the now identified Elaine. "Do you ever hear from Elaine?" he inquired casually, as if he was commenting about the weather. Davidson was surprisingly candid, at least as far as Richard could have expected. "No, not a word. She just left and never got in touch again. We got divorced by mail one day maybe two or three years after she left and that was it. In fact, I don't know where she lives now." Thinking of Andrew, who might have or likely did figure importantly in her decision to leave, Richard asked if she could be aware of where he and Andrew currently lived. "I doubt it. I mean, we moved three times since she left although if she wanted to know, I guess it would not be hard to find out." Richard then followed with the obvious question. "If you wanted to, would it be hard for you to find out where she lived now?" Davidson looked a little thoughtful for a moment and then replied with an edge of bitterness in his voice. "Not really but I really don't care." They were turning onto Belcourt. He wanted to continue to delve further into the history of the Stewart/ Elaine but time and propriety would prevent additional investigation. By the time Richard had turned into the driveway at 240 Belcourt and Stewart Davidson had disembarked from the car, he had abandoned the idea of quizzing Davidson further. The two of them said good night and Richard drove home.

Richard sat in his car in the driveway on Lakeview Avenue, considering the evening's conversations with Stewart Davidson. He was fairly certain that he could not continue to involve Davidson in any further pursuit of his investigation of Davidson and his ex-wife, if that what he was in fact doing. He wondered about the possible explanation for the decision of Davidson's ex-wife to leave him and their son Andrew. It seemed counter-intuitive. It made no sense to Richard that his ex-wife would leave her handicapped son with her alcoholic husband rather than take him away from her alcoholic husband. Was Elaine so distressed with the situation with her husband Stewart that she was willing to abandon her handicapped son as well or was her handicapped son part of the problem as well? Richard sat in his car in his own driveway turning the situation over in his mind. The trail would now inevitably lead to the former Elaine Davidson, wherever and whoever she was. He didn't think he would be going to any more AA meetings with Stewart Davidson or anyone else for that matter.

VISITING THE COURT HOUSE

It was two days after the last Tuesday meeting that Richard, after a short internet search, decided that he would look for the current location of the former Elaine Davidson through the record of her divorce from Stewart Davidson. He still did not know what he would do with that information once he found it. He would have to visit the reading room of the Supreme Court of Justice on the second floor of the Ottawa Court House on Elgin Street. The record that Richard sought would not be available online, an apparent eventuality he discovered after a confusing journey through various Ontario Government websites. He concluded that he would have to search the archives in which all Certificates of Divorces issued by the Ottawa Court were filed. He was reasonably certain that Stewart Davidson had divorced Elaine, current name unknown, over the past decade or so. He therefore decided that he would have to search pretty well all the divorce records available in the reading room of the Court House from 2008 to the present. He was worried that Stewart Davidson had not been entirely reliable in discussing his history with his former wife Elaine and that his search would be that much more difficult than it would otherwise be.

The Court House in Ottawa was located on Elgin Street near the new City Hall and the old teacher's college building. Both the Court Hall and the City Hall were relatively new buildings, built almost thirty years ago while the teacher's college building, which was now part of the City Hall, it's educational responsibilities having ended and been transferred to the University of Ottawa in the mid-1970s, was built in 1875, seemingly as an Edwardian castle, at least to Richard. He recalled lining up on Elgin Street in the early 1970s, his intention to register for teacher's college, his Bachelor of Arts degree pointless and worth next to nothing from an employment perspective. At the time, he thought that he would have made a good teacher although he never got the opportunity. When he arrived to arrange for registration, the actual line was several blocks long and did not seem to be moving too quickly. He stood in line for almost an hour, spending his time speaking to several people both in front and behind and smoking, half a dozen cigarettes consumed. After that hour, during which time he spoke to two women who prompted him to reconsider his plans to move in with his current girlfriend, who still had another year of university remaining, he also reconsidered his plans to remain in the lineup any longer.

By the time he left the lineup, it was nearly four blocks long, past the next most significant street, Somerset, one street east of Cooper, where he had been living since he moved out of the residence at Carleton University several months back, he had decided that teacher's college was definitely not in his future. It appeared to Richard that there would be little, if any prospect that graduating from teacher's college would result in a teaching career, being that there seemed to be an excess of competition for future positions, the lengthy lineups he had just seen not likely limited to Ottawa. He recalled discussing the depressing lack of future careers with his university classmates, other students on the edge of obtaining their useless degrees. Besides, he had realized that he did not have the funds to support himself, his girlfriend, and two years in teacher's college. On the way to his bachelor apartment on Cooper Street, he already had plans to start looking for a job that afternoon.

—

He made his first visit to the Court House in Ottawa on a Friday, three days after his most recent AA meeting with Davidson. He had an interesting experience in the elevator from the parking garage to the main rotunda of the Court House, a large lobby that looked like it could have hosted a state funeral visitation. He had parked the car in the lot under the building and entered an elevator car with six other people, four young men in black suits and pony tails, looking for clients a lawyer friend later told him, a teenager with high end headphones and an older man, a judge wearing the required robes, and carrying a stack of papers. He carried a scent of cigarette smoke. The young man removed his head phones and, without warning, started to berate the judge, almost pushing the man against the wall.

Two of the young men in black suits intervened, trying to place themselves between the judge and the teenager, the latter suddenly yelling about a prosecution against his father. By the time the elevator arrived on the ground floor, one of the guys in a black suit may have had a new client and the judge looked a little uncomfortable. Richard, free of the minor fray, presented himself to the reception desk while three of the guys in black suits walked toward the cafeteria which was situated directly across the bank of court rooms on the east side of the building, the fourth black suit escorted the kid in the headphones to one of the lobby benches, and the judge disappeared toward the end of the lobby. The man behind the reception desk nodded as Richard approached and remarked. "Happens all the time. People are always disappointed with judges. I wouldn't worry about it." He then looked up, smiled and asked how he could be of service. Richard was alone in front of the reception desk.

"I am interested in records of divorces at least over the past ten years or so." he asked. The receptionist replied by pointing to a sign that advised "Archives – Second Floor". As Richard headed back to the elevators, he heard the man wish him good luck. He took the elevator to the second floor and was immediately facing two large doors and a security guard sitting at a small desk with a cellphone to his ear. Behind the doors and the security guard was presumably the archives. On seeing Richard emerge from the elevator, the security guard slowly put down a cellphone and greeted him with a stare and a partial grimace. He leaned over the desk with his hands folded and continued to stare. He was wearing a white City of Ottawa badge with his name Mike Brennan inscribed on it. Richard stepped forward and stated his purpose in being there.

"I am interested in obtaining a divorce record." explained Richard, "I understand it may be in the archives here."

"Well, you're right. That's the archives." Brennan pointed his hand behind his left shoulder. "You'll need to fill in a form if you want to look through the archives." Brennan handed over a one page form on which, aside from the usual informational requirements, asked for the names of the divorced people and the reason for the request for the record. Those two questions presented Richard with an anticipated dilemma. While he had the names of the divorced, that is Stewart and Elaine Davidson, which should have been sufficient unless the form asked for Elaine's maiden name. On the other hand, he was having trouble formulating an acceptable reason for his visit to the archives. He had sat down on a bench to the left of the elevators and started to fill in the form. When he came to the perplexing question, he had decided on that elusive of answers, i.e. basically a slight variant of the truth. In the three lines below the question, he wrote: "Seeking the record for an ill friend." He left it at that. He got up from the bench, walked across the hall and handed the form to Mike Brennan. He felt like he was back in university, handing in his answers to a final examination. Brennan just placed the form in a paper tray and waved him into the archive room. "It's open, the lights go on automatically." said Brennan, never getting out of his chair. Richard walked past him, opened the door, and, as promised, the lights went on.

It was a large room, more befitting a warehouse than an office room. There were ten rows of racks, each of which held five shelves each. Each shelf held large cardboard boxes in which divorce certificates were catalogued by month for the years since 1979. Richard had learned from various websites that any record prior to 1979 was available from the Archives of Ontario as opposed from the Court House. At the head of each rack were small signs indicating the years for the cardboard boxes held by that rack. He had already calculated, more a guess than a calculation actually, from the information provided by his AA friend Davidson, that he would have to look through the boxes from 2003 to the present, a span of fifteen years, likely hundreds of boxes and thousands of filed certificates. It could take years to look through them all although he was relieved that he did not have to look through every box in the place. He also noticed that there was another sign, this one over the doors, announcing to the inquisitive, he would imagine that most of them were lawyers and infuriated ex-wives, that the room was open to four o'clock in the afternoon, after which time he presumed that Mike Brennan's shift would end.

It was eleven o'clock in the morning. He stuck his head out of the archive room to ask Mike Brennan when he went to lunch. Brennan told him that he would be replaced at his post by a guy he called Tim within the hour, suggesting that he could go to lunch at any time between then and four o'clock in the afternoon when the room closed for the day. Richard turned back to the room and stood for a moment considering which of the ten rows he should start looking for the former Stewart and Elaine Davidson. He had already concluded that he should start with the year 2003, meaning that he would have to start in row five, which was the middle row, the one facing him from where he was standing. He walked straight to the middle of that fifth row, stopping at a small sign for the certificates filed during 2000-2005. The box for the year 2003 started on the third shelve of that row. Unfortunately, the certificates were filed by month, although, fortunately, within each month, the certificates were filed alphabetically. Therefore, he would have to start the monthly documents from the file for January 2003.

There was only one certificate for January 2003. It concerned a couple named Connolly, Keith and Nancy, who were granted divorce without dispute after two years of separation. Richard was pleased to see that separate addresses for both parties were recorded on the certificate, the only detail in which Richard was ultimately interested. After looking through the certificates for February 2003, he had started to realize that the particulars of some of the divorces made interesting reading, sort like screenplays for a series of soap operas. He had started to flip through the certificates for February at random without apparent reason. The second certificate in February 2003 concerned a couple named Langlois who listed several reasons for their divorce, listing a variety of unfortunate behaviours sure to interest tabloid admirers; adultery, alcoholism, cruelty and domestic violence. He was sufficiently curious to look through three more certificates, couples named Davis, Gallagher and Moore, all of whom were divorced for pedestrian reasons like desertion, separation and something called lack of reasonable arrangements, no hint of the more inflammatory grounds like alcoholism and sexual perversion. It took him less than twenty minutes to go through the certificates for the remainder of 2003, perhaps a total of less than a hundred divorces, not stopping to examine any document detail aside from their names, arranged of course alphabetically. He decided to move on to 2004, the batch for that year appearing to contain less than the number of certificates filed in the previous year. A quick perusal of the certificates and then he would break for lunch. As expected, he did not find a certificate for the divorce of Stewart and Elaine Davidson.

He was sitting alone in the Court House cafeteria having a bowl of soup and a sandwich when a rotund young man in a navy blue suit and wearing a pony tail joined him at his table. He was carrying a leather file folder and a coffee in a disposable coffee cup. He sat down. "I noticed that you were up in the archive room looking through the divorces." Richard looked at him with a blank look on his face. "Yes I was. How do you know?" he asked the rotund pony tail. The latter smiled, put down his coffee cup and his file folder and reached across the table to offer his hand. "I'm Matt, Matt Balfour. Like most people in this building, I'm a lawyer, mainly handling divorces. I saw you going into the room just as I was just leaving." Richard didn't recall seeing Mr. Balfour leaving the floor although he could have slipped out as he was talking with Mike Brennan. "And...." Richard said as he gingerly shook Balfour's hand. He withdrew his hand and explained. "I was just curious, that's all. I thought that maybe you were a competitor, researching the files for clients." Richard shook his head. "I'm not an attorney. I wasn't researching for clients, I was looking for a friend." Attorney Balfour nodded, got up from the table, said "Just checking." and walked away. Richard then watched him leaving, puzzled about the entire conversation, as short as it was. He wondered about what kind of information a lawyer would want or even could collect for current clients from information available in that room on previous clients. He speculated about the possibility for a few moments before he started back to the second floor. Maybe Balfour was looking for an address of a former client, sort of like he was. Maybe the former client had neglected to pay his bill. He followed Balfour out and was soon passing Mike Brennan sitting at his desk on the second floor in front of the archive room. He looked like he was about to put his head down on the desk and take a nap. Richard gave him a wave, which he didn't return, and went back to search the filed certificates. He would be resuming his hunt in the box for the year 2004.

While he was certain that there was no explanation, the year of 2004 happened to be a year in which a lot of couples had managed to finalize divorces, their certificates crammed into the year's box like pressed meat. They were almost glued together, so much so that Richard practically had to use his teeth to separate the certificates from each other. January, the first month he examined, was so prolific that Richard estimated that maybe the Court would have had to work overtime to process all the divorce applications that were on the dockets. Even more intriguing was that at least two certificates were stapled together, for reasons unknown. Richard decided to uncover that reason. So he undid the staples, picking them apart carefully. He assumed that no one would notice that they had been separated, notwithstanding curious attorneys like Matt Balfour. Not surprisingly, the first stapled certificates referred to the same couple, Jack and Irene Clapworthy, the reason being that the grounds for the divorce, which was eventually granted on January 19, were modified three times, from adultery to alcoholism to desertion. Although hardly an expert, he had decided that there could not be a reasonable explanation for their obvious indecisions, unless one or both of the former partners were in need of therapy of some sort. Richard briefly wondered whether either of them, or maybe even both of them, were AA members. The other stapled certificates recorded the divorce of Lorne and Betty Gallagher, as recorded on one of the certificates, and the divorce of Lorne and Carol Gallagher, the change in the latter respondent's name, another inexplicable development. The grounds for their divorce was adultery although, like all divorces, the certificate did not identify the individual committing the adultery, unless of course both of them were fooling around.

Richard went through March and April, both of which were comparatively light, without a glimmer of interest. In the May certificates, he came across a couple named Sawchuk who lived on Cooper Street, an Ottawa street he had lived on when he was living with his university girlfriend Linda. While he realized that the Sawchuks, Steve and Jackie, had lived only one block away from his old place on Cooper Street, he also realized that it was highly unlikely that they had lived there at the same time, the fact that he and Linda had moved away more than forty years ago. It was a peculiar little historical coincidence that sometimes appeared in one's life thought Richard, the kind of thing that happened randomly. If his project of searching for Stewart Davidson's former wife and presumably Andrew Davidson's mother was not confidential, he would have shared it with Jean, even though he would have to mention Linda, which always made his wife uncomfortable, even though he hadn't seen his former roommate for more than fourty years.

He sped through the months of June, July and August until he came across a couple named Davidson in the September batch. Hope dashed, however, when she saw that their names were Norman and Anita. Their grounds for divorce as stated on the certificate was "boredom", a justification which had not been listed on any other divorce certificate he had examined and was not likely to be listed on any future certificate he was to examine. He almost dismissed it with a laugh but also realized that the grounds that the Davidsons cited were closer to the truth that any other justification he had seen recorded on the certifications he had reviewed. He had guessed, given the stated reason for their divorce that the former Davidsons were middle aged and beyond and that "bored" was not an exaggeration in describing a relationship they had decided to end. He took a moment to contemplate not only his own marriage, which was hardly in danger of collapse, but the marriages, mainly of friends and relatives, of which he was familiar. He wondered how many of them could qualify as boring. He knew that his own martial relationship was hardly uninteresting but thought about the years ahead. The next divorcing couple were the Franks who cited the old standby excuse adultery as their grounds for their decision, hardly "boring" but entirely predictable. He continued to sweep through the files for the reminder of the year 2004. He found nothing noteworthy.

He would have to pay more attention now that he was moving into the files for 2005 and more recent years, remembering Stewart Davidson's casual admission that he and Elaine had been divorced for over ten years, suggesting to Richard that he would have to start searching a little more carefully from 2005 on, just to be on the safe side. The first six months of 2005 revealed little, if anything he had not seen before. A few dozen uninspiring divorces, running the gambit from desertion to separation to an old standby "irreconcilable differences", a few suggestions of adultery and one, a couple named Govan, enumerated practically every possible ground for divorce that one could think of. It was, however, the second certificate he came across in the month of September that caught more than his passing attention. It certified the divorce of James and Ellen Baxter and indicated unusual grounds for their decision: untidy housekeeping and incompetent cooking. He wondered how failure to satisfactorily perform two relatively pedestrian activities in any marriage could lead to divorce. However, the more he thought about it, the more understandable it appeared to be. In fact, he was surprised he had not seen such justifications previously. He also thought that maybe general house keeping could start appearing on some of the certificates.

It was a couple of hours later. He had finished examining the filed certificates for the years 2005 and 2006 when he suddenly found Mike Brennan standing behind him. It was four o'clock in the afternoon. The archive room was closing for the day. He would have to come back on Monday. He had spent five hours in the room. It had been boring, almost pointless but occasionally had its moments of entertainment, if not enlightenment.

FINDING THE CERTIFICATE

It was the next Tuesday that Richard appeared in front of Mike Brennan and the archive room on the second floor of the Court House. He had not appeared there neither on the weekend, when the room was closed, nor the Monday, when the sudden visit of Jean's cousins occupied the entire day. He would start with the filed certificates for 2007. His enthusiasm for the search had yet to regain the heights it had reached when he had first started last week. He was quite frankly bored. He was hoping to come across a certificate or two that would incite his interest, like the unusual details that he had uncovered in several of the certificates he had reviewed on Friday. Mike Brennan, who was on the telephone when Richard arrived on the second floor, waved him into the room, the door having been unexpectedly open, as if Mike Brennan had been waiting. Richard stood in front of the box marked 2007 and started looking.

Review of January and February's certificates passed without notice, every one of them recording entirely pedestrian fundamentals, including of course the grounds supporting the divorces. He counted them. Of the twenty six certificates that he had briefly appraised in the months of January and February, fifteen of them recorded separation as grounds for their divorce, five of them recorded desertion, the less voluntary lack of definition of the latter, three recorded lack of reasonable arrangements, of which there was no definition, another for something the couple called malaise, which Richard interpreted to be another term for plain boredom, and one each for alcoholism and the most interesting of the grounds, adultery. Richard wondered if there was a possibility that there was some way one could obtain more information on such cases. It would make for some interesting reading although if details of divorces were so publicly available, the archive room would have to strengthen its security and increase its size. Further, perhaps the archive room would become a significant source for one or more of the tabloids. Either that, or a screenplay for a reality television show.

Richard reached the objective of his search around eleven o'clock on Tuesday morning. The document certifying the divorce of Stewart and Elaine Davidson recorded the grounds for the action was separation, which Richard immediately discounted, finding it difficult to believe that the disrepair in their relationship with each other and their relationship with their son Andrew was as simple as a case of separation. No, whatever prompted their divorce was almost certainly far more interesting and complex. Richard thought that any possible scenario would have to involve Andrew, the son who the two divorced parents Stewart and Elaine shared and likely fought over for years. He noted that they had married on September 7, 1978 and were divorced on March 5, 2007. He also noted that the former Mrs. Elaine Davidson was living in an older Edwardian apartment building called Ambassador Court on Bank Street in Ottawa when her and Stewart Davidson were divorced. For their part, Stewart along with Andrew, who he assumed was staying with his father after they separated and divorced, remained on a street called Glencairn in Ottawa South. He knew where Stewart and Andrew were now living and he hoped to discover where the former Elaine Davidson was now living. He now had a place to start. He copied down Elaine's address at the time of the divorce and happily left the archive room, saying goodbye to Brennan on the way out by slapping his desk, and was in the elevator and then the parking lot within minutes.

He stopped for lunch at the Royal Oak pub on Bank Street near MacLaren, read the paper and had a salad and a draft. He was itching to tell someone, particularly Jean, but knew that he could not let the information out to anyone, particularly an individual like his wife for example, who might think him someone less than mentally healthy, the possibility of obsession a prominent diagnosis. Sitting there in that pub at around one o'clock that Tuesday afternoon, he contemplated, as he often did, the possibility that his interest in finding the former wife of Stewart Davidson of 240 Belcourt Avenue was more than ordinary obsession, perhaps verging into something akin to compulsion, which seemed at least to Richard, like a psychological condition more unfortunate and perhaps more damaging. He concluded, however, that he would have to continue to look for the former Mrs. Davidson, whoever she was and wherever she was.

For a brief moment, he thought of his previous plan whereby he would somehow discover Elaine's maiden name, a name that he might find in marriage records, another run through another archive somewhere. But still, he needed her location, that is what he was looking for and, when he thought about it, setting the start of that chronology further back in history, a more difficult task he thought than starting his search in 2007, the date of the divorce, or maybe thirty years before that, the year of their marriage. Anyway, he would start to investigate her current whereabouts at the Ambassador Court the next day, perhaps call on the janitor. He left the pub, leaving a hefty gratuity and headed home to take a nap.

The custodian's name was Albert Langlois and he answered the buzzer at Ambassador Court with a scratchy, old man kind of voice. Richard explained that he was looking for a woman, a former tenant hoping that he could help him in locating her current address. Mr. Langlois seemed initially rather reluctant, asking for the tenant's name and his relationship to the former tenant in a halting, quiet voice. He also sounded a little frightened, Richard imagining that Langlois might have thought he was a police officer, a private detective or a debt collector. On the other hand, perhaps Albert Langlois was frightened all the time, a man who might well have regarded paranoia as a job requirement. It was a wild guess, based entirely on the shaky tone in his voice.

Richard was speaking through the speaker, standing on the first step in the doorway, right underneath the sign which identified the building as the "Ambassador Court". The steps were of well worn stone, the top two having formed into depressions reflecting over a century of use, countless tenants walking in and out of the stately address, wearing down the steps until they were as smooth as marble.

"Who was the tenant? When did she live here?" asked Langlois through the speaker. Richard asked to enter the building, thinking it would be more effective, if not more convenient to speak to Langlois face to face. "Okay, I guess. Apartment 106." He did not sound certain but he buzzed Richard in anyway. Richard opened the lobby door and was inside the first floor corridor. The door to Apartment 106 was open and Albert Langlois, a close to elderly man who was tall and thin with a furrowed, hollow eyed face, a stoop and ill fitting dentures, was standing in the doorway. He was standing in front of an elderly woman, presumably his wife, a short, rotund lady wearing a frightfully coloured house dress and holding the handle of an old fashioned vacuum cleaner laying at her feet. Albert the custodian stepped out of the doorway of his apartment and introduced himself. "Hello, I'm Albert and this is my wife Helen." he said, sweeping his hand with a thumb behind him in her direction. Richard reciprocated. "I'm Richard Matthews and I'm looking for a woman who may have been a tenant of this building some time ago." He offered his hand and Albert stepped closer and shook it. He was holding a light bulb in his other hand. He smelt a bit like turpentine. Richard looked behind Albert and offered Helen a broad smile, to which Albert's wife seemed to put her entire body into returning the expression. "Well, Mr. Matthews, Helen and I have been looking after this place for maybe twenty years....right Helen? And we were and still are usually pretty close to our tenants."

"Well, Mr. Langlois, her married name was Elaine Davidson and after her divorce in 2007, I believe she moved into this building. I'm sorry but I never did find out her maiden name, the name she was likely using when she moved into this building. As I say, she had just been divorced and was moving from where she and her husband were living."

Momentarily, Langlois had a blank look on his face. He then gave the only answer he could in the circumstances. "I can't remember anyone like that. Do you, Helen?" Albert again looked over his shoulder. The woman hunched her shoulders and Albert followed suit. There was a disturbing silence during which all three of them could actually hear two ladies in the lobby complaining about the weather. Albert then offered a suggestion, which would have been entirely predictable to most people but seemed like a revelation coming from Albert. "You should speak to Mrs. Cartwright. She works for the company that owns the building, you know, my boss, the landlord. She would have the rental applications, probably going back quite a long time, surely back before 2007. You should contact her." Richard smiled and asked for her telephone number. Albert turned and went back into his apartment. He did some rummaging through an old fashioned, roll top desk that was standing just inside the door. He found what he was looking for, returned to the door and handed him Joanne Cartwright's card. Richard took it, put it into his pocket, and shook Albert's hand for a second time, thanking him. He was outside the Ambassador Court before he took the card out of his pocket and examined it. It introduced her in embossed black letters.

Joanne Cartwright
Leasing Management
Ford Real Estate
160 Elgin Street, Ottawa

On the back of the card, telephone and fax numbers as well as the coordinates for Facebook, e-mail and the company website were included. Richard checked his watch. If he left then, he would arrive there well before lunch. It was the Place Bell building and was situated, conveniently enough, right across from the Court House. Richard knew the building. In fact, he often went to meetings there when he was working for the government. He drove over to the location, parked on Nepean Street adjacent to Place Bell and walked through a side entrance. He went past several places, a small restaurant, a convenience store, and a men's wear store that years ago used to be high end. In fact, Richard wondered how a place like that could possibly still stay in business, the emergence of other men's wear stores and the replacement of business suits with casual wear among government employees obvious explanations for those doubts. Richard had concluded that customer loyalty was stronger than he might have thought.

Richard arrived at the circular reception desk in the lobby, behind which were three building officials dressed in uniforms, almost like doormen, responsible for security it seemed. The building, although it was likely built sometime in the sixties and definitely looked that way from the outside, had the internal presence, the inside architectural atmosphere of a much older structure, cavernous and almost forbidding, like an office building that had been constructed maybe thirty or forty years previously. Its marble floors, wide corridors, high ceilings, and dark panelled walls, all of which were dimly illuminated by old fashioned chandeliers almost gave the place the look of a church.

As Richard approached the reception desk, he was struck by the silence of the building, only the faint echoes of footsteps disrupting the quiet. He approached the desk and one of the building officials looked up from a newspaper to greet him. He smiled and looked relieved, apparently happy to be of service. Richard asked for directions to Ford Real Estate, an unusual request for modern office buildings where their offices were principally identified by digital display signs. The official, a beefy man whose name tag only identified him, as he had guessed, as being employed by a firm called Sampson Security, told him that Ford Real Estate had a small office on the 12th floor, in Room 1252 precisely. The official then asked Richard to sign in. He did and the building official, after taking a brief look at the sign in sheet, then pointed to the elevators behind him. Richard thanked him and headed toward the 12th floor.

The building official had been right. Once on the 12th floor, he found room 1252 in the far north east corner of the building. He knocked on a plain maple door with only the number 1252 on it, no Ford Real Estate, no Joanne Cartwright, nothing else. A tall, thin, bespectacled woman in maybe her mid-forties answered the door. The building official, who may not have ever visited room 1252, Ford Real Estate, or Joanne Cartwright, had been right. Ford Real Estate was housed in an extremely small office, just large enough for a small desk, two vinyl padded folding chairs, a metal filing cabinet, and two telephones. Ms. Cartwright barely had room to step around the desk to answer the door, almost bumping into him. Richard briefly wondered how a larger person would manage. Richard and Ms. Cartwright introduced themselves, the latter acknowledging the close quarters. She offered him a chair and asked if she could help him. Richard simply explained the purpose in his visit, with understandably counterfeit details and apologizing at least twice for the unusual nature of his request.

"I'm sorry, I know this isn't about real estate or anything but it is important that I find out if a woman named Elaine, whose married name was Davidson, moved into the Ambassador Court on Bank Street sometime in the winter or spring of 2007. She moved in because she was just divorced and probably rented her apartment under her maiden name. My wife and I were neighbours a long time ago, long before she and her husband were divorced, and am interested in returning to her some things, mainly jewellery and some expensive silverware, that my wife borrowed from her maybe twenty years ago. My wife recently passed away. So I am in the process of moving out of the old place. In packing up the place, I came across her things, at least I think they were her things, and want to return them to her."

"And you don't know her maiden name?" Ms. Cartwright expressed some surprise. "No, never did know it." answered Richard.

"I suppose that can happen. But why don't you ask her ex-husband?" asked Ms. Cartwright, shrugging her shoulders slowly.

Richard shrugged his own shoulders in response and made his excuse. "I have tried but I simply don't know where he is. Apparently, he has moved a lot since the divorce." Ms. Cartwright leaned over that small desk of hers. "So I thought I'd try Mrs. Davidson. Besides, the things I found belong to the former Mrs. Davidson, not her husband." Ms. Cartwright leaned back in her chair and waited for Richard to continue his spiel. "I know it might seem a little improper, maybe even unethical, but I'm asking you for her maiden name, or whatever name she may have been using when she rented a place in Ambassador Court."

Ms. Cartwright nodded and put her hands together as if she were about to initiate prayer. "Okay. I think I can do that." With that assurance, she rose from her chair, turned and opened the second drawer of the filing cabinet behind her. "I don't know if I can find her rental application, that is if she ever submitted one, but we have only twelve units in that building and there couldn't have been too many applications in 2007." She looked back at him and started looking through the second drawer, flipping through the rental applications. "Let me look here." After about a couple of minutes, she stopped and pulled a sheet of paper out of the cabinet, turned, sat back down at her desk, laid it down, and identified the applicant, as someone named Elaine Sherwood.

"Is her previous address shown on her application?" asked Richard who was now leaning his elbows on Ms. Cartwright's desk. He was obviously attempting to read Elaine Sherwood's rental application.

Ms. Cartwright smiled. "Her application shows every address where she has lived in the last thirty years or so. Her last address was on Glencairn Avenue in Ottawa South. It shows that she lived there with the Stewart and Andrew for more than twenty years. Before that, she lived on Northview in Nepean and before then, a couple of streets downtown, namely Cooper and Lisgar Streets." Ms. Cartwright did not have to report any residences beyond Glencairn Avenue. Richard could barely contain himself. In one of his conversations he pursued with Stewart Davidson during their trips to and from the meetings at the old Holy Conception on Bronson Avenue, he had mentioned that the Davidsons were living on Glencairn Avenue when he and Elaine divorced. He had found Stewart's ex-wife and more importantly, Andrew's mother. Her name was Elaine Sherwood. He now had to find her.

LOOKING FOR ELAINE SHERWOOD

Riding down in the elevator from the 12th floor office of Ford Real Estate, Richard was almost intoxicated with anticipation of finding Elaine Sherwood/Davidson that he had forgotten to thank Ms. Cartwright or even to bid her farewell. He was out the door of Room 1252 to the elevator on the 12th floor within what seemed like seconds. By the time he stepped into the elevator, it had occurred to him that his lack of grace in leaving Room 1252 was regrettable. For a moment, he thought of returning to the 12th floor and apologizing to Ms. Cartwright. He dropped the idea by the time he had reached the first floor and had stepped out of the elevator. No one else had boarded the elevator. It had therefore been a quick trip. He was past the reception desk, the beefy officer still reading the newspaper, the small restaurant, the convenience store, and the men's wear shop. He was out of the building and was standing on Nepean Street within minutes.

On the drive home, before Richard thought about the method of locating Elaine, he was troubled by the thought that the Elaine Sherwood had rented an apartment at the Ambassador Court more than ten years ago. She could have married again and changed her name a second time. He doubted that. Even if she had, he would find it difficult to believe that any modern woman, even one past middle age, would take the name of a second husband. He just didn't think she would. To locate Elaine Sherwood, he decided that the best way to find her would be to utilize Facebook, a convenience that he continued to use despite recent news stories questioning its use. He found that the modern version of the old telephone book, the Canada441.ca website, could be marginally helpful but hardly a sure thing. The website only provided the names, the addresses and the telephone numbers of people with the same surnames but, unlike Facebook, no further details, no education history, no work history, no pictures. Furthermore, and more importantly, it apparently only provided the telephone numbers of customers with landline telephones, the identification of people with cellphones not available to the curious.

Besides, Richard had managed to come across a number of people with whom he had not been in touch with for years, if not decades, mainly out of curiosity rather than anything approaching necessity. Richard managed to come across five long lost people through Facebook, including two ex-girl friends, two old classmates, and a boyhood friend whom he hadn't seen for maybe sixty years. There were a number of other people who he found navigating through Facebook, practically all of them individuals who were included as "friends" of people who were included as either his "friends" or "friends" of other people. It was like having a digital private detective on retainer. In fact, while Richard was not a frequent participant in using Facebook, unlike a lot of his fellow users who had hundreds of "friends" and who posted daily messages, videos, and pictures on almost everything that happened to them or anyone else for that matter, he figured that he was savvy enough to use it to locate Elaine Sherwood, that is of course if she was on Facebook, a possibility for which he had no estimate. If exploring Facebook turned out to be fruitless, a particular possibility since not everyone was a participant, especially if they were middle aged and older, he would have to pursue other avenues, such as contacting and talking to people who might know or might have known Elaine Sherwood, either in the Ambassador Court or, more importantly, on Glencairn Avenue.

The next morning, the trail of Elaine Sherwood now warm, he sat down in front of his laptop, logged on and got started searching for her Facebook profile. Amazingly enough, at least it seemed amazing to Richard, Facebook showed eleven Elaine Sherwoods with profiles. Six of them lived in the United States, two lived in Great Britain, and one each in Australia, Brazil and Canada, the latter profile identifying the individual as a recent graduate of the University of Toronto with a Master's in

Business Analytics, whatever that was. It was disappointingly obvious that he was not going to find Elaine Sherwood through Facebook. For reasons limited to curiosity only, he briefly explored the recently graduated Elaine Sherwood's profile. She reportedly had over a hundred Facebook friends, not an extraordinary number by any measurement, one that was well within the average. He wondered whether the majority were friends in real life, the number of friend requests to him by total strangers the standard for the observation. Regarding the latter, Richard would usually receive a friend request every second week or so. He never knew the motivation for such requests, not having made or even contemplated making such a request. It wasn't as if any of these people, including himself, were celebrities or had any hope of becoming celebrities. Richard personally knew all of the 75 or so friends that he had gathered over the two years and assumed that most other individuals that had Facebook profiles personally knew their friends as well. He did, however, find it difficult to believe that they were personally acquainted with all of the countless friends that were recorded on their profiles. Several of his Facebook friends supposedly had hundreds of friends, an impressive circle of friends for people who were not in the public eye. Perhaps some of these individuals were a lot more popular than he would have thought.

In any event, not familiar with any of Elaine Sherwood's friends, having failed in his bid to find her or her friends through Facebook, he realized that there were two only individuals who he could now rely upon through Facebook, her former husband and her son's worker. Regarding the former, while chances were not particularly good that Stewart Davidson had maintained or still maintained a Facebook page, it was nevertheless possible. So, as he did with his former wife, he found multiple profiles for Stewart Davidsons, not as many as he had with Elaine Sherwood but six people with the same name as his target. Four of them lived in the United States while the other two lived in Canada. All six of them were much younger than his Stewart Davidson, pretty well eliminating that avenue of inquiry. In that context, he had been told, by whom he could not recall, that sometimes people established several profiles for themselves, for reasons that were likely to be nefarious in some way. Richard thought about it for a while, ruminating about any such reasons, the pursuit of money and sex being possibilities but exactly how was beyond his speculation.

Richard then went on to Andrew Davidson's care worker, a man named Douglas Kane, a name that his employer, Stewart Davidson, nonchalantly provided to Richard during their first meeting, when Richard and Margie were caught trespassing on the Davidson property at 240 Belcourt Avenue. He could barely remember the name, which was not particularly surprising since Davidson only mentioned the name that once and never again, even during their conversations in the car to and from their AA meetings. Actually, it may have seemed to be almost a miracle that he could recall the name at all although the circumstances under which Davidson mentioned Douglas Kane were memorable enough anyway. In fact, Richard could almost recall his conversation as if he were reading it from a play, which was not surprising since the entire episode was, at least for a while afterwards, frightening. He had thought that Davidson had considered informing the police regarding the incident. Fortunately, that thought faded over time and was completely gone by the time Richard ran into Davidson at his first AA meeting. He had been fortunate he thought.

He was not so fortunate, however, with locating Mr. Kane on Facebook. He plugged his name in Goggle and was provided with five Douglas Kanes, not one of whom was even being close to the person that he could imagine could be the Douglas Kane that was Arthur Davidson's health care worker. Of the five profiles, three belonged to middle aged men, clearly disqualifying them from further consideration, and the other two, while young enough to be Douglas Kane, health care worker, claimed to be university students. He noticed, however, that one of the younger Kanes had not posted anything for four years. He then concluded that anyone who hadn't posted for so long was basically unapproachable. He also concluded that he should contact the other Kane, university student. At least that Kane was FB active and could be contacted as a connection. His message was simple.

"My name is Richard Matthews and I am looking for Elaine Sherwood, formerly Mrs. Elaine Davidson, ex-wife of Mr. Stewart Davidson and mother

of Andrew Davidson. It is a personal matter and I would appreciate any information you may have on her."

After he sent the message, he immediately realized that it was a little glib, too curt, leaving too much to supposition. It was, after all, a digital missive from one total stranger to another, for reasons that are not only unclear but possibly questionable. The only other time he attempted such an unusual message, at least he knew the individual to whom he was attempting to communicate. It was a girl from the old neighbourhood who was surprisingly connected to a Facebook friend with whom he had gone to high school. He had sent the girl, now a woman in her late sixties who he had not seen or heard from in more than fifty years, a simple message identifying himself for reasons other than old time's sake. She responded enthusiastically, which was not unexpected since both her and Richard lived across from each other for several years when they were both in grade school. They exchanged friendly banter over several messages, including expressions of mutual regret that their relationship, which had been romantic in the way eight year old boys and girls can be, had not lasted until adolescence. It was a strange interlude that lasted several days before the episode drifted happily into history, becoming another chapter of a childhood that continued to be memorable, at least to Richard.

—

Richard had continued to walk Margie but avoided going down Belcourt Avenue, not wishing to accidentally run into Stewart Davidson. His search for Elaine Sherwood had convinced him that he didn't really need to continue to explore his relationship with Stewart Davidson, a decision that he had already made before he had started to search for her in any event. He had dropped a note into the mailbox of 240 Belcourt. The note explained to his former AA acquaintance, if not fellow AA member that he no longer wanted to continue to attend the meetings, claiming that he felt that he could overcome his dependence on alcohol without the consolation of Alcoholics Anonymous meetings, a particularly ironic explanation in view of the fact that he was only pretending to be an alcoholic in the first place. By the time he had finished the note, he wondered, for only a moment, whether anyone else at the AA meetings he had attended was playing the role of an alcoholic, recalling a movie in which one of the characters joined a variety of self help groups for the companionship, if nothing else.

He was also familiar with a relative of a friend who liked to go to meetings of such groups for the free food. In that event, he had decided that he would avoid Stewart Davidson, in so far as he could, for the immediate future.

Richard took several days off from pursuing the matter of Elaine Sherwood, during which time he formulated a plan for the next stage of his search. He thought he had no option other than to canvas Elaine's old neighbourhood for people who might remember her, may still be in touch with her or, most importantly, may know where she currently lived. On his walks with Margie, he still took care to avoid Belcourt Street and Stewart Davidson. For reasons that he could not quite explain even to himself, he was actually worried about Stewart Davidson's opinion of him and his decision to stop going to the AA meetings. He knew he would be hard pressed to expand upon the note that he had slipped into the Davidson mailbox. Accordingly, he had gotten into the habit of continually rehearsing an explanation for resigning from AA and its meetings, hoping that he would never have to use any excuse he could devise, his principal one being that the combination of meditation, yoga and vegetarianism was an adequate replacement therapy for his phantom alcoholism. He was also prepared to claim that it had been his wife Jean's idea, a fairly predictable justification to say the least.

LOOKING FOR ELAINE SHERWOOD II

The next Monday, Richard drove down to Glencairn Avenue in Ottawa South, initially just to get a perspective on the neighbourhood in which Elaine and Stewart Davidson had lived with their son Andrew for twenty years. It was a nice, traditional suburban street right out of a situation comedy from the 1960s, brick cottages and bungalows behind tidy sidewalks and nicely manicured front and back lawns. Most houses were equipped with garages. The street reminded Richard of the old family home on Columbus Avenue in Pointe Claire. The vintages were similar although it was obvious to Richard that the houses on Glencairn Avenue were likely much more expensive than the houses on Columbus Avenue. The other notable observation that Richard made was that there was only one recently constructed "monster" house on the street, a significant departure from the many such houses that had recently been and were still being constructed around his place on Lakeview. It seemed curious to Richard that two similar locales in the same city, barely five kilometres apart, should have have such different real estate characters. The only explanation he could fabricate was that the people on Glencairn were much longer term residents there than his neighbours on Lakeview Avenue and environs. When he thought about it, which he did as he sat in the car in front of the Davidson's old address at 64 Glencairn Avenue, it was fairly obvious. On Lakeview, he and Jean had witnessed more than half of their original neighbours replaced by younger families who were moving into much larger homes than their predecessors had owned. He and Jean had often discussed their observations regarding the increase in the number of children that were now living on Lakeview relative to two decades ago when they had originally moved there. Now there were dozens. Back then, there were maybe half a dozen, including their own two kids. Children, large houses and expensive cars; those were the characteristics of the neighbourhood in which they now lived. Glencairn Avenue did not appear to be so distinguished although Richard did notice that one of the houses on the street, their being several dozen, had a BMW of recent vintage parked in its driveway.

In addition to his brief ruminations on the nature of the residents of Glencairn Avenue, as he was sitting there in a parked car, he reviewed his plans for his search for anyone on the street who might have known Elaine Sherwood/Davidson when she and her husband lived there. He thought that he would start by talking to anyone on Glencairn who would answer the door, preferably anyone who was old enough to have resided on the street when the Davidsons lived there, who were likely retired and therefore likely to answer the door at this time of day. He decided to start next door to their old address. He got out of the car and walked up to the front door. The house was a two story brick edifice that looked to be of the same general vintage as the other houses in the area. It featured what appeared to be a recently installed bay window in the front of the house, a new roof, and a red front door three steps led up to a concrete porch. There was a well tended lawn in the front of the house surrounding a large maple tree, a paved driveway leading to a wooden garage that looked to be about as old as the house. A Canadian flag was hung from a pole and a stone walk snaked up to the elevated front door. He climbed up the three steps and rang the bell. An elderly woman leaning on a walker answered the door immediately, as if she had been waiting for him. She was profoundly wrinkled, had pure white hair, was bent over her walker, was attired in an oversized blue and white house dress and was wearing nylon stockings rolled down to her ankles, and old slippers that were almost falling off her feet.

"Hello," she said, in a quivering voice that could have belonged to a cartoon character, "who are you?"

Richard took a step forward, one foot now on the door jam, put his right hand out and answered. She looked at her hand and sort of waved it, barely touching his hand. "My name is Richard Matthews. I am an old friend of the Davidson family who used to live next door to this address but I understand they moved more than twenty years ago. I have just moved back to the city and am looking to contact them, particularly Elaine Davidson who was a good friend of my wife. She is very ill and she has asked me to find Mrs. Davidson. She wants to see her before she gets any worse. We have been out of the country for years and lost touch with them."

The old woman looked confused. "The Davidsons?"

Richard smiled in a certain sympathetic way, an affectation that he often employed when speaking to the elderly. The old woman returned the smile although she still appeared confused. "Yes, the Davidsons. I thought I would start to look for them at the last place I knew they lived, which was next door." Richard then stepped into the house, his sympathetic smile still obvious on his face.

The old woman tried to look up. "I didn't know them. I only moved in with my son and his family a few years ago. They have lived here for a long time. They probably knew and might know where they went after they moved from next door."

Richard then asked for the family's telephone number. "Okay. Why don't I call your son tonight? Maybe he knows where they went after they moved."

"Okay." said the woman.

Richard nodded and asked for the telephone number. She shook her head and motioned him into the house. He stepped around her, spotted the telephone handset in the living room underneath the bay window, picked it up and found the telephone number. He then walked past the old woman back toward the front door. He patted her on the arm and headed toward the door. His hand on the front door, he turned back toward the old woman and gently asked. "What is your son's name?"

She smiled and looked up. "David Gibson, his name is David Gibson." Richard thanked her, smiled for the last time, left the house, got into his car and drove home.

He waited until seven o'clock that evening. He had dinner with Jean who then went to her yoga class, a fortunate situation since he could speak to David Gibson without worrying about Jean overhearing. He was still determined to ensure that his search for Elaine Sherwood remained a secret. If his interest with Andrew Davidson and his family become apparent, an interest that he was convinced was no longer evident to Jean, she would return to believing her husband had been and remained obsessed with the man in the window on Belcourt Avenue. So he was pleased that his telephone call with David Gibson would be confidential. He didn't want her to know and he didn't want to have to explain if she did.

He sat on the sofa and dialed the Gibson telephone number. A man answered. "Hello, Mr. Gibson?" asked Richard. Without waiting for a reply, he continued. "My name is Richard Matthews. I visited your place this afternoon. I spoke to your mother. I hope I didn't scare her or anything."

David Gibson acknowledged Richard. "Yes, she told me and I don't think you scared her. Fact is we are always worried that mother isn't scared enough. She will open the door for anyone it seems."

"I'm sorry. As I say, I didn't mean anything. I was just inquiring about the Davidson family, who I understand used to live next door." Richard explained, almost an apology.

Mr. Gibson continued. "So you were looking for the Davidson family who used to live next door, right?"

Richard sounded enthused, almost talking too fast. "Right, that's right. I am looking for Mrs. Davidson in particular. I haven't been able to contact her. I don't know where she is. I know that she and Mr. Davidson were divorced when they were still living here, at least I think so. Then, she went back to her maiden name, Sherwood. Her name is Elaine Sherwood, unless of course she got married and changed it again."

David Gibson interrupted. "I knew the Davidsons got divorced. Everyone knew that that's why they moved. But, sorry, I didn't know where they went. All I know is that the son, Andrew, went to live with his father while Elaine ended up living by herself."

It had occurred to Richard, and maybe anyone else who knew about the circumstances of the Davidson divorce, the question of why neither

Stewart or Elaine kept the house when they split. David Gibson, perhaps anticipating such an inquiry, which was pretty well obvious to most people, explained. "If you're wondering, and everyone did, they had to sell the house to settle the financial aspect of the divorce, which wasn't very friendly. Where they went after that we don't know. I'm sorry."

Richard was understandably disappointed. "Well, thanks. I thought you might know something about where they went."

There was a delay on the telephone. Then David made a suggestion. "You might want to talk to the Martins. They live a couple of doors across the street at number 57, the first house after the turn off Riverside. They've lived there for more than thirty years. Louise Martin was pretty close to Elaine Davidson."

Richard hurriedly interrupted and finished David's thought. "And she may know where she went."

"Exactly and you might get lucky." concluded David Gibson.

Gibson was about to conclude the call when Richard asked an obvious question, at least to him. "By the way, did you ever notice anything strange about their son, Andrew.?"

There was another pause on the telephone. "Well, the whole neighbourhood knew that Andrew was mentally handicapped. It was a problem, you know, his behaviour was a bit odd sometimes, disruptive, sometimes almost dangerous. He liked to throw things, said strange things, sometimes just wandered off, he had to be watched most of the time."

Richard was just about to say goodbye when David Gibson added another observation about Andrew Davidson. "One more thing. Andrew always like to stand looking out a window on the second floor of the Davidson house. It was strange, eerie, Andrew just staring out that window in a trace. Nobody knew what he was looking at and why. He was a weird kid who did weird things. The window thing was just one of those things, maybe the strangest."

Richard decided that he would call on Louise Martin the next day. He assumed that, like David Gibson's mother, she was an older woman, long retired and likely to be at home pretty well all the time. That night, as he was seeking slumber, an ambition that he often pursued with some difficulty, he contemplated the history of his pursuit of the mysteries of

Scott Vessey and Andrew Davidson and their mothers, wondering, as he had previously, the basis for his apparent fixation, both then and now. Although he had regularly raised his fascination with Andrew Davidson with Jean when it had first emerged, he soon found himself abandoning discussion of the matter with her, deciding to hide his fixation. Still, now that he was so far in another search, he had begun to renew his desire to discuss the matter with someone, as along as it wasn't Jean, who would probably think him disturbed, someone who could provide him with an explanation. He thought, at least occasionally, of consulting a psychiatrist, maybe a psychologist, maybe Doctor Rowen, a psychologist whose license was revoked after he was caught having affairs with two of his female patients, both of whom were allegedly under the age of consent.

He had visited Doctor Rowen twice, both times to help him overcome his problems with anxiety, a difficulty that had bedevilled him ever since he had threatened to disembark from an airplane while it was still aloft. From then until he retired, after which time that particular problem surfaced only occasionally, a variety of tranquilizers were sufficient to control his nerves. He now thought himself cured, at least of that particular condition, only to be replaced he suspected by another mental problem, his obsession about two guys in two windows. He would lie in bed and stare at the ceiling, just like he imagined Scott Vessey and Andrew Davidson would stare out their windows, wondering if he had been crazy all along, preoccupied, haunted, select the diagnosis. His conclusion, one to which he had arrived every sleepless night for the last week or so, was simple: find Andrew Davidson's mother. It was his sedative for every one of those nights.

His other preoccupation during his sleepless nights was his apparent decision to gradually abandon watching Andrew at his window. Since his encounter with Stewart Davidson at his first AA meeting, he had made an effort to avoid observing Andrew Davidson. While he still walked Margie down Coolbreeze after he had begun his search for Andrew's mother, he never once took the opportunity, as tempted as he was, to look beyond the backyard of 233 Coolbreeze into the second floor window of the house at 240 Belcourt. He never even thought of asking Andrew's father about him, aside from casual, perfunctory questions about his health during their drives downtown. He never knew why he didn't continue his observations. Maybe he was waiting until he had something important to give him.

—

The next morning, after providing Jean with one of his usual array of excuses, he left for Glencairn Avenue to call on Louise Martin at number 57. He didn't have to rehearse his line of patter, his spiel. He was now an expert at approaching people who might know the location of people they might know. He wondered whether he could ever develop a career as a private detective looking for missing persons, a kind of geriatric Hardy Boy. He contemplated the fantasy for about fifteen minutes before he found himself turning off Riverside Drive onto Glencairn Avenue. The Martins lived just past the left turn off Riverside, a two story brick cottage that looked to be of the same vintage and design as the Gibson house across the street, the only actual difference being that the Gibson house had a red front door with green coloured roof shingles while the Martin residence had a white front door with rust coloured roof shingles.

He parked the car in front of the Martin house, walked up the stone path, stood before the red door, and rang the bell. After waiting for less than a minute, a man's voice came from behind the door.

"Yes, who is it?" the voice was thin, tentative, leery. It was apparent to Richard that the residents at 57 Glencairn were leery of strangers ringing their doorbell, their suspicions likely based on their custom of consulting the peephole in the door, a habit that seemed to be more prevalent among older people than anybody else. "Mr. Martin?" asked Richard hopefully.

"Yes." answered who Richard presumed to be Mr. Martin. He still sounded a bit unsettled, like he doubted Richard was a legitimate visitor.

His voice volume up, Richard introduced himself. "Mr. Martin, my name is Richard Matthews and I was referred to your wife by the people across the street, the Gibsons – they're at number 62."

The door opened a crack. Mr. Martin's face was now somewhat visible. Richard could see that he was short, bald, had stubbly skin the colour and composition of parchment, and had watery blue eyes which appeared to be on the verge of tears. "You mean, you want to speak to Louise. Why?" he answered, the door opening wider. Richard could now see that Mr. Martin was wearing a dressing gown and flip flops.

Richard moved closer to the door. "I'm looking for a woman named Elaine Sherwood. She used to live across the street from you with her husband, Stewart Davidson. Mr. Gibson told me that your wife and her were friends back then. I was wondering if Louise was still in touch with Elaine and maybe knew where she was living now."

"The Davidsons? You know the Davidsons?" asked Mr. Martin.

Richard sort of shrugged his shoulders dismissively. He was now standing on the porch, Mr. Martin having moved into the hallway. "No, not really. But my wife worked with Elaine. She was close to her. She knew the Davidsons lived in this neighourhood but lost touch with Elaine after they divorced and moved."

Suddenly, an elderly female voice emerged from further down the hallway, behind Mr. Martin. It was obviously Louise Martin. Richard saw a sizable halo of white hair astride a short woman wearing a mauve house dress decorated with large white flowers. Despite a tiny upper body, hunched over and supported by almost elephantine legs which required a walker, she was remarkably supple. She was able to manoeuvre around her husband effortlessly, almost pushing him aside, and beckoned Richard further into the house, motioned him into the living room. "Mr. Matthews, right? You want to know if I'm still in touch with Elaine Davidson, I mean Elaine Sherwood you said, if we still stayed in touch after all these years."

"That's right." said Richard. "My wife, who used to be a good friend of hers, wants to see her again. She's ill, you know, and wants to see her again, just once if she could."

Louise Martin rolled herself into the living room to join him. He was now sitting, as was Mr. Martin, to whom he had not yet been introduced. Louise then sat down on her walker. "Poor woman. I think I remember the family. They lived across the street. They had a handicapped son. Right, Henry?" At first, Henry shrugged and then he added an important detail. "I remember the boy. He was strange. He liked to stare out of their window, upstairs."

Richard was feeling a little more optimistic. It was obvious that Louise Martin knew Elaine Sherwood, almost certainly when she was still a Davidson and he thought it possible that she might have been in touch with her after the Davidsons split and the family moved out of the house on Glencairn. Richard was steering Louise to his search for Elaine.

"So, Louise, have you or Henry seen or heard from Elaine since the Davidsons left the street?" asked Richard, a hopeful smile surfacing on his face. Louise looked at Henry, then at Richard and then at nothing in particular.

She looked perplexed and then answered. "The last time I saw Elaine was in the Rideau Centre, maybe five year ago or so. I was shopping with Henry, my daughter Allison and two of my grandchildren. I just ran into her. She was with a lady who she introduced as someone who lived in the same retirement residence. I can't remember her name or the name of the residence. Do you remember, Henry? You were with me." Henry, who didn't appear to be listening to his wife, just shook his head and slowly threw up his hands in supplication. "Anyway, we didn't talk long. She just introduced me to her friend."

Richard lowered his head for a moment. When he looked up, he looked disappointed. Louise said she was sorry and added an important speck of memory. "You know, I think she said that she was living in the west end." Richard's disappointment faded. He smiled and rose from the Martin's sofa. "I hope I haven't taken up too much of your time."

Louise offered her own smile. "No, no, not at all. I hope we were helpful.", a curious comment since they had not been helpful at all. "And oh yes, good luck with your search."

A WEST END RETIREMENT RESIDENCE

So five years ago, Elaine Sherwood was living in a retirement residence located in the west end. Richard had thought that the Martins, particularly Louise, would be giving him an answer and for several moments during his visit to her house he thought that they had. He was disappointed and frustrated. Maybe he was growing tired of chasing Elaine Sherwood. To regain his commitment to the search, immediately after his visit to the Martin house, he had taken Margie for evening walks on two consecutive evenings, intending to confirm that Andrew Davidson was still making his appearances at the second floor window. On that first night, Richard surreptitiously crouched down in the backyard of 233 Coolbreeze near the garage watching the second floor window of 240 Belcourt. He must have been huddled in that backyard for twenty minutes before he ran out of treats for Margie and had to head home before she got too agitated. Andrew did not appear during the twenty minutes Richard invested in that first evening's stake out. But during his second evening's surveillance, he spotted Andrew in his customary place almost as soon as he took up a position by the garage behind 233 Coolbreeze Avenue. He was just standing there, hypnotized as he usually was, staring into the backyard as if he was looking for something. Now that he was assured that Andrew was still staring from his window, they turned to leave when they encountered Mr. Pat Bissell, the man in the baseball cap who lived further up Coolbreeze and whom he met when Richard and Margie were checking out Andrew one evening several weeks ago. Bissell was standing at the end of driveway. He gave Richard and Margie a quick wave and waited for him.

"I see you are still checking out Andrew in his window." Bissell observed casually, as if he had been expecting him that evening.

"Yeah, you got me." explained Richard, who walked Margie down the driveway to greet Bissell. They reached the bottom of the driveway. He fed Margie another treat and they both stood there. "I haven't been around lately. For the first time in weeks, I went by last night. Margie and I huddled in the backyard for maybe twenty minutes and he didn't appear. But tonight, well tonight, he's in his usual place." Richard then shrugged and gave Margie another treat. Bissell returned the gesture. "I don't see him much anymore either, not that I'm looking for him. I mean, I don't go by here that often anyway. And when I do, I don't look up at his window every time, just occasionally."

Richard didn't know what to say. He offered Bissell a quick nod, looked down at Margie and turned to head home. "Well, you know he's still in the window, not every evening as far as I can see, but still there." And with that observation, he and Margie left Pat Bissell standing in front of the house at 233 Coolbreeze.

Like before every specific step in his investigation, he had formulated a plan for his search for Elaine Sherwood at retirement residences in the west end of the city. He would simply contact each of them by telephone, claiming if asked that Elaine Sherwood was a relative or a friend. He was almost dumbfounded when he discovered, after a quick Google investigation, that there over fourty retirement residences in Ottawa, half of which looked to be located in the west end of the city. And he didn't even bother to even look up the nursing homes, of which he assumed there were quite a few as well.

He initiated his telephone research with Amica in Westboro, one of the most prestigious retirement residences in the city he thought. Since it was located in their neighbourhood, he and Jean drove by it frequently. Richard would usually comment, suggesting that Amica's bar, pool table, and lobby, all of which were visible from the outside, were features that motivated Richard to extract a promise from Jean that when the time came, they would live out their retirement in Amica. Within an hour, beginning with the call to Amica, he had spoken to representatives of a dozen residences, seven women and five men, all of whom were absurdly cheerful and all of whom said that they had never heard of Elaine Sherwood. He started to wonder whether Louise Martin had been correct in directing him to a west end retirement residence. After a short break, he resumed his telephone search. The first place he called, was Valley Stream, a relatively new facility conveniently located several hundred metres directly across Baseline Road from the Queensway Carleton Hospital. The lady at the front desk cheerfully answered the telephone but then hesitated way too long before responding to his inquiry about Elaine Sherwood. Richard was on the line for several minutes before the lady at the front desk, who had introduced herself as Mary Someone Or Other, got back on the line and asked him to drop by the residence, saying that the director of the facility, a woman named Gertrude Ross, wanted to talk to him in private. Momentarily stunned, Richard said that he could visit her that afternoon and asking for an appointment time. Mary suggested two o'clock that afternoon.

For the next couple of hours, Richard continued to wonder about the reason for the request by the director of the Valley Stream for a meeting about Elaine Sherwood. By the time he arrived for his meeting with Gertrude Ross, he had abandoned wondering about the purpose of the meeting, having concluded that it likely foreshadowed something distressing. He was worried. Maybe Elaine Sherwood had been a resident but had disappeared. Maybe she had changed her name again. Maybe there was another Elaine Sherwood. Maybe, maybe, maybe, the word was reverberating through his head like a persistent migraine. By the time he walked into the director's office, he was anxious, likely in need of a tranquilizer, maybe he needed Doctor Rowen again. He was immediately impressed with both the external and internal decor of the Valley Stream Retirement Residence. It was obvious that the facility had been built quite recently. It was a rust coloured brick structure with five floors spread out in two wings around a central building. The place had a large lobby in which maybe a dozen sofas and an equal number of chairs were scattered under four chandeliers. There were three large tables in the rear of the room at which residents and visitors could obtain refreshments, snacks, newspapers and magazines. There were also big screen televisions on the west and east walls of the lobby. To his immediate right as Richard walked into the place, he took note of the dining room, a few stragglers still eating lunch, two residents sitting at one table talking while three others were sitting by themselves. Staff members were scurrying about preparing for the next meal. To the left of the front entrance was a counter that looked like a hotel reception desk. Behind the counter and through a short corridor, Richard could see what appeared to be a glassed-in medical office. Richard walked up to the desk and asked the woman behind it for Gertrude Ross, mentioning their appointment. She smiled, picked up the telephone and announced his arrival to Director Ross. She then told him that her office was off the lobby to the left past the elevators. Richard had to be nimble to move through a crowd of walkers and wheel chairs to get to her office. He noticed that a lady in a one of the wheel chairs was completely bald and was wearing overalls and two different shoes, one a slipper and the other a canvas loafer. She smiled like some sort of cartoon character. She also seemed to be talking to herself. No one else but Richard seemed to notice. The door to Ms. Ross's office was open. She was waiting.

Ms. Ross, an plain looking woman in her fifties, was wearing a navy blue suit decorated with a small gold brooch, greeted him with a firm handshake and a serious expression. He noticed that Ms. Ross was not wearing any makeup, an observation that temporarily made him feel guilty. She motioned him into one of the two chairs that stood before her desk. He sat down on the edge of the chair that happened to be to the right front of her desk. Ms. Ross adjusted her chair closer and straightened up with her elbows on the desk and hands clasped together in front of her, almost in prayer. She reminded Richard of his second grade teacher Miss Decarie.

She looked straight at Richard. It was almost a stare, a sympathetic stare that suggested that sad news was forthcoming. Richard moved his chair closer to her desk. "I am told you are looking for Elaine Sherwood." she stated.

"Yes, I am." answered Richard. "My wife Jean is an old friend who she hasn't seen for years. Jean's sick and wants to see Elaine, you know, while she is still able." She paused for a moment and looked thoughtful, her head tilting toward the ceiling and then down to the surface of the desk, seeming to process the circumstances facing Richard, planning her next remark. "I'm sorry to hear that, Mr. Matthews." She looked up again and her face came closer to him. "I don't know how to tell you this but...." There was a pause and Richard leaned forward again. Ms. Ross was now almost whispering. "I'm sorry to tell you this but your wife's friend passed away almost three years ago." A longer pause this time. She was still looking at him, still earnest, almost reverential. "She had been living here for almost two years. She seemed to be in good health. And then all of sudden she had a heart attack, just after lunch one day. I was here that day. It was awful. No one had any idea, any inkling. It's a terrible thing to say but she just dropped dead, just collapsed without warning." Richard sat there, stunned into shock, his search for Elaine Sherwood apparently over. He let out an audible sigh although Ms. Ross did not react. They both just sat there, staring at each other. Ms. Ross broke the temporary trance. As the director, she had obvious experience with relating unfortunate news.

Predictably, Richard was not going to allow the story of Elaine Sherwood's demise to be discussed without further comment. After all his effort to find her, his disappointment and maybe even strange kind of sorrow with the news that Elaine Sherwood was in fact dead was so obvious to Gertrude that she was almost close to tears. Richard was dazed, sitting there deliberating. He then asked an inappropriate though obvious question, even though he had found his missing person and really did not have to investigate further.

"Who took care of the arrangements when she died, you know for her funeral?" Still looking for clues, it was possible Richard could have concluded that her former husband Stewart Davidson and their son Andrew were either responsible for the arrangements for Elaine's departure or had at least appeared for its celebration. Although he had not had much time for rumination about his investigation or its purpose, he had come to believe that he would be satisfied if he knew that her ex-husband and her son were involved in the acknowledgement of her passing. It would finally finish his investigation, it would conclude his crusade.

Gertrude Ross leaned back in her chair and looked away for a moment.

She then turned back to face Richard. "Her sister Colleen took care of things." she informed him.

In his research, Richard never came across her sister Colleen. He didn't even know that she even had a sister. "I didn't know she had a sister." he told Ms. Ross.

Ms. Ross nodded her head and offered him a grimace. "I'm not surprised. She has lived in Toronto for a long time and only visited Ottawa occasionally, maybe once every couple of months. She did, however, partially support Elaine's stay with us."

"There wasn't anyone else?" asked Richard.

Ms. Ross shook her head. "Not that I knew of. Understandably, I spoke to Colleen a lot at the time of her passing. She was the executor of her will and so pretty well made all the arrangements. She was up here for a couple of weeks."

Richard was more than curious. He had to ask the question. "Do you know if her ex- husband, a man named Stewart Davidson, and their son Andrew attended the funeral or the visitation, that is if there was a funeral or a visitation."

Gertrude leaned back in her chair. "Well, Colleen made sure that there was an obituary, which was understandably short since nobody here knew much about her and that there was a visitation and a funeral but I don't think either her ex-husband or her son – I have never met either of them – attended either function but they may have. I wasn't introduced to everyone."

"Did a lot of people attend?" asked Richard, casually.

Gertrude shook her head. "Not really. Maybe three dozen or so and maybe half of them were residents from Valley Stream. We hired a bus for the residents for both the visitation and the funeral. I assume that the rest were either former neighbours – I was introduced to some of them – and, well, I wasn't introduced to the rest of them and can't tell you anything about them."

The two of them sat in silence. Richard then asked Gertrude Ross about her final resting place. Richard did not know why he asked. He could not think of anything that could be gained by knowing where her remains were interred. He assumed that she had been cremated, as most of the deceased these days are. In the silence, he contemplated the possibilities. Perhaps her remains had not been interred but were in her sister's possession somewhere, which seemed unlikely since the sisters did not appear to be close. Perhaps her remains were scattered somewhere, another unlikely eventuality. Gertrude resolved that matter when she reported that Elaine Sherwood's remains had been interred in the Pinecrest Cemetery, which was less than a kilometre away from Valley Stream, proximity to her final living residence a likely explanation.

A VISIT TO THE PINECREST CEMETERY

It had come to him in something that could have been a dream, late one night as slumber was eluding him, an apparent inspiration that in the end wasn't an inspiration at all. It was the only the alternative left. The idea came to him, more like it was left to him several days after his meeting with Gertrude Ross. He had continually thought about the information that he managed to gather about Elaine Sherwood, so much so that it had become almost a psychosis. Fortunately for him, he did not confide any of his reveries with Jean. Yes, he had located her but she had passed away. His original idea, locating Elaine Sherwood and somehow untangling the mystery of her son Andrew by doing so, had now been rendered moot by the death of the key to the plan itself. Waiting for sleep that night, he came to the only conclusion he thought he could. He would visit her grave at the Pinecrest Cemetery.

The next morning, after a nice breakfast at a local diner where he had his usual repartee with one of the two waitresses who always brought him his poached eggs, one slice of brown toast, coffee and a copy of the *Ottawa Sun,* he arrived at the office of the Pinecrest Cemetery, a small one story building behind a circular driveway. He parked his car in the lot to the left of the entrance, nodded to a security guard standing by the front door, and entered the building. There was a large lobby, a chapel to the left, a meeting room to the right, and in the centre of the room, a receptionist sitting at a small desk behind which there was an office equipped with a door that had a full length glass insert on which was inscribed "Director" in gold lettering. Richard walked straight up to the receptionist, who appeared to be busily navigating on a laptop. The receptionist, a fresh faced young woman with carefully applied make up and blond hair swept up in a ponytail, looked up from her explorations and quietly greeted him.

"Good morning, may I help you?" she asked quietly, in a serious tone. He felt like he was in a church which, in a way, he was.

Richard took a couple of steps closer. "Hello, my is Richard Matthews. I'm looking for the grave of a recent decedent. Her name is Elaine Sherwood and I understand that she was likely interred here about three years ago."

The receptionist offered him a gentle smile. "Of course, let me check the registry." She then looked down on her laptop, found the registry site and typed in the name of Elaine Sherwood. She leaned in to take a closer look at the screen and started to look through the names. "You know there are over 15,000 graves in Pinecrest." she remarked. "You know, at one time, everything was just paper files, it must have been a terrible thing to find anybody's file. Now, it is so easy" She looked up beyond her laptop and gave Richard an answer. "Here she is. Her plot, ID number 9010812, is located in Section R, C-9."

Richard leaned back in his chair. "Thanks, that was pretty simple. And how do I get to her plot?" he asked.

"No problem. I can print you a map." she answered. A couple of keystrokes and a sheet was coming out of a printer. The receptionist then handed him the map. Richard took the map and studied it. "Thanks again." Richard then got out of the chair and headed toward the entrance, holding the sheet of paper in his hand like a treasure map.

—

Within less than five minutes, Richard Matthews was standing over plot number 9010812, in Section R, C-9. He looked down at a bronze memorial placed in the ground, a flat marker so inscribed.

Elaine Lindsay Sherwood
June 3, 1944 – October 12, 2014

ANOTHER VISIT TO THE HOUSE ON BELCOURT AVENUE

It was the day after he had visited the plot at the Pinecrest Cemetery. That morning, he had printed a photograph he had taken the previous day with his cellphone. It was a picture of a bronze memorial, a flat marker identifying the final resting place of Elaine Lindsay Sherwood. He sized the photograph to 4" by 6", typed the word "Mother" at the bottom, and laminated it, having purchased a machine several years ago for the purpose of preserving his photographs, something that camera stores, drug stores and even convenience stores used to provide years ago. He placed the photograph in an envelop, sealed it, and took it on his walk with Margie.

For the first time in weeks, he and Margie walked down Belcourt Avenue. He stopped in front of 240 Belcourt Avenue, walked up to the front door, and placed the envelop in the mail box. The envelope was addressed to "Andrew Davidson". Inside was the photograph.

Printed in the United States
By Bookmasters